The Quilted Heart

Three Novellas in One

OTHER BOOKS BY MONA HODGSON

HISTORICAL FICTION

Prairie Song

The Sinclair Sisters of Cripple Creek

Two Brides Too Many
Too Rich for a Bride
The Bride Wore Blue
Twice a Bride

CHILDREN'S BOOKS

Bedtime in the Southwest (Northland Publishing)
Real Girls of the Bible: A 31-Day Devotional (Zonderkidz)
The Princess Twins and the Puppy (Zonderkidz I Can Read)
The Princess Twins Play in the Garden (Zonderkidz I Can Read)
The Princess Twins and the Tea Party (Zonderkidz I Can Read)
The Princess Twins and the Birthday Party (Zonderkidz I Can Read)
The Best Breakfast (Zonderkidz I Can Read)
Thank You, God, for Rain (Zonderkidz I Can Read)

For a complete and current listing of Mona's books, including
any out-of-print titles she may still have available, please visit
her website at MonaHodgson.com.

Praise for
The Quilted Heart Series

"Like a warm breeze ripples across a lake, *Dandelions on the Wind* offers a gentle crossing in this first-in-a-series novel. Mona Hodgson gives readers characters we care about, a bit of intrigue, love, and a satisfying ending that promises more in the second series book. Well done!"

> —JANE KIRKPATRICK, best-selling author of *Where Lilacs
> Still Bloom*

"Filled with true-to-life characters and fascinating historical details, *Dandelions on the Wind* is a heartwarming story of second chances in the turbulent days immediately after the Civil War. Don't miss this, the first of Mona Hodgson's The Quilted Heart trilogy. If you're like me, you'll be waiting eagerly for the second."

> —AMANDA CABOT, author of *Waiting for Spring*

"*Dandelions on the Wind* is a sweet tale about the merging of two hurting hearts. The characters drew me, and I can't wait to read more about their lives…and their love!"

> —TRICIA GOYER, best-selling author of thirty-three novels,
> including *The Memory Jar*

"In *Dandelions on the Wind*, Mona Hodgson weaves a tale of broken promises, wounded hearts…and the power of forgiveness—a heartwarming reminder that we walk by faith, not by sight. Maren is a heroine you'll cheer for!"

> —CAROL COX, author of *Love in Disguise* and *Trouble in Store*

"Mona Hodgson's *Bending Toward the Sun* captures Saint Charles following the Civil War so well. Quaid returns home—a man changed by the war. Emilie is a delight—a young woman pursuing her education, who knows her own mind. And even though the war has changed so many things, this story reminds us that some things, like love, never change."

—DORRIS KEEVEN-FRANKE, archivist, Saint Charles
County Historical Society

"Mona Hodgson has written a warm, tender tale of family loyalties and forbidden love. When Emilie's father objects to her seeing the handsome McFarland boy, recently returned from war, the couple struggles to do the right thing. But they are about to discover that God has another plan. Filled with charming characters and godly themes, this heartwarming story is pure delight."

—MARGARET BROWNLEY, *New York Times* best-selling
author of A Rocky Creek Romance Series and the Brides
of Last Chance Ranch Series

"With believable characters, an historic setting, and a gripping love story, Mona Hodgson gives the reader an uplifting account of a time when our country was recovering from a dark period and looking forward to a brighter future."

—MARTHA ROGERS, author of the Winds Across the Prairie
Series and the best-selling *Christmas at Holly Hill*

Dandelions on the Wind • *Bending Toward the Sun*
Ripples Along the Shore

The Quilted Heart

Three Novellas in One

MONA HODGSON

WATERBROOK
PRESS

THE QUILTED HEART
PUBLISHED BY WATERBROOK PRESS
12265 Oracle Boulevard, Suite 200
Colorado Springs, Colorado 80921

All Scripture quotations and paraphrases are taken from the King James Version.

This is a work of fiction. Apart from well-known people, events, and locales that figure into the narrative, all names, characters, places, and incidents are the products of the author's imagination or are used fictitiously.

Trade Paperback ISBN 978-0-307-73114-2
eBook ISBN 978-0-307-73115-9

The novellas included in this compilation are *Dandelions on the Wind, Bending Toward the Sun,* and *Ripples Along the Shore,* all copyright © 2013 by Mona Hodgson.

Cover design by Kelly L. Howard; cover photo by Scott T. Smith/CORBIS

Published in association with the literary agency of Janet Kobobel Grant, Books & Such, 52 Mission Circle, Suite 122, PMB 170, Santa Rosa, CA 95409-5370.

Published in the United States by WaterBrook Multnomah, an imprint of the Crown Publishing Group, a division of Random House LLC, New York, a Penguin Random House Company.

WATERBROOK and its deer colophon are registered trademarks of Random House LLC.

Library of Congress Cataloging-in-Publication Data

Hodgson, Mona Gansberg, 1954–
    Dandelions on the wind / Mona Hodgson.—First edition.
        pages cm.— (The quilted hearts novella ; 1)
    ISBN 978-0-307-73143-2 (electronic)
    1. Single women—Fiction. 2. Danes—United States—Fiction. 3. Veterans—Fiction. I. Title.
    PS3608.O474B75 2012
    813'.6—dc23

                                                    2012042772

Hodgson, Mona Gansberg, 1954–
    Bending toward the sun / Mona Hodgson.—First edition.
        pages cm— (The quilted heart ; novella two)
    ISBN 978-0-307-73144-9 (electronic : alk. paper) 1. Young women—Fiction. I. Title.
    PS3608.O474B46 2013
    813'.6—dc23

                                                    2013001084

Hodgson, Mona Gansberg, 1954–
    Ripples along the shore / Mona Hodgson.—First Edition.
        pages cm— (The quilted heart ; novella three)
    Includes bibliographical references and index.
    ISBN 978-0-307-73114-2 (alk. paper)—ISBN 978-0-307-73145-6 (electronic) 1. Young women—Fiction. I. Title.
    PS3608.O474R57 2013
    813'.6—dc23

                                                    2013008382

Printed in the United States of America
2014—First Edition

10 9 8 7 6 5 4 3 2 1

The Quilted Heart 1

DANDELIONS ON THE WIND

MONA HODGSON

*With love to my Aunt Marion, Aunt
Pauline, and Aunt Nellie May,
all living well with Retinitis Pigmentosa(RP)*

*Thy word is a lamp unto my feet,
and a light unto my path.*

—PSALM 119:105

Saint Charles, Missouri, 1865

Never mind that four months had passed since General Lee's surrender. Maren never walked the apple orchard or the wheat field without careful watch for bushwhackers and jayhawkers. Four-year-old Gabi held tight to Maren's hand while they followed Gabi's grandmother to the field. When Mrs. Brantenberg's walking stick sprung a branch in her path, the child's gaze darted up the lane toward the orchard then back to the farmhouse and across the hillock to the five acres of wheat.

"Are they coming again, Miss Maren?" Dread strained Gabi's voice.

Maren drew in a deep breath in the hopes it would remove any tension from her own voice. "The war is over, little one." *We should be safe.* "God is with us. Like *Oma* said, 'Fear is not of the Lord. We cannot live in fear. We must trust God.'"

Gabi gave a quick nod, then began swinging Maren's hand at her side.

Fear is not of the Lord. We cannot live in fear. We must trust God.

Maren willed her shoulders to relax into the child's playful arm swinging. Still, she'd heard too many stories about raiders from the women in the quilting circle to let down her guard. To believe the fighting would ever end. The memories of the Union jayhawkers traipsing through the orchard picking apples and taking the steer from the pastures remained fresh in her mind too. She glanced toward the cabin at the far corner of the property, past the orchard. Now empty. She'd only heard about the Confederate bushwhackers who had raided the farm last year, but little Gabi remembered.

Maren fanned the side of her bonnet against her ear to cool the onslaught of hot August air. Thankfully, she saw no sign of trespassers today. And if any outlaws did show their faces, Mrs. Brantenberg had her stick ready with a stack of sorrows backing it up.

Mrs. Brantenberg stopped at the edge of the field. This close, Maren could see that two women didn't do as even a job of planting as she and her father had in the old country.

Gabi stepped up to the three-foot-high lawn, giggling. "They have whiskers like the cats do." Her hands brushed the tips of the wheat stalks.

Bent, the widow plucked one head and rolled the grains between her fingers.

Maren did the same on the thinner area, where the stalks didn't reach as high. The grain was soft and green inside. She didn't need to taste it to know it'd be bitter. "Still a ways to go here."

When a covey of bobwhites exploded from within the crop, Gabi cried out and fell to the ground.

Maren bent over the child. "Just thieving fly-by-nights. They learned their lesson, didn't they?"

Gabi nodded. "They scared me."

"Didn't do my heart any good either." Mrs. Brantenberg patted her chest. Then, smiling, she pressed the tip of her stick to the ground. "The wheat on the north end turned golden first. It's more likely to be ready in just a few more days."

Gabi's little hand slid into Maren's. Together, they tromped around the stand of shimmering stems, the *whiskers* tickling Maren's arms.

This wasn't the home Maren expected while traveling on the boat from Denmark four years ago. But back then, she'd still had more of her sight. Eight months ago, when the family that had taken her in gave up and moved away, Mrs. Brantenberg brought her out to the farm and provided her work in exchange for room and board. The widow, her granddaughter, and the quilting circle were Maren's family here in America, but she missed her mum, her sister, and her little brother, left behind in the old country.

The promise to bring her family to America had disappeared, right along with Orvie Christensen. Lying in bed at night, all she thought about was going home to Denmark. But the only jobs she'd been able to find during the war barely covered her living expenses, with nothing left over to save for the cost of travel. Yet how could she stay not knowing how long she'd have vision enough to work on the farm? She needed to make the long passage home while she could see well enough not to be a burden.

About twenty yards from the north end, Mrs. Brantenberg stopped and they repeated the testing process. This time, when the grain separated between Maren's fingers, she bit into a kernel and nodded to the widow.

Gabi stretched onto her tiptoes. "Is it sweet?'

Mrs. Brantenberg pulled another head from the stock and handed it to Gabi. "What do you think, *Liebling*?"

The *little one* rolled a kernel out of its sheath and bit into it like she'd seen Maren do. "Not sweet like Mr. Heinrich's rock candy. Tastes like dirt."

Mrs. Brantenberg tittered. "Well, most of us agree then—this section is nearly ready." She waved along the northern edge. "Monday, the three of us will begin harvesting."

Gabi's stomach growled and she giggled. "The bear in my belly is hungry now."

They all laughed. Even in the midst of work and careful watch, the child had a knack for easing their tension.

"It has been too long since breakfast. Gabi and I will fix us all an early supper while you tend the animals."

"Yes ma'am."

As the trio walked back toward the farmhouse and barn, the sinking sun began casting shadows on the path. Maren's deteriorating sight robbed her of colors in low light, leaving everything tinted in gray. Now she knew the trouble her father had suffered in his blindness. Her own stomach growling, she picked up her pace, hoping to reach the familiar inner yard before there was too little light to define the path. They'd worked in the vegetable garden right through the noonday mealtime, and she had chores yet to do before she could settle into the house for supper.

At the arbor, Mrs. Brantenberg and Gabi headed toward the house while Maren continued to the chicken yard. She needed to find a job in town where she could earn enough money to start saving for her return to Denmark. But they had the wheat fields to harvest this month, and then the twenty acres of apples would be ripe a few weeks after that. How could she even think of leaving the widow and dear Gabi alone out here?

"Shoo. Shoo." She spoke the words as much to her own thoughts as she did to the chickens pecking at her bootlaces. She reached into the scrap bucket hanging on a nail and tossed handfuls of potato peelings and grain in a wide arc. The cackling chickens scattered to be first to the bounty.

Inside the stifling hot coop, Maren dodged the roost and reached into the first of the five nests along the back wall. After all the eggs were gathered, she felt for the pole and ducked under it, taking the most direct route out of the smelly henhouse. Protecting her face with her hand, she stepped into the chicken yard, through the gate, and into the ruts leading to the barn. The parching wind stung her eyes and whipped her apron.

She folded one of the double-hinged barn doors and clamped it open, then stepped inside, squinting against the near darkness. The strong, sweet smell of the hay filled her nostrils. The cow scent was strong too, but not so sweet. Both reminded her of the farm her family had lost in Copenhagen. And the farm Orvie had promised her in his letters.

After Maren hung the basket of eggs by the door, she climbed the wooden steps to the hayloft. Cows bawled and horses whinnied below. Hay needed to be tugged from a stack and tossed over the edge into the swinging mangers at the stalls, then repeated on the other side. When she'd flung hay into Duden's and Boone's stalls, she dropped a couple forkfuls onto the center of the barn floor. At the top of the ladder, Maren brushed her hands together to dislodge any remaining hay stems from her woolen gloves before climbing down. Her plan was to feed the hogs and mules, milk the two cows, and then go inside for supper. She had planted her boots on the first two rungs of the ladder when a raspy baritone voice split the still air.

"Good day, ma'am."

Maren jerked and her boot slipped, causing her chin to strike a step. Wincing, she released her grip and fell backward. Fear caught a scream in her throat. The fresh pile of hay on the floor broke her fall, but still she landed flat on her back. She fought to recover her breath and gather her wits. A staccato heartbeat pounded in her ears. She didn't associate the deep voice with anyone who belonged on the farm.

Blinking, she willed her eyes to focus in her limited circle of vision. Brown curls swerved every which way on the head of a man she did not recognize. Scrambling to right herself, she edged toward the wall near the cow stall.

"Ma'am." A Union accent. Not one of Mrs. Brantenberg's German neighbors. "Are you well?"

"Yes." She felt along the wall for a makeshift weapon. When she found the shovel, she lifted it off its nail and held it across herself.

"I mean you no harm."

Holding the shovel steady, Maren widened her shoulders and raised her smarting chin.

"I apologize. I didn't—"

"Didn't what, sir?" This man may be harmless, but he was no less a nuisance. "You did not mean to burst into my barn and cause me to take a topple?"

"You're not Mrs. Brantenberg." It wasn't a question.

Did he know Mrs. Brantenberg, or had someone in town told him to expect an older woman?

"I am Maren Jensen." She couldn't make out his facial features in the shadows, but she did see one arm in a sling. That could be a ruse. "And you are?" Silence ticked off the seconds.

He removed his cap and moved closer. "People call me Woolly."

While repositioning her heavy weapon, Maren blinked to focus her vision. Her employer had never mentioned anyone named Woolly. If he wasn't a troublemaker, he had to be a drifter looking for work. And with her own work to finish, she had no time to waste. "You'll find Mrs. Brantenberg at the house."

"Thank you." His voice held a pleasant tone, although it sounded a bit gravelly, like he'd been out in the wind for a long spell. She should be nicer to the gentleman, but she couldn't afford to be. Chores were obligatory. Niceties with strange men were not.

He turned to leave the barn and quickly faded into the darkness. Maren lowered the shovel and listened as the door closed behind him. If she ever did have a home of her own, it wouldn't sit beside a well-traveled road. Especially not during or immediately following a war.

Woolly felt like the prodigal son in the New Testament. Except it was his daughter, not his father, he was coming home to. He followed the path from the barn to the front of the brick Georgian-style plantation house. Its fluted porch columns needed whitewashing. The shutters framing the double-hung sash windows needed attention too. When the wind caught his kepi, he pulled the cap tight onto his forehead. The smell of fresh bread wafted on the breeze, taunting his hunger. He couldn't say how long it'd been since he'd dined on anything but hard-tack or bully soup.

Now that he was home, he had a lot to catch up on. But this wasn't a Bible story, and he wasn't a beloved son.

He stopped at the bottom of the steps. If nothing else, perhaps his mother-in-law would let him stay long enough to meet the little girl he and Gretchen had created on this very farm, and to make a few repairs around the place. He owed her that much. And more than he could ever repay. He couldn't change the past four years. Not for Mother Brantenberg. Not for his daughter. Not for himself.

"Oma!"

The strained little voice drew his gaze to the window for a glimpse of sunny round cheeks framed in heaps of brown curls. Like his own. Tears stung his sleep-deprived eyes.

"A man, Oma."

"*Bleib hinter mir, Liebling.* Behind me." He recognized the voice, and the endearing term. Mother Brantenberg was protecting her *little one.* His little one.

He removed his cap, then spoke through the closed door. "Greetings, Mrs. Brantenberg."

The door opened just wide enough for him to see the woman's face. She gasped. "It is you." Her color matched what was left of the whitewash on the door that stood between them, and her foot didn't budge from its crossed position behind the door. Mother Brantenberg studied him, her gaze resting on the cloth that tethered his left arm to his neck. "You are hurt?"

"I got my arm caught in a rope whilst loading a barge and pulled my shoulder out of place."

His mother-in-law opened the door, but she hadn't spoken of his identity. He so desperately wanted the child hiding in the skirts to know her father had returned home. But at least for now, he was only a visitor. Inside, good smells and memories of happier times hit him, and his stomach rumbled while his heart wrenched.

He glanced from the woman to the child, who stepped out from behind her. He held out his right hand to her. "And who is this?"

The little one leaned against her grandmother, dipping her chin and peering up at him with wide eyes. "I am Gabi."

Short for Gabrielle—the name he and Gretchen had discussed for a girl. Gabi's face was a sweet miniature of her mother's. "What a lovely name." He hoped his smile hid the pain.

"Thank you." Gabi curtsied like a princess, then pointed to the soiled cloth that cupped his elbow. "Does it hurt?"

"It isn't so bad anymore. Thank you." His daughter was already four years old, and so grown up. He turned to his mother-in-law. "The arm should be workable in another day or two. I can start on repairs soon. Harvest?"

His mother-in-law huffed. Wrinkles framed her face. She still wore her hair parted down the middle with a braid, now white, encircling her head. But her eyes had dulled.

"Mister." Gabi's sweet voice cut into his thought. "What's your name?"

"Woolly." Mrs. Brantenberg rested her hand on Gabi's head. "His name is Woolly."

That's what Gretchen had called him the first time they'd met on her father's farm.

Gabi swayed side-to-side like she had music in her. "Woolly like a lamb?"

"Yes." He pointed at his head. "My hair is curly like lamb's wool."

"Mine too." Gabi patted her hair.

Woolly nodded, afraid to speak, sure the truth would come out before Mother Brantenberg was ready to reclaim him as family.

Mother Brantenberg glanced toward the washstand at the top of the staircase. "It is time to wash for supper, Liebling."

Gabi offered him a forlorn glance, and sighing, she marched up the stairs.

His mother-in-law studied him. "I did not expect your return."

"I have come to see my daughter. I should never have left you." He glimpsed the staircase and the little round cheeks pressed between the white oak spindles. The light in Gabi's eyes pierced the darkness in his heart…until he returned his attention to his mother-in-law. Mrs. Brantenberg looked as if she'd just gulped camp coffee. A look that said he'd not be staying for supper.

2

Maren sat on the stool with her hands under a cow, squirting milk into the bucket. She groaned and reached to touch her face. Her chin stung where she'd bumped the step. Her haystack landing had made a mess of her. All thanks to Mr. Woolly. But it wasn't his fault she hadn't seen him enter the barn. Although he smelled like a month on the road, he had been a gentleman, asking after her welfare and apologizing for the disruption.

Maren finished the evening milking and carried the pail and the basket of eggs to the house. By now Mrs. Brantenberg would've given the drifter a loaf of bread and a sausage and sent him on his way. She set the bucket of milk on a bench just inside the kitchen door. Facing the stove, she focused her thin vision. Mrs. Brantenberg scraped a tin spoon across a cast iron skillet. "Forgive my tardiness," Maren said. "A man came looking for you and caused a stir in the barn. Did you speak to him?"

"He will have supper with us." Her employer's voice lacked its usual melodious quality.

Maren drew in a deep breath. The savory aroma of Mrs. Brantenberg's gravy mingled with the smell of a-month-on-the-road clothing. He was there in the kitchen. Resisting an impulse to touch her sore chin, she placed the basket of eggs on the counter and turned toward the table.

He stood.

"Mr. Woolly."

"Miss Maren."

"You will surely enjoy Mrs. Brantenberg's *Schnitzel* and *Brötchen* rolls."

He nodded. "I have, thank you, and they're indeed worthy of the long journey."

He had? When?

Mrs. Brantenberg banged the spoon on the skillet. "Rutherford Wainwright has been here before." Her voice remained emotionless.

Certainly not in the last eight months. Maren would have remembered him. But the name did sound familiar. When she'd learned the war had ended, she'd overheard Mrs. Brantenberg mention the name *Rutherford* to the shopkeeper in town. "Rutherford Wainwright." Her son-in-law's name. "He is Gabi's *PaPa*?"

Mrs. Brantenberg blew out a long breath, which answered the question. Her son-in-law had returned.

"Mr. Woolly is my PaPa?"

Maren spun toward Gabi's voice. When had the child come into the room? They hadn't told Gabi her PaPa had returned from the war, and she'd blurted it out. If only the deafening silence could swallow her.

Mrs. Brantenberg nodded, silent.

The man took slow steps toward his daughter. "It's true, Gabi. I'm your PaPa." His voice held tenderness that made Maren's heart ache. He knelt and lifted Gabi's chin.

The child darted from the kitchen, leaving her PaPa on his knees.

"Liebling." Mrs. Brantenberg's call didn't stop her, and soon the child's footsteps on the stairs echoed throughout the house.

The man stood, his jaw slack.

Mrs. Brantenberg crossed her arms, rigid. "She is likely afraid of you. You look a fright, and you smell worse."

Maren glanced toward the kitchen doorway. When neither of them uttered a word or showed any signs of budging, Maren slipped out of the kitchen and up the wooden staircase to the first door on the left. She tapped on the closed door, then opened it.

"Gabi."

The child's sobs pierced her heart. She prayed for guidance and walked toward Gabi's bed. A little girl needed her PaPa. And unlike many fathers, Gabi's had returned from the war. So why had the child run from him? Gabi had told her more times than Maren could count that her PaPa would one day come home. Now that he had, his daughter lay on her bed, curled in a ball. The man did look like a bear just come out of hibernation, but Maren had rarely witnessed fear in Gabi. Not even when thunder rattled their bedroom windows and frayed Maren's nerves. Gabi only needed time to get to know her PaPa. But judging by Mrs. Brantenberg's cold reception of the man, he may not be here long enough.

Tears threatened to clog her throat, but Maren eased onto the edge of the bed and rested her hand on Gabi's quaking shoulder. "I am here, little one."

Clutching her cloth doll, Gabi looked at her. "My PaPa came back."

An ache gripped Maren's chest. "Yes." Remembering the comfort in her own mother's tender touch, she stroked the child's tear-dampened hair. "You said he would return, and he did."

Gabi scooted to the edge of the bed beside Maren, her legs dangling over the side.

"Are you not happy your PaPa is here?"

❦

His daughter's silence widened the ache in Woolly's chest. He'd failed Gretchen. She'd died giving him a daughter, and he'd walked away. He wasn't sure he could bear to stay, but he had to get to know Gabi. He drew in a deep breath and peeked into the room.

The young woman from the barn stroked his daughter's curls. "A lot of men went away to fight in the war. Many did not come back," she said.

"Like Miss Hattie's PaPa." Gabi's voice quivered, causing his chest to tighten. He'd heard about Mr. Pemberton, and thousands of others.

"Yes. But your PaPa came home to you. You cannot forgive him for leaving you?"

Gabi covered her face with her hands. "I c-cannot."

It wasn't his mother-in-law who would turn him away, but his own child. He'd been foolish to hope anyone could forgive him.

Her shoulders quaking, Gabi threw the doll on the floor, then buried her face in the woman's lap, sobbing. "He l-left 'cause of me. I killed my *Mutter*."

His insides ripping, Woolly rushed into the room and knelt on the rag rug at his daughter's knee. His hand trembling, he lifted her chin with his fingertip. Her moist blue eyes were heavy with sadness.

"Little one," he said, "you didn't kill your mother. It wasn't your fault she died. Your mama loved you very much." He patted the tears from her cheeks. "She would rub her big belly and sing to you. We both did."

"Mutter liked music?"

"Yes, very much." He swallowed hard against another painful memory. "God needed her in heaven. She couldn't stay with you. With us." He fought the lump forming in his throat. "She left you here as a good-bye gift."

Gabi's long lashes were clumped like new grass after a spring rain. "A gift from Mutter?"

He nodded. "Yes." Gretchen hadn't been given a choice in the matter. He had.

"Why did you leave me?"

He turned away from her pleading eyes. He'd been so shortsighted. Why had he abandoned his baby girl when she was all he had left?

"I was sad," he said. "I didn't think I could live here without your mother. I missed her so."

Miss Jensen slipped her arm behind Gabi and looked him in the eye. "But you were happy Gabi was born?"

"Yes! We…I wanted a baby girl who looked like her mother."

Gabi snuffled and peered at him. "I look like Mutter?"

"You have her sparkling blue eyes and her sweet nose." He tapped its rounded tip. "When she died, I was afraid I wouldn't be able to give you the care you needed. That's why I left you with Oma. And why I went to fight in the war. I knew she would take good care of you. But I never stopped missing you." He extended his free arm and his daughter fell against his chest, soothing the ache.

Miss Jensen brushed tears from her smooth face. "Oma is waiting."

He scarcely had time to stand before Gabi's small fingers wrapped around his. His daughter's tender touch weakened his knees as she pulled him toward the door.

At the top step, he glanced back at Miss Jensen, now an angel in his eyes. "Thank you."

He didn't deserve to feel this good.

3

Maren unfurled the napkin on her lap, then focused on the child seated across from her. Gabi's smile had no room to grow on her sweet little face.

While Woolly seated himself to her right, Maren contemplated the man's return to the farm. She didn't want to like the child's father. He had walked away from his newborn daughter. Away from his widowed mother-in-law. And so much bad had happened here since he left. His presence may not have changed the circumstances much for Mrs. Brantenberg, but she wouldn't have had to face it alone.

Woolly knew the farm. He belonged here with his family. Maren understood Mrs. Brantenberg's reserved reaction to his sudden homecoming, but still, she'd watched the man and his daughter find their way back to one another. Once his arm was healed he'd be of much greater help with the harvests than she would. And, with Gabi's father at her side, the little one would no longer require Maren's attention.

The fact remained that in his grief, he'd abandoned his mother-in-law...left her to mourn one loss atop another. Would Mrs. Brantenberg find it in her heart to forgive him and let him stay, or would she send him away?

Maren hoped he'd stay. For their sake, and for hers.

Woolly could very well be the answer to her prayers. His presence here would make leaving the farm easier, could free her to find a paying job in town. Allow her to dream anew of going home...to Denmark.

When Mrs. Brantenberg bowed her head, they all did the same. Thankfully, her blessing was brief. Maren set a hunk of hard bread on her plate, then handed the basket across to Mrs. Brantenberg.

"Butter for your bread, Miss Jensen?"

"Yes. Thank you." Maren reached for the edge of the bowl. Instead, her hand plopped into the middle of the soft, warm butter. She should have taken the time to focus her vision before reaching for the dish. But she had placed too much trust in her peripheral vision in candlelight. Embarrassment seared her ears.

Gabi giggled.

Mrs. Brantenberg clicked her tongue, silencing her granddaughter.

Maren wiped her hand on her napkin.

"PaPa, did you know that Miss Maren's eyes don't work right? She uses her hands to see."

She hadn't used her hands on purpose.

"I didn't know."

The man must think her an idiot. She didn't wish to know if he was staring at her, so she turned the other way.

When he brushed her forearm with the bowl, she focused her vision and scooped butter onto her plate and passed the bowl to Mrs. Brantenberg.

"Now I understand."

Her stomach soured. What exactly did the man think he understood? Losing his sight, not being able to see a sunset? Pressing her tongue behind her front teeth, Maren smeared butter on her roll, then willed her eyes to focus on his whiskered face.

"I'm sorry."

Now he was offering her condolences…pity? That was what drove Orvie away, wasn't it? Pity. She smeared butter on the bread's crusty surface. "It's not your fault I cannot see."

"No." He raised his coffee cup to his mouth. "I meant to say I'm sorry I thought you were…uh, a bit *touched*."

She straightened in the chair. "You thought *me* crazy?"

Woolly spooned potatoes onto his plate. "You could've told me."

"You were the intruder, sir. I was alone in a barn with a stranger, and you would have me say I am going blind?" She set the butter knife on her plate too loudly and took the potato pan from him. "You didn't tell me you belonged here."

"You and PaPa are like the barn cats." Gabi giggled.

"Liebling." Mrs. Brantenberg reached for her coffee cup. "Eat your supper."

"The cats sound like they are fighting when they play."

The man's chuckle stung Maren's ears. She had only just met him, and in little more than an hour the situation had gone from bad to good, then to worse. She stood and set her wadded napkin on the chair. "Pardon me. This evening belongs to family." And she had left what remained of hers in Denmark.

∞

Woolly stood. He couldn't scold his daughter for her embarrassing statement. It wasn't his place to reprimand her anyway. Not when he'd left her in his mother-in-law's care. Furthermore, Gabi had drawn her conclusion in innocence.

Mrs. Brantenberg tapped her mug with her fork. "I cannot abide wasted food."

The pink rounds on Miss Jensen's cheeks had spread and deepened into a strawberry red. She slid into her chair.

Woolly sat just as quickly. No need to vex his mother-in-law any further.

When Mother Brantenberg scooped a spoonful of cut-up schnitzel onto the bread in the center of Gabi's plate, his daughter picked up her fork and looked at him, a smile firmly planted on her sweet face. At least someone in the house was glad to see him.

Woolly bit through the crisp surface of the bread into the soft, aromatic center. He may not deserve Mother Brantenberg's home-cooked meal, but he intended to enjoy every bite nonetheless. Scooping potatoes onto his fork, he glanced sideways at Miss Jensen. The young woman sipping her water seemed thousands of miles away. He'd recognized the Danish accent. She was obviously unmarried and living here. He'd seen evidence of that in Gabi's bedchamber—a dressing gown in a size too generous for his daughter draped over a bedpost. Her understanding of English made it obvious her immigration hadn't been recent. Good chance she was one of the countless war widows. Probably answered to *Miss* because of her familiarity with Gabi and Mother Brantenberg. His guess was that her thoughts were of Denmark.

Woolly savored another bite of Mother Brantenberg's pork cutlet schnitzel, his mind whirling like windmill blades in a stiff breeze. The meal was as familiar as yesterday…as foreign as the unknown future.

Miss Jensen set her glass on the table, her brow creased. "Wherever will he sleep?"

Woolly straightened in the chair. He'd sleep anywhere but the cabin. He looked up at Mother Brantenberg. She was staring—not really at him, more like through him.

"I'd like to stay in the barn, if I may." He hadn't considered his mother-in-law would have someone here. Miss Jensen obviously lived in the house as part of their family. He was a man who'd come home to three females living in the house, and one of them was a single woman not related to him. A woman who assumed Mrs. Brantenberg would let him stay. He wasn't so sure.

Her voice devoid of sentiment, his mother-in-law spoke over the rim of her coffee mug. "As you wish."

"It stinks in the barn." Gabi pinched her rounded nose, then smiled at him. "But Snowflake is all woolly and warm, and she lets you snuggle."

He couldn't help but chuckle. Somehow his daughter had managed to maintain a measure of innocence in the madness of the past four years.

"Thank you." He'd happily spend the night in the barn. He'd seen the buckets and a wooden tub in there. He knew where to find the water pump, and he was well overdue for a bath.

"The Ransoms are gone." Mother Brantenberg stared at him, her gray eyes laced with sadness.

He nodded and set his fork down. "I stopped at the empty cabin when I first reached the property." His throat suddenly dry, he gripped his coffee cup.

"The bushwhackers came last year." Mother Brantenberg rolled her lips. "You weren't here. They drove the Ransoms away in the dark." Her voice quivered.

His stomach knotted. He had taken part in night raids. The memories of families being rousted heaped more self-loathing on him.

"I couldn't stop them." Her shoulders sagged.

His arms on the table, Woolly made himself look her in the eye. "I'm sorry."

So sorry, for more than he could ever say. For not listening to Gretchen. For his wife's death. For selfish grief. For war. And acts of war. For thinking he could escape the worst of the pain by leaving. And now he regretted his return. Understandably, his mother-in-law hadn't welcomed him home with open arms and even seemed sorry to see him. All he'd done was bring her anguish back to the surface.

Less than thirty minutes later, Woolly carried a pillow and a woolen blanket tucked under his sling. A lantern dangled from the other hand, flickering in the moonless night, casting dim light on the whitewashed barn. A swirl of memories sped his steps. Stealing kisses from Gretchen out behind the barn. Her PaPa catching them and making him muck out the corral right then, under the heat of a lecture. A June wedding under a canopy of oak leaves. Then came the vise he felt in his gut the night his wife died. The fear he felt when he was sent to Arizona Territory to quash the Indian uprisings. The image of the Apache girl about Gabi's age. Her black hair framed a face scarred by the horror of the raid on her village. On her family.

Woolly stepped into the muggy warmth of the barn and closed the door. The animals had bedded down for the night. The lantern illuminated the shovel Miss Jensen had wielded like a club when he'd startled her. The young woman had pluck. Had to have a hardy bit of it to cross the seas to America and work the farm, all the while losing her eyesight.

As he climbed the steps to the loft, new images filled his mind. A little girl with a big smile had hugged his neck, an aging woman who'd been like a mother to him served him a hot meal, and a woman who was going blind seemed able to see into his daughter's heart.

But was he home?

He would try to accept responsibility for his family, if Mother Brantenberg would give him the chance. He'd sat at the familiar dining table with the mother-in-law who once loved him and the daughter who never knew him. All of that was far more than he deserved.

∞

Maren lowered herself onto the edge of Gabi's bed, her mind filling with memories. The child's sobs, her PaPa rushing into the room and kneeling at her bedside. His declaration that his daughter had been a gift; that he and his wife sang to their unborn child.

Her thoughts turned to Orvie as she pressed her hand to her empty midsection. She scolded herself for dwelling on the past and expectations that would never be fulfilled. She'd not heard a word from Orvie in four years. Didn't even know if he still lived.

"Miss Maren?" Gabi pulled the quilt to her chin.

Maren brushed soft brown curls from Gabi's forehead, then willed her eyes to focus on the child's little round face. The lantern she had lit on the side table cast a golden light around bright blue eyes. "Yes, little one?"

Gabi worried her bottom lip. "Oma's nose was red, like when she's angry. Does she not like PaPa?"

Maren swallowed hard. To say the man hadn't received a warm welcome from Mrs. Brantenberg would be an understatement. An indication that she didn't like him. Not a suitable response to share with a four-year-old girl whose most fervent prayer had been answered. "Your Oma was surprised to see him. A lot of time has passed."

"Four years." Gabi pressed four fingertips to Maren's arm.

"Yes." Maren shifted, pressing her knee into the side of the horsehair mattress. "Your grandmother needs time to know how she feels." She tucked the cotton-edged quilt at Gabi's shoulders, hoping the action would tuck in the child's thoughts for the night as well.

"Will she let PaPa stay?"

Maren met Gabi's persistent gaze. "I don't know, little one," she said, "but tomorrow is a new day." Neither did she know if Woolly intended to stay.

A yawn bunched Gabi's cheeks. "Good night, Miss Maren."

Maren brushed her lips against Gabi's forehead and stood. "Sweet dreams."

Surely the child's dreams would be sweet, having been reunited with the father she had never met.

Maren whispered a prayer over Gabi and lifted the lantern off the table. A long list of questions circled her mind as she descended the staircase toward the kitchen. Dare she ask them?

Inside the kitchen, she hung the lantern on a hook and pulled a clean dishtowel from a shelf. She joined Mrs. Brantenberg at the cupboard. "She will sleep soon, if not already."

"*Danke.*" Mrs. Brantenberg handed her a wet bowl.

Crickets chirped outside the open window. The plow horse nickered at the corral fence. All of them much quieter than the question tugging at Gabi's heart and echoing in Maren's head. She dragged the towel through the inside of the bowl.

A plate slipped from Mrs. Brantenberg's hand and splashed into the dishpan. Instead of retrieving it, she looked at Maren, her lips pressed. "I should be thankful he is alive." The woman's words came out flat. "I should be happy Gabi has her PaPa."

But she wasn't?

"I am." Mrs. Brantenberg sighed and turned toward the night outside the window. "I want to be."

"God has given you the chance to be a family again." Even as she said it, Maren knew it wasn't the family any of them had imagined in the beginning. Mrs. Brantenberg didn't have her daughter back. Gabi didn't have the mother who had borne her. And Woolly was without the wife who had given him a beloved child.

"I loved him like my own son." Mrs. Brantenberg brushed wisps of gray hair from her face with wet hands. "I lost my dear husband Christoph, Gretchen, and Rutherford—all three. Gabi was all I had left."

Maren longed to say something to ease her employer's anguish. But if the right words existed, she surely wasn't acquainted with them. She had considered the newborn daughter without her father, but not the grandmother suddenly living without her daughter *and* without her son-in-law. With a baby to raise. Then her beloved friends and helpers had been run off under the cover of darkness. Mrs. Brantenberg had loved and lost so many. No wonder the man's abrupt return was causing the dear woman such tumult.

Swallowing regret for all of them, Maren added the bowl to the stack. "And now that he has returned?"

"I do not know what to think, or feel. Or if I even can." The widow handed Maren a wet coffee mug. "How could he have walked away? Tell me that."

Maren lifted her shoulders and let them fall. She didn't know what she would do in Mrs. Brantenberg's stead. If Orvie returned after four years with a change of heart, could she forgive him and utter their postponed vows?

"If he wants to stay, will you let him?"

The widow's chin quivered. "I should."

As Maren wrapped her towel around the cup, another question wrapped itself around her heart. If Mrs. Brantenberg didn't let Woolly stay, would he want to take his daughter with him?

4

Black feet bleeding and heart pounding, he ran as fast as he could through a dark forest. Dogs barked as shots rang out behind him. Children wailed. Tree limbs slapped his body, raising welts. Until…the crow of a rooster stopped him. Woke him.

Woolly bolted upright, his hands clasping the splintered edges of a cot. Sweat drenched his long johns. A nightmare, but different from all the others. He rubbed his eyes. Where was he? The deep breath he drew filled his nostrils with the pungent blend of hay and horse manure, and an even deeper realization dawned. He was in the barn on the Missouri farm, safe. Gabi was safe. Mother Brantenberg had survived the war.

He pulled his knees up and rested his elbows, cradling his head in his hands. The fighting may have ended, but the wounds had cut deep, leaving him to doubt they'd ever scar over.

⌘

In the corral an hour later, Woolly pulled a bristle brush through the old plow horse's mane. Dawn's first light sketched crisp shadows against the side of the barn. A robin trilled in the oak between the barn and the house. The very tree where he and Gretchen had carved their initials the day he'd asked her to marry him, six years ago. The same tree he'd sat under, praying while she lay dying...birthing his baby girl.

How could he have left sweet Gabi and his bereaved mother-in-law? And the Ransoms. Only God knew where they ended up. Were they even alive? If only he'd been here. He should've protected the women and families in his life.

Snorting, Duden stomped the ground near Woolly's foot. He jumped back, remembering the gelding's spirited response to having his mane brushed. That's all Woolly was doing too—snorting and kicking at the ground, and neither action brought him any closer to peace. "Whoa, boy." He patted the horse's withers and stroked his back. Woolly wanted to stay, to do what he could to make Mother Branten-berg's life easier. Although he knew words would never be enough, he needed to talk to her. But even if he could convince Mother Branten-berg to let him stay, with Miss Jensen living here, he held no hope of moving into the house with his family. As the horse calmed, so did he. Sleeping in the barn didn't matter, not if he was home to stay.

Setting the brush to the horse's tail, Woolly looked up in time to see Miss Jensen walking the path toward the barn. Her steps set at a snail's pace, the young woman looked neither left nor right, apparently focused solely on her destination. He thought to call out to her, but decided the distraction would likely not be welcomed.

❧

When Maren arrived in America, she was surprised to find that Thursday quickly became her favorite day of the week—the day the quilting circle met on the farm. Before immigrating, to her mother's dismay, Maren had little interest in textiles and could barely work a needle. But since her move to the farm, she'd come to cherish the company of women who gathered here for stitching and companionship.

This morning, Maren was intentionally running late. A man had slept in the barn, and it wouldn't have been proper for her to enter it in the dark. If at all. But she had morning chores and didn't wish to delay breakfast. The first rays of morning sun at her side, she stopped outside the open barn doors and poked her head inside. "Mr. Wainwright?"

No answer. She hadn't thought to look for the man outside.

Blinking and squinting to force her vision, Maren listened for any hint of his presence. Usually the sheep, cows, mules, and horses greeted her with impatient calls for breakfast. Not this morning. Instead, the sound of their chomping was nearly deafening. The feed had been dropped.

Maren reached to the hook for the egg basket and found it heavy, with nine eggs nestled inside. The bucket she kept by the hogs' grain bin was gone, and apparently Woolly was too. The milking bucket still sat empty outside the cow pen, so she grabbed it and the stool, settled beside Bootsie, and ran her hand down the cow's side to the udder. "Morning, girl."

The Jersey greeted her with the turning of her head. Hay stuck out of her mouth like uneven whiskers, and Maren couldn't help but giggle as she positioned the bucket. "I see you have been well fed this morning." She squeezed with one hand and then the other, creating a staccato rhythm with the milk spray. The man had certainly lightened her early morning workload. She could easily grow accustomed.

"Miss Jensen." The now-familiar voice filling the barn didn't startle her in the least.

Neither did the footfalls approaching the cow stall. "Miss Jensen, it is Woolly."

Maren angled toward the gate and willed her eyes to bring him into focus. Shafts of light spilling in through the gaps in the barn-boards spread like thin fingers across the barn. The sling was gone from his arm. "Good morning, Mr. Wainwright." He wore a yellow work shirt, and he had tamed his hair under his cap.

"It is a fine morning."

"Was it you who gathered the eggs and fed the animals?" Not that she didn't know the answer, but she didn't want to assume.

"I was pleased to help."

"Thank you." Bootsie shuddered, and Maren returned to her task under the old cow.

"I may not be able to mend fences or shore up the barn just yet, but I want to do more to help around here."

"So long as you do no further damage to your arm." Woolly obviously intended to stay. That meant Gabi would too. "In the old country, PaPa would have suggested a mint poultice." Her words followed the rhythm of the milk splashing into the bucket.

"My shoulder is better today. Thank you." He rested his elbows over the rail between them and looked at her. "Your chin? How is it faring?"

She resisted the impulse to touch it. "Slightly sore, but fine. Thank you."

"Mother Brantenberg wasn't pleased to see me. Do you think she'll let me stay?"

The milking rhythm continued. She wanted to tell Woolly that Mrs. Brantenberg had to let him stay, that he had to persevere until the widow softened toward him. She wanted to tell him that what he did—whether he stayed or left—could change the course of her life.

"I don't know." And, even if she did, it wasn't her place to second-guess the woman who had been so kind to her. Like a mother, in many ways.

Maren stilled her hands and looked up at him. He was staring at the far wall, looking broken in spirit. "You want to stay?"

When Bootsie swung her head, Maren had to regain her balance on the stool.

Woolly burst out with a laugh. "She doesn't appreciate the distraction."

Shaking her head, Maren resumed her task. She understood the cow's frustration and lack of patience. She also agreed that the man was distracting.

"To answer your question…yes, I want to stay." He slid his worn boot onto the lower rail. "I want to be a father to Gabi, or at least try."

"Then you must persuade her that you belong here."

"Yes ma'am."

Mrs. Brantenberg had a good heart, if he had the patience to wait for her to come around.

Finished with the milking, Maren carefully lifted the bucket from under the cow and stood. She hung the stool on a hook, then walked to the open stall gate, the gate where Woolly now stood. He smelled of soap and fresh hay instead of years on the road, and he'd trimmed his beard.

"How long ago did you arrive from Denmark?"

"I left there nigh onto four years ago." And she would rather not say why. She stepped through the gate and closed it.

"A corporal I met had come from Denmark."

Orvie Christensen? She wanted to ask, but what good would it do her to know? Even if he were alive, he didn't want her. If he did, he would've married her...come home to her.

Woolly held his hand out to her. "May I take that inside for you?"

"Yes, of course. Thank you." In the exchange of the milk bucket his hand brushed hers, sending a shiver up her cotton-clad spine.

At the barn door, Maren lifted the basket of eggs off the hook and stepped out into the morning sunlight. Curious, she looked at the man beside her. She knew what it was like to be away from home for four years and had thought a lot about what it would be like to return. That's what Woolly had done. "How does it feel to be home?"

He removed his cap, then set it back on his head. "Like I'm waking up from a long, restless sleep. A sleep filled with night terrors."

Maren slowed her steps. The man could be intense, and she didn't know how to talk to him. His experiences in battle would no doubt make her struggles here seem small.

"The first of this year, the army sent me to Arizona Territory to protect the settlers from Cochise and the Chiricahua Apaches. The warriors had burned out a settlers' camp." He scrubbed his cheek. "The whole tribe paid the price. A little girl lost her parents and two brothers in the raid." He blew out a deep breath. "I was at the creek when I heard whimpering. The child, about Gabi's age, cowered in the reeds." Another deep breath, this one accompanied by a fluttering exhale. "Her family got killed in the raid ordered by our lieutenant."

Maren blinked back tears. "That poor girl." *And this poor man.* He knew personal sorrow in losing his wife and had seen even more pain in two different wars.

"My child still had a father, and she needed me." His voice cracked. "And I didn't know it at the time, but I needed her."

"You were blinded by your grief."

He nodded, bouncing a brown curl at his forehead. "I was."

Although the sun had risen bright this morning, the night's chill persisted. Maren pulled her cape tight. "Family is important."

"You left your family in Denmark?"

"My mother, my older sister, Brigitte, and my younger brother, Erik."

"Is it too personal for me to ask why?"

"I left Denmark because of a letter." *And because of a longing for a family of my own.*

Maren stilled her steps and met the man's gaze. "You mentioned you met a corporal from Denmark."

"I did. An Orvie Christensen. Said he lived here in Saint Charles for a short while."

Maren nodded, swallowing the bitter bite of regret. "Mr. Orvie Christensen's uncle lived in Silkeborg and was a carpentry apprentice with my PaPa."

"You knew the corporal?"

She drew in a deep breath. She'd already said too much, but felt compelled to answer the question arching Woolly's eyebrows. "I met him here, after I arrived in America." She drew in a deep breath. "When PaPa died, we all did our best, but my little brother was sick and we couldn't keep the farm. Orvie Christensen heard about our fate and sent me a letter. He was ready to marry, and he sent money for my passage."

Maren climbed the steps to the porch and paused outside the kitchen door.

He glanced down at her empty ring finger. "You married him?"

She slowly shook her head. "I was a mail-order bride who arrived with postage due. My blindness worsened during the trip and when I told Orvie, he couldn't—"

"See past his own nose?"

She nodded and covered her mouth, but a giggle still escaped.

Orvie Christensen had never done her chores. Nor had he ever made her laugh. Woolly was a good man, who belonged in the house with his family.

"I worked as a nanny for a family in Saint Peters until they gave up on trying to subsist in battle-torn Missouri during the war and returned to Philadelphia. That's when Johann Heinrich at the dry goods store talked to Mrs. Brantenberg, and she took me in to help with Gabi and the farm."

"She'd already lost the Ransoms?"

"Yes. The month before."

"She's a good woman."

"Yes." Like a mother, at times.

Smiling, Woolly held the kitchen door open for her.

Mrs. Brantenberg slid a ham butt into the oven, then turned as they entered the kitchen. "I see you found him."

"Yes, uh—"

"I was in the corral, brushing the plow horse."

"He had fed the animals and collected the eggs."

"Oh?" Mrs. Brantenberg's voice carried surprise...or was it satisfaction?

As Maren and Woolly set the basket and bucket on the worktable under the window, he leaned toward her, mere inches from her ear. "Orvie's loss. The man is a fool."

At a loss for words, she moistened her lips. Woolly Rutherford was quite likable. She turned toward the table and silently counted the place settings. Four.

He was staying, at least through breakfast.

5

Breathing in the rich aroma of fresh baked *Milchbrötchen*, Emilie Heinrich pulled her favorite teapot from the kitchen shelf in the upstairs apartment over their dry goods and grocery store. The sausage was cooked and on the table. Another two minutes and the breakfast rolls would be ready as well. Just in time for PaPa's timely morning appearance. She poured steaming water over imported Earl Grey. In Saint Charles's German community, a tea drinker was a rarity. Among Germans anywhere, actually, but Emilie preferred the soothing taste of tea to the stout coffee boiling on the stove.

Emilie was sliding the pan of bread from the oven when she heard the door click open on PaPa's bedchamber. At six feet tall, he was in the habit of ducking his balding head on his way under the door frame, even though here he had several inches of clearance. *"Guten Morgen, Tochter!"*

"Guten Morgen, PaPa. It is a good morning." Thursday—Mrs. Brantenberg's quilting circle day. Emilie filled his favorite mug with coffee, then carried it and the bread rolls to the table.

PaPa took the mug from her and planted a soft kiss on her forehead before seating himself.

She draped a small cheesecloth square over her cup and poured tea through it, then carried her cup to the table and slid onto the chair opposite him. Wearing his white tucked blouse under a red dragon vest, Johann Hermann Heinrich was one of the most dapper men on Main Street, and one with a reputation for kindness and fairness. Yet he remained alone, with only her to care for him. Not that she minded. She loved him and had a full life caring for their household and working in the store. She'd never understand why her mother left him, and for a steamboat captain, no less. At least that's what she'd heard. She was only two when it happened.

PaPa sniffed the fragrant air, pulling her thoughts back into the present. *"Hunger ist der beste Koch."*

Hunger is the best cook.

"And my stomach and your good cooking have the timing down to a science."

Nodding, Emilie pulled the napkin from her plate and spread it on her lap.

After a brief prayer, PaPa gulped coffee and set two breakfast rolls on his plate.

Emilie added a sausage to her own plate, then handed him the dish.

"It's Thursday." He stabbed a thick sausage with his fork. "Are you going out to Mrs. Brantenberg's farm today?"

Emilie broke open a roll, feeling its warm steamy freshness on her face. "I'd like to, if you're sure you don't need me in the store."

He slathered apple butter on his bread. "We're not expecting any deliveries today, are we?"

"Mr. McFarland said it would be tomorrow."

"Then I should do fine." He stuffed the sausage into the roll and raised it to his mouth. "You'll tell the widow about that new cloth we got in Monday?"

"I will."

Swallowing a big bite, he glanced at the mantel clock. "I think it's time I hire some help."

"Help?" It'd always been just the two of them. "For the store?"

"Yes. You're a young lady now, and you've been working too hard." He looked at the stove, then toward the door that opened up to the staircase. "It's time I freed you up for other pursuits."

Other pursuits? Her eighteenth birthday was only a couple of months away. He couldn't be thinking what she thought he was thinking, could he? While many of her girlfriends from school and church were being courted and wooed, she'd kept too busy for such nonsense. And when such thoughts did tug at her, she dismissed them, knowing PaPa couldn't manage without her help. Thinking about his welfare was what kept her levelheaded about any romantic notions.

"You need to think about your future."

"My future?" She'd assumed her future would look much the same as her past and present...living here, cooking and cleaning, working in the store, and managing the record books.

"Yesterday, when I went to the bank..."

Emilie nodded, her mind racing. If he did hire help, perhaps she could consider adding a social aspect to her life. Something besides Mrs. Brantenberg's quilting circle. Not that men were lined up to court her. But it would be nice to—

"I went to Lindenwood Female College."

"What a good idea!" She reached for her teacup. "Making a friendly sales call now and then is smart business."

He smoothed the tails hanging from his tight bow tie. "I spoke with President Barbour. We both agreed that you'd be a valuable asset to the growing student body."

Emilie sprayed tea into her hand. Wiping her hands on her napkin, she peered up at her father. "That's the future you were talking about?"

Nodding, he poked the last bite of bread and sausage into his mouth.

"You want me to go to college?"

"You're already a smart young woman. But with the higher education Mrs. Sibley's school offers, well, there would be no limit to what you could do." His smile didn't quite reach his blue eyes.

She knew how to order inventory, check in orders, barter for garden vegetables and fresh eggs, and keep an accurate ledger. What else did she need to know? Emilie stood and carried his empty cup to the stove. Her father wasn't thinking about anything even remotely close to what she was thinking. If she had her way, she'd live on a farm...like Mrs. Brantenberg's. "I have much too much to do to add one more requirement to my calendar."

"That's precisely why I plan to hire help." PaPa reached over and pulled a booklet out of a drawer in the sideboard. He handed it to her then reached for his full cup. "The entrance examination on September 21 is simply a formality."

Emilie drew in a deep breath. "I'll look at this when I return from the farm this afternoon."

"You're riding out with the Pemberton women?"

"Yes. Hattie and her mother should be here any minute." She stacked their empty plates and carried them to the cupboard.

"I had best open up." Standing, he gulped his second cup of coffee.

"I'll clean up and be right down."

When he pulled his apron from a hook and closed the door behind him, Emilie stared at the table.

Mrs. Pemberton lost her husband in the war; Hattie, her father. Emilie knew she had a lot to be thankful for. And she was. Her own father was one of the few men able to remain in Saint Charles without dire consequences. But what made PaPa think a female college was the best thing for her? Now or for the future?

Woolly drove Mother Brantenberg's wagon into town just as shopkeepers set out their wares and flipped the signs on their doors, showing they were open for business. He liked Saint Charles. It, too, had been marked by the ravages of war. Shops owned by Southern sympathizers lay plundered and empty, and empty lots marked the former locations of their homes. But the city hadn't lost its quaint charm…tree-lined streets, brick buildings with white gingerbread trim, and cobblestone sidewalks. Martial law was in effect, but it didn't seem to have dampened the spirit of the townspeople.

He pulled Mother Brantenberg's horses to a stop in front of Higgins Lumbermill and stepped down from the wagon. Thanks to his bum shoulder, he couldn't start the work on the fence or the barn yet. But he *could* stock up on the necessary supplies and have them at the ready. Perhaps that would help his mother-in-law see that he was serious about staying, and that he intended to earn his keep.

"Woolly? Woolly Wainwright, is that you?"

Removing his hat, Woolly turned toward the female voice approaching from behind. At the sight of her, he gulped hard. He hadn't seen Mary Alice Brenner in more than four years. Not since—

"It *is* you!" Gretchen's best friend stood in front of him, a small child attached at each hand and her middle swollen as Gretchen's was toward the end. Tears filled her eyes. "I was so sorry. I still miss her terribly."

His lips pressed against a wall of his own emotions, Woolly nodded and looked at the children. A boy and a girl, close to Gabi's age. "Twins?"

"Yes. Thomas and Alice." A shadow crossed Mary Alice's round face. "Born that next week."

The week after Gretchen died. He knew what she meant. He'd measured most everything in accordance with his life with Gretchen and his life without her.

"I didn't know you were in town. If you were even alive." She met his gaze, her brown eyes still rimmed with tears. "I quit asking Mrs. Brantenberg about you."

"I should've written."

Her nod was curt. "Yes. She was worried sick… We all were." She glanced at the horses, the same ones Mrs. Brantenberg had when he'd first met Gretchen. "You're back out at the farm?"

"Yes." But he couldn't say for how long. "And Tom, he's well?"

Nodding, she glanced down at her swollen belly. "He came home a couple of months before Lee signed."

Woolly's ears warmed in a blush. A poignant memory pricked his heart, and he looked away.

"Have you heard the talk about a wagon company goin' west out of Saint Charles?"

He shook his head. "But I just got back yesterday, and this is my first trip into town."

"Tom heard there's a guy comin' to lead a wagon train to California in the spring."

Another memory clamped his throat. When they first married, he and Gretchen talked about going west.

"We're planning to go."

"The baby?"

"Will be several months old by then."

Things don't always happen the way they should. Keeping the cynicism to himself, Woolly glanced at the giant wheel sticking out of the side of the mill, spinning away under the force of the creek water.

"Tom plans on homesteading in the San Joaquin Valley. Says there's nothing but miles and miles of fertile farmland with plenty of water and mild winters." Mary Alice blew a sprig of hair away from her eye. "Maybe you should think about it. You and Gabi and Mrs. Brantenberg."

His mother-in-law couldn't look him in the eye and was barely able to speak to him. He didn't know if she'd even let him stay. He didn't dare bring up going anywhere else, but he nodded anyway.

The twins squirmed and Mary Alice looked him in the eye. "I'm glad you survived too, and happy to see you."

"Thank you."

"I best get on with my shopping."

He nodded. "Tell Tom I said hello."

When she toddled off with the children in tow, Woolly strolled around the building and through the yard stacked with fresh-cut lumber. He breathed in the sweet scent of pine and the rich aroma of hardwoods. It'd feel good to have a hammer in his hand and be able to fix something. Even if it was only a fence or a barn door.

"Why, if it isn't Woolly Wainwright come home." Matthew Higgins took quick strides toward him and stuck out his meaty arm for a handshake.

"Hello, Matthew. Good to see a familiar face." He and Christoph Brantenberg had bought more than one wagon load of lumber and cut trim from the man in those first years.

Twenty minutes later, after greetings and reports to Matthew Higgins and a couple of customers, Woolly stood in front of a bunk of pine board and looked up at the burly owner.

Matthew studied the sawdust-packed floor, his mouth twisted.

"Is there a problem? I'm not in a rush. If you have someone else needin' it, I—"

"It's not that." He cleared his throat. "I'll need cash."

Woolly's spine straightened. Earlier in their conversation, he'd seen Matthew sell a smaller order on credit to another farmer and bundles of stakes to a vineyard owner with nothing but a signature. He hated to admit it, but it did make sense that folks would either pity him or distrust his honor. After all, he had left his newborn daughter with a grandmother mourning the loss of her own daughter.

He drew in a deep breath. "I'm buying the supplies for the farm. Mrs. Elsa Brantenberg's farm. She has an account."

Matthew looked at the empty space around them, then leaned forward. "Not anymore, I'm afraid," he said, his voice just above a whisper. "I'm sorry. But I have my own accounts around town to settle, and I need to know I have the money to pay my own debts."

"She hasn't been paying her bills?"

Matthew shook his head. "Not here, anyways."

He'd just bought gifts at the dry goods store, and Heinrich hadn't mentioned anything about Mother Brantenberg failing to pay her debt in his store. Of course, Elsa and Johann's history dated back thirty years to their school days in Germany. Best of friends, he wouldn't refuse her credit.

No wonder Mother Brantenberg hadn't welcomed him home. He'd already cost her too much.

6

Every time the ladies take too long to get here." Little Gabi sat on a stool in the kitchen, her arms crossed and a pout on her cherubic face.

Maren pulled a tray of almond paste cookies from the oven. "I agree, little one." She, too, looked forward to the Thursday gatherings at the farm. Her friends Hattie Pemberton and Emilie Heinrich, who lived in town, would be arriving soon. Hattie had a knack for delivering local news with flair, but this week the big news was right there on the farm. Or would be when Woolly returned from town. Maren set the tray of cookies on the cooling shelf at the open window, then wiped perspiration from the back of her neck.

At the sound of a wagon rumbling up the road, Maren removed her apron and Gabi scrambled off the stool. Catching up to the child at the front door, Maren breathed in the sweet scent of the geraniums that hung in baskets from each corner above the porch. With all the work to be done, she hadn't spent much time enjoying the porch. She glanced to the right, toward the barn, remembering the gift of Woolly's help with her chores that morning.

"Orvie's loss. The man is a fool."

Woolly's statements had been so matter-of-fact, and spoken so closely she had felt his breath on her ear. Then following a quiet breakfast, he'd left toward town with the wagon.

Jewell Rafferty's wagon was the first to roll to a stop at the far trough, outside the barn. Jewell's two daughters and her son scrambled over the tailgate, and Gabi ran to greet them. An unfamiliar young woman, who had been seated beside Jewell, carefully placed her feet over the side plank and onto the wheel spokes.

Mrs. Brantenberg stepped out of the barn, her arms full of hay. *"Herzliche Grüße."* The widow flung hay on the ground in front of the dapple gray.

"Thank you. Warm greetings to you as well. It's good to be here." Jewell wrapped the reins over the hitching rail and stepped into Mrs. Brantenberg's hug. The older woman viewed an embrace as the fee for membership into the quilting circle. Mrs. Brantenberg was fond of saying hugs were an important part of binding their hearts together.

Jewell turned toward her guest. "This is my sister from Pennsylvania, Mrs. Caroline Milburn."

As soon as Jewell made the introductions, Maren remembered having heard about Caroline Milburn last month in the circle. Mrs. Brantenberg had been praying for the young woman...they all had. She looked to be about Maren's age, twenty-one or close to it.

Maren decided to leave the first hug to Mrs. Brantenberg. "Welcome, Mrs. Milburn."

"It's a pleasure." The newcomer's voice sounded small. "Please, call me Caroline."

Mrs. Brantenberg gave Caroline her welcoming hug. "Do you quilt, dear?"

"No ma'am. Jewell spent more time in the house than I did as a girl."

Giving the pump a few quick strokes, Maren added more water to the trough. "Mrs. Brantenberg is a good teacher."

Caroline adjusted the bonnet on the pile of red curls swept back into a loose bun at her neck. Maren wanted to tell the young woman they were praying for her...for her husband, but instead she followed Mrs. Brantenberg's lead and kept silent about it. They would give Caroline a chance to get used to all the new faces.

When two more wagons rolled up the road, Maren went to the barn and returned with armfuls of hay. Hattie Pemberton drove the lead wagon, with Emilie seated between her and Mrs. Pemberton. The elder woman still wore her mourning bonnet.

"Maren!" Hattie stepped down from the wagon first. A simple summer bonnet was never enough to suit the fifteen-year-old. Not when she had her deceased grandmother's hatboxes to draw from. Today, Hattie wore a bright-green straw hat with a brim that bounced out past her shoulders, while a train of lace and ribbons trailed her back.

Emilie, wearing a simple skirt and shirtwaist with a calico bonnet, stepped down and offered her hand to help Mrs. Pemberton to the ground.

Maren greeted her friends with her own hugs, taking care not to collide with Hattie's bonnet. The Beck women arrived last. The elder Mrs. Beck sat beside Mrs. Webber up front. When the surrey came to a stop, Mrs. Lorelei Beck climbed down from the backseat. The senior ladies took a bit longer to step down, backing down the proper metal steps. After greetings and hugs all around, Maren gave each of the horses something to nibble and made sure they had plenty of water, then the parade of women made their way to the house.

Within a few minutes, all introductions seen to, Mrs. Brantenberg settled into a caned rocker by the window in the sitting room. A Hexagon Flowers quilting top draped her lap and spilled onto the braided-rag rug at her feet. Maren sat in a wooden armchair on the other side of Jewell and Caroline, thumbing through a stack of colorful squares.

Mrs. Brantenberg folded her hands and looked across the room to where Hattie smoothed an appliqué onto a block. "Hattie, this week, I do believe it is your place to ask the good Lord's blessing upon our time together."

"Yes ma'am." Hattie played with a brown curl at her shoulder.

Mrs. Brantenberg folded her hands and bowed her head. "Remember to thank the Lord our God for our newest member, dear."

The activity in the room stilled. Without being too obvious, Maren tried to sneak a glance at Caroline Milburn. The newcomer sat on a sofa beside her sister Jewell, a Double Hourglass quilting top spread over their laps.

At the conclusion of Hattie's uncharacteristically brief prayer, Caroline pressed a handkerchief to her face.

Mrs. Brantenberg lifted her head. "We've all been praying for you."

Maren nodded along with the other women.

Caroline sniffled. "I shouldn't have come."

"*Unsinnig.*" Mrs. Brantenberg wagged her finger. "That's nonsensical. You are among friends here."

Jewell captured her sister's hand. "I thought it would be good for her."

"You received word?" Mrs. Pemberton's voice was flat.

The newcomer shook her head, her lips pressed, taking in a quivering breath.

The poor woman hadn't heard from her husband, Colonel Milburn, in the four months that had passed since the South surrendered.

"It can take a man awhile to travel if he was deep in the South," Mrs. Brantenberg said, her tone as calming as a mother's song. "And some stayed on to fight in the Indian wars."

Caroline shook her head. "The last word from him"—her words were slow and heavily weighted—"his regiment was being sent to Georgia."

"To one of the last battles?" Mrs. Pemberton reached up and pressed her mourning bonnet against her cheek.

Mrs. Brantenberg looked at Caroline. "You've written to the Department of War?"

"In June, I did. They haven't responded." Caroline worried the handkerchief on her lap. "I couldn't bear to be alone any longer, so I came to Saint Charles. I should've stayed in Philadelphia."

Maren brushed a tear from her own face. Most of the women in the circle were doing the same thing, or shuffling and clearing their throats. Hattie lost her father to the war. Jewell's husband had returned missing a leg. And now Colonel Milburn hadn't come home at all. Mrs. Brantenberg was one of the more fortunate ones—her son-in-law had survived the war and returned home yesterday.

"Here, in this quilting circle, none of us are alone." Mrs. Brantenberg pulled thread through a needle. "Not in our sorrows, nor in our triumphs."

"While you are waiting for word, there is still hope that he is alive." Mrs. Webber had lost her husband early in the war. In the time since, she'd been a comfort to several widows in town.

Mrs. Brantenberg shifted the quilt top on her lap to get to the square at hand. "We will wait with you and continue to pray for his safe return."

The word *continue* struck Maren. Hattie had told her about praying with Mrs. Brantenberg for Mr. Wainwright's return, but Maren hadn't seen any evidence while she was living on the farm that those prayers had continued. She also noticed there had been no mention to the quilting circle so far of the prodigal son-in-law.

Emilie turned squares to make a block for the Shoo-Fly baby quilt she was making. "I saw Mary Alice in the store yesterday. She said she was seein' the doctor this morning. Probably won't be comin' out until after the baby's born, which is why I'm working on the quilt for her baby today. That, and soon I won't have much time for it." She sighed, looking at Maren. "I don't know how often I'll get to be here. If at all."

"Is it the store?" Hope rose in Maren. "Business is booming again?" Perhaps now there would be work enough for her in town.

"Business is good. But my father has decided I should go to college."

"College?"

"Lindenwood." Emilie pulled her needle high, setting her start-stitch.

"I've heard it's a wonderful school." Lorelei Beck folded her hands on the pile of fabric on her lap. "As a matter of fact, I wanted to go to the female college before I met Arvin." She smiled at her mother-in-law.

"Gretchen"—Mrs. Brantenberg looked at Caroline—"my daughter, gone to be with the Lord, was part of Mary Sibley's book club."

Emilie nodded. "Well, PaPa thinks higher education is the answer for my future."

"Your father doesn't want to give you in marriage?" Hattie's question hung silent in the air.

"He didn't say that in so many words, but he's keeping me busy enough that—" Emilie gulped. She'd been so thoughtless grumbling about her father when Hattie had recently buried hers. "I'm sorry. This must be hard for you to talk about. Fathers and daughters."

Hattie shook her head, biting her upper lip. Something she did when fighting emotion. "We've all lost someone, if not to the war, to... something else. I'm glad you have your father. Mine started early talking about the day I'd find a young man who had a house big enough for all the hats Granny gave me." Hattie looked behind her at the hall tree where her chic hat hung. "I was only thirteen."

Mrs. Pemberton was the first to laugh with her daughter. "I'd forgotten about that." She held her hand to her mouth. "But she's right. He objected to having to house all of his mother's hats when she came to live with us." Another laugh. "I think she gave them all to Hattie out of spite."

Maren laughed, seeing that even Caroline Milburn had joined in.

The laugh felt good. And her friend Hattie certainly had a gift—for gab, Mrs. Brantenberg would say, but also for mirth.

"And I think it's time we change our topic," Hattie said, feigning frustration. "Since we recently sent off that bundle of quilts to the army hospital, I wanted to propose that our next project be making quilts for the new mental hospital." She looked at Mrs. Brantenberg, who nodded. "Mother and I have been reading about all the good work they're doing for those suffering such illness. Not all are as fortunate as Oliver Rengler to have a brother like Owen to look after him."

Emilie held up her hand. "I'll make a Scrap Squares quilt."

"You can count on me for a Log Cabin quilt." Mrs. Pemberton reached for another block from the table beside her.

"Wonderful!" Hattie said. "Mother's already working on a Soldier's Cot quilt for the hospital, and I'll make a One Patch."

Maren had just opened her mouth to chime in when Gabi rushed into the sitting room. "Excuse, Oma." Leaning on the arm of Mrs. Brantenberg's rocker, Gabi glanced toward the children wiggling in the doorway. "When will PaPa bring your wagon back?"

At the reference to Woolly, Mrs. Brantenberg stilled her needle and bent toward the child. "He didn't say when." She fluttered her hand like a bird wing, shooing the girl. "Why don't you children get the wheelbarrow out of the barn and fill it with kindling?"

Gabi spun toward the other children. "We can see who will find the most."

"Gabi's father is in town?" Hattie jerked toward Maren. "Our town?"

Maren nodded.

"Elsa?" Mrs. Webber fairly shouted. "Whatever were you saving such wonderful news for?"

"For my turn." Mrs. Brantenberg slanted a glance toward Caroline. It made sense that she didn't want to share such information when Jewell's poor sister was still waiting for news.

"Well, consider it your turn."

Their circle leader clasped her hands on her lap. "It's true that Rutherford—many of you know him as Woolly—has returned. Gabi's father is back."

A shiver raced up Maren's spine. *Returned. Back.* But was Woolly *home*? Mrs. Brantenberg hadn't used that word. A mindful decision or a mere omission?

"This is wonderful!" Jewell lifted her needle in the air, pointing it at her sister. "It renews my hope that Phillip is still on his way home to you."

Caroline nodded. "I hope so. And I'm happy for you and your family."

"His return is an answer to little Gabi's prayers, and mine." Hattie's voice quivered. "When did this happen?"

"Yesterday afternoon...in time for supper." Mrs. Brantenberg's voice was as devoid of emotion as her expression. "Rutherford has gone to town today. I'm not sure when he'll be back."

Back. Again, she hadn't said *when he'll be home.* The word choice had been intentional. Mrs. Brantenberg no longer considered the farm his home.

And if he didn't stay, Maren had little hope of ever seeing her homeland again.

7

A snort startled Woolly, and he opened his eyes under a canopy of green leaves. One of the two horses tied to an oak branch offered another snort.

Woolly sat in the bed of the wagon, surrounded by stacks of boards, a barrel of nails, and flour sacks. How long had he slept? The memories of his visit with Miss Jensen early that morning and seeing Mary Alice Brenner in front of the lumber mill began clearing the cobwebs from his mind. Stretching, he realized he should've left his arm in the sling a bit longer—it might have kept him from doing too much with his wrenched shoulder while he was in town. He'd best get back to the farm while there was still light enough for the horses to find their way home.

He untethered Boone and Duden, backed them up to the wagon's doubletree, and hooked the traces. Although he'd rather live and work on the farm and be close to Gabi, his mother-in-law's silence made it clear she didn't want him there. He'd gone into town to look for employment, but with so many former slaves flooding the workforce here, there wasn't much work available for him.

Thankfully, when he'd mentioned going into town to get supplies, Mother Brantenberg offered him the use of the wagon if he'd pick up a few supplies for her. He deserved the cold shoulder she'd turned his way, and if all she could offer him was the treatment of an employee, that would have to do.

Woolly goaded the horses onto the main road, and the wagon rose out of the bottomlands, through the stands of birch and sycamore trees lining the small German family farms common to the area. Some farms still had a look of abandonment and disrepair, but most showed signs of a new postwar hope and vitality. He remembered the first time he'd made this trip from town. He'd stepped off a steamboat in Saint Charles and walked into Mr. Johann Heinrich's dry goods store looking for work. He had done farm work for his folks growing up in Virginia, and that's all he knew. Johann told him of Christoph Brantenberg who was looking to hire a farmhand and sent him this direction. That June day, he'd found work and met his future bride.

This trip he had a lot at stake—a future with his daughter, his gift from Gretchen. He was rehearsing what he'd say to his mother-in-law as her apple orchard came into view. At the intersection, he reined the horses onto Brantenberg Lane. The now-empty log cabin he and Gretchen had lived in sat at the corner of the Brantenberg property. The day he left for the war, he'd hired George Ransom, a freedman up from Mississippi, to work the farm. And now the family was gone, chased away by raiders.

It hadn't taken long for the cabin to sag. The roof probably wouldn't make it through the winter, and it was in better shape than most of the farm.

Thinking about what Mary Alice had said about the land in California, he had a notion to go west in the spring. But now wasn't the time to entertain such thoughts.

When he glimpsed Mother Brantenberg walking to the barn, Woolly's pulse quickened. Fortunately, the horses were anxious to be home and sped their gait. He parked the wagon beside the barn and hopped down from the seat. He'd unload it later.

Before he reached the barn door, Mother Brantenberg stepped back outside, swinging a bucket. Her wooden work shoes pounding the dirt path, she marched past him to the watering trough outside the corral.

Woolly walked up beside her. "The place needs some repairs. I purchased some supplies." He chose not to mention the conversation with Higgins about her financial state.

Mother Brantenberg glanced at the wagon. "Lumber." Her gray eyebrows arched. "Higgins gave you credit?"

"I used money I saved from the army." That he should've been sending home to her. "I want to help around here."

She scooped water from the trough and poured it over the pump head, then hung the pail on the spigot and began to pump the handle.

He removed his cap, praying for the right words.

She stilled her arm and the flow of water tapered to a drip. Her lips pressed, she peered at him. "Did you expect a hero's welcome?"

"No ma'am." He drew in a deep breath. "I didn't know what to expect."

Her jaw set, Mother Brantenberg turned toward the vegetable garden.

If a soft answer turned away wrath, what then of no answer? Even if Mother Brantenberg's silence didn't necessarily hold wrath, it knotted his stomach. But his mother-in-law had never been one to rush her words. She'd once said that while some folks liked to chase their words about a room, she preferred to hold them close until they were ready to be let loose. He should count her silence a blessing.

He rested his hand on her arm. "You have done very well by Gabi. Done for her what I couldn't do."

She looked at his hand, but didn't move away. Instead, she met his gaze, her eyelids wet. "You left us alone."

"My thoughts were filled only with my sadness."

"What of my thoughts?" Her voice cracked. "You weren't the only one who was sad."

She didn't want him here. And he couldn't help but wonder which would be the more difficult—staying, or leaving again.

Maren stood at the dry sink longer than was necessary to complete her chores. She'd scrubbed the top of the pine cupboard. She'd reorganized the shelves on either side of the window. She'd even washed the glass and straightened the gingham curtain. Woolly had finally returned from town. The reason for her sudden interest in the tidiness of the kitchen was out in the yard, and she had a perfect vantage point. She could make out his silhouette as he climbed from the wagon and approached Mrs. Brantenberg at the watering trough.

The prodigal son-in-law and the woman he left behind were finally talking. Maren would eavesdrop if she could, but they were across the yard. Sure as the day was hot and muggy, she desired to hear what Woolly had to say to his mother-in-law. And Mrs. Brantenberg, would she finally say more than five words to him? Would she listen?

"Miss Maren?" Gabi's sweet little voice startled her. The child stood at her side, stretching onto her tiptoes with her chin pushed up toward the window. "Is it my PaPa?"

Clearing her throat, Maren stepped back from the cupboard. "Yes. He returned from town with the supplies."

"I will go help him." Gabi turned to leave the room.

Maren caught the back of the child's dress and stopped her. "Wait, dear one! Your grandmother is at the pump with your PaPa, and they need time to talk."

Gabi nodded. "Oma has to let him stay." She swayed back and forth with her hands clasped at her chest as if in a prayer.

Maren agreed with that prayer.

"I waited and waited for my PaPa," Gabi said.

Maren stroked Gabi's soft brown curls. "I know. You did."

They both needed a distraction. "We have time to practice our music before dinner." She followed Gabi to the sitting room. The child pulled her recorder from a cloth sack on the piano and positioned her small hands on the holes in the wooden tube then wrapped her lips around the mouthpiece on the end. When Woolly could hear his daughter playing the recorder, he would certainly be proud of her. The thought transported Maren back to Copenhagen, to memories of evenings and Sundays gathered at a hearth in her family's farmhouse. *Moder,* brother, sister, and her singing while *Fader* played the flute. Yes, a girl needed her father, and Gabi was blessed to have hers here.

Swallowing the emotion that always came when she thought of family, Maren pulled her flute box from the bottom shelf of the bookcase. While Gabi blew into the recorder, practicing her chords, Maren pieced the wooden flute together and added the metal and ivory head. The instrument was one of the few items she'd brought with her from the old country.

∞

Woolly added the last of the pickets to the stack at the side of the barn. A list of things he should've said—meant to say—to Mother Brantenberg taunted him. But when he stood before her, words seemed an empty offering. She was right…he hadn't considered her sadness. Only his own.

He had already unhitched the horses and fed them. All that was left to do was to carry the flour sacks into the pantry and deliver Gabi's surprise. He patted his shirt pocket where he'd tucked the other two gifts. It wasn't proper that he give Miss Jensen a gift so soon. For now, he'd hang on to her surprise.

Music met him at the kitchen door. Pure notes from a flute and the hesitating notes of a recorder. Mother Brantenberg had marched off to the garden upon ending the conversation between them, and he'd just seen her bent over collecting squash and beans. The harmony must be coming from Miss Jensen and his daughter. Tears of joy pooled his eyes as he quickened his step to match his racing heartbeat. He didn't want to miss a note of the music.

He opened the door and quietly stepped into the kitchen. "Home, Sweet Home." A song he'd heard much on the marches from one battle to the next until it was banned from Union army camps. He'd recited the words to motivate himself as he became too weary to take the next step toward home. And now, though it seemed a bittersweet taunt, he'd never heard a melody so charming. He set the flour sacks on the table and followed the music on light steps. At the doorway to the sitting room, he paused and listened.

Mid pleasures and palaces though we may roam,
Be it ever so humble, there's no place like home.

Mid verse, the flute's music ceased. The recorder continued, at the hands of a less experienced musician.

"Mr. Wainwright?"

He peeked around the doorframe to see Miss Jensen standing beside the piano, a smile teasing her lips. He removed his hat and entered the warm room. "How did you know?"

"You were humming along."

He hadn't realized he was humming. Nor had he realized that Miss Jensen had developed especially keen hearing, no doubt due to her failing eyesight. A good thing to keep in mind.

He approached the piano where she and Gabi stood. "Please continue. It was beautiful."

The grandfather clock sprang to life, sounding its hourly cacophony, a wholly unwelcome intrusion.

Miss Jensen began pulling the flute apart. "I'm afraid I've lost track of time, and I'm due to start dinner."

"Does Oma still have music time after Sunday dinners?"

"We do. Yes." Gabi's smile brightened her eyes, the shade of bluebonnets.

"I'll look forward to it."

Miss Jensen placed the flute parts in the box, then looked at him. "You're staying then?"

"I plan to."

"I want you to." Gabi set her recorder on the piano bench and gave his leg a hug. "You have to."

Emotion clogging his throat, he reached into his pocket and felt around for the right gift. "Little one, I brought you something from town." He handed her the paper-wrapped present.

Her eyes widening, Gabi seated herself on the piano bench and unfolded the paper. "It's an ornament, Miss Maren!" The metal angel dangled from her finger as if it were hanging on the branch of a Christmas tree.

Miss Jensen stepped toward them and held the angel to her face. "It's lovely." She returned the ornament to Gabi then set her flute box on the bottom shelf of the bookcase.

"PaPa, did you bring Miss Maren a present too?"

"I did." The words were out before he could stop them.

"You did?" Miss Jensen blinked feverishly. Was she trying to focus her vision, or had he made her nervous? "You shouldn't have. I don't even know—"

"Yet, you've cared for my daughter very well." Woolly reached into his pocket and handed Miss Jensen the other paper-wrapped package.

Seated on the sofa, she carefully pulled the paper layers back as if it were an onion. Her lips pressed in concentration, she raised the gift into the light.

Gabi sat beside her. "It's a whistle," she said. "That's a lovely gift too."

Miss Jensen nodded while Woolly's insides tightened. He shouldn't be giving her gifts at all. She barely knew him.

He paced from the sofa to the piano and back. "I thought..." He stopped in front of her. "It's in case some lunk should come trespassing and startle you in the barn. I would come running."

Her face turning a lovely shade of pink, Miss Jensen draped the silver chain over her open hand. She clasped the copper whistle with her other hand and looked at him with a focused gaze that could pierce the darkest night.

Woolly watched as she lifted the chain over her head, the whistle resting on her lace bib. She held the copper trinket in her fingers. "Thank you. It is a lovely and...practical gift."

He hoped Miss Jensen never needed to use the whistle to summon help, but he felt better knowing she was wearing it around her neck.

Woolly smiled. "You're welcome." He had to find the strength and means to stay on the farm. Despite Mother Brantenberg's objections, she needed him. So did his daughter, and even Miss Jensen.

8

Sunday morning, Woolly drove the wagon to Immanuel Lutheran Church with Gabi singing a happy song beside him. The reins slack in his hand, he directed Boone and Duden onto Salt River Road. Behind him, Mother Brantenberg chattered to Miss Maren about various women in the quilting circle.

Seemed wrong not to go to church, but going didn't feel right either. At the breakfast table, Gabi asked if he was driving the wagon or if Oma would still drive. Naturally, they'd assumed he would join them. It's what the Brantenberg family did on Sundays, even when it no longer felt like a family.

Mother Brantenberg announced that he would certainly drive, and he couldn't say no. Didn't know if he could ever again deny either of them. After his mother-in-law stomped off to the garden Thursday evening, he was nudged by a sudden memory of her asking him to stay after Gretchen died. The very next day with nary a word, he'd left her alone with his newborn.

"Dear, are you all right?"

Certain the endearing term wasn't meant for him, Woolly glanced at the backseat. Mother Brantenberg rested her gloved hand on Miss Jensen's arm. Concern laced her gray eyes.

"Oh. Fine. Yes. Thank you." The tentativeness in the young woman's voice didn't pair well with her answer.

"You're as quiet as a church mouse. You were all through breakfast too."

"Just thinking, I suppose."

His guess was that her thoughts were of family and Denmark. Now that he was here to help Mother Brantenberg with the farm and Gabi, the young woman might think of returning home. And if she weren't here, his help—his presence—on the farm may be better appreciated.

Miss Jensen sighed. "Also, I'm enjoying the ride and the cooler temperatures. It'll make the wheat harvest a more pleasant task tomorrow."

"At the farm?"

"You didn't tell him?" Miss Maren's voice rose.

He looked at Mother Brantenberg.

"With your sore arm and all, I saw no point in it."

"So, it's my arm causing you to treat me like an outsider?"

No answer came. Even Gabi fell silent on the last mile into town.

As he reined the horses to a stop at a hitching rail in front of the brick church, he was glad to see that some things hadn't changed. Pastor Adam Barklage greeted parishioners at the doorway. His steps reluctant, Woolly wrapped the reins, then moved around the horses and offered his hand to Mother Brantenberg.

Her feet on the ground, his mother-in-law let go of his hand. "Pastor Barklage will be pleased to see you."

Woolly wasn't so sure. He had plenty disdain for himself. How would the pastor and his parishioners not feel the same? They all knew of his abandonment. He was swinging Gabi to the ground when he heard his name.

"Woolly Wainwright!" The pastor rushed down the steps toward him, his hair now thinning on top and gray at the temples. "Why, it is you! I'd heard you were back."

"Pastor Barklage." Woolly reached to shake his hand, but quickly became enveloped in a welcoming embrace.

"If you aren't a bright spot in a bleak aftermath." The pastor studied him from hair to shoe. "One of the few in our congregation who's returned in one piece." He clapped Woolly's shoulders and gave them a good shake. "Happy to have you home, son!"

Home. He wasn't sure which hurt the most—his shoulder or his heart.

"Thank you, sir." Woolly looked at Mother Brantenberg, the little girl at his side, and then at Miss Jensen. "It's good to be here." And on some levels—the shallow ones—it *was* good.

After a barrage of warm greetings from the other parishioners, Woolly told Gabi he'd wait for them outside. He watched as the ladies proceeded inside, chatting with the others. About halfway to the chancel, Miss Maren seated herself on the aisle next to Mother Brantenberg.

Sitting on the step just outside the door, he could hear a young woman's clear soprano voice rise and fall in "A mighty fortress is our God, a bulwark never failing." The hymn had played over and over in his mind on the battlefield, but never so sweetly as with a Danish accent.

∞⧓∞

After supper, Woolly's baritone laugh and Gabi's giggles wafted into the kitchen from the sitting room, stirring Maren's dreams of home and family. She dried a plate, her thoughts being swept back through time. In her first year here, she'd dreamed of Orvie Christensen changing his mind, returning from the fighting, and marrying her despite her failing sight. She wanted a husband…children of her own. But when Orvie walked away and never looked back, she let those hopes fall by the wayside. No man would want her now, and she couldn't blame them. All she wanted to do was to return to her mother and siblings…to be a part of their lives.

"You'll soon have those flowers rubbed clean off."

"Oh dear." Maren added the dry plate to the stack.

"Thinking again?"

"Yes ma'am, I am."

Mrs. Brantenberg handed her another wet plate. "I'm doing a lot of that myself lately."

"Your son-in-law coming home has stirred your thoughts, I'm sure."

"Most of them memories I'd rather forget."

"And the good memories are not powerful enough?"

Mrs. Brantenberg looked straight at her, a gray eyebrow raised. "Is that something I said at the circle?"

"Yes ma'am. You said, 'God would have us give more power to our good memories and see the weakness in the bad ones.'"

Huffing, the older woman dunked a bowl into the dishpan. "Your thoughts are of your family in Denmark?"

Nodding, Maren turned toward the singing and laughter coming from the sitting room. "I love you and Gabi, and so appreciate you opening your home to me. But, yes, I do miss my family."

"Maren." Mrs. Brantenberg patted Maren's arm, leaving her sleeve damp with dishwater. "Not all men are as narrow-minded as Orvie Christensen."

"I could be completely blind in a matter of a few years. I wouldn't wish myself upon a man who needs a wife who can work beside him."

"Don't shortchange yourself, dear—you are a hard worker. And many women with full eyesight don't have half the heart you do."

Tears stung the backs of Maren's eyes. "Thank you." It squeaked out on a whisper. She would surely miss this woman and Gabi—and all of her quilting circle friends—when she left Saint Charles. Yet she had no choice but to do so. A hard worker or not, the day would come when her limitations would catch up to her. She took the wet bowl from Mrs. Brantenberg and dried it thoroughly.

"You think I'm being unfair to him? That I should've welcomed him home with open arms?"

"It's not my place to say."

"I asked." The widow stilled her hands and waited for an answer.

"Grace cannot be earned, only given."

"Did I say that too?"

Maren nodded, trying not to smile.

Mrs. Brantenberg lifted the washtub to the window and flipped the remaining water outside. "I talk too much."

"I think it's just easier to trust someone else's wise counsel."

She wagged her curved finger. "Your heart is not only full, dear, but perceives more than most eyes can see."

"Oma. Miss Maren." Gabi's voice split the silence as she dashed into the kitchen, skidding to a stop in front of Maren. "PaPa said it is time for the music. You and Oma need to come."

Maren had scarcely removed her apron when Gabi captured her hand and pulled her through the doorway of the sitting room. She focused on the glow in the fireplace, then on the man on the settee. Smiling, he stood and brushed a wild curl from his temple.

That's when she realized she was fingering the silver chain at her neck. Woolly had given her the present, and the whistle now lay between her chemise and her shirtwaist. Her neck warmed at the thought. She'd not heard of a nanny who had ever received such a gift. She should never have accepted it, especially when she had plans to end her care of Gabi soon.

"Without a flute and a piano the band is incomplete." He glanced at Mrs. Brantenberg, then pulled the bench out from the piano.

The older woman held up her hand, pointing a finger upward, and spun toward the staircase. In silence, the three of them watched her disappear from the second-floor landing. Before Maren could think of small talk, Mrs. Brantenberg descended the stairs with something in her hands. As she drew closer, Woolly's breath caught.

"My zither? You kept my zither?"

Nodding, Mrs. Brantenberg handed Woolly the instrument. "Now, the band will be complete."

He held it as he would an infant, counting toes and fingers. Silent, he wiped his cheek with his sleeve. Also silent, Mrs. Brantenberg rested her hand on his arm.

Maren's own eyes brimmed with tears, her heart full of joy for them.

Woolly looked at Mrs. Brantenberg. "It's been too long. Thank you."

She nodded and turned to the piano.

Maren pulled the box from the bookcase and assembled her flute while Mrs. Brantenberg seated herself on the bench.

"We'll start with 'Love Divine, All Loves Excelling.'" Mrs. Brantenberg tapped an A-note on the piano. Gabi chimed in on her recorder and Rutherford strummed the zither. His profile against the light streaming in from the window revealed a tall forehead, a straight nose, and a square chin beneath a neatly trimmed beard. She could see a man described in the Viking mythology of her childhood.

Maren joined in. When her memories tried to carry her back to the good days in the old country, she shook them off so she could enjoy this moment.

9

Maren held a sickle in one hand and Gabi's little hand in her other. With barely enough daylight to see the path at her feet, she followed Mrs. Brantenberg and Woolly toward the wheat field. The chill in the morning air wouldn't last, but right now if she had a hand free, Maren would raise the collar on her coat.

Gabi swung Maren's arm, her steps cheerful despite their extra-early start on the chores. The difference between this walk out to the field and the cautious one last week was as stark as the sunlight casting a glow on the heads of the wheat stalks.

"Miss Maren." Gabi tugged her hand.

Slowing her steps, Maren looked into the child's sweet face. "Yes, little one."

"I am really happy PaPa is here with us."

Maren couldn't help but giggle when she nodded. "I am happy too, little one."

Woolly looked over his shoulder at them, his bright teeth revealing a warm smile.

Of course she was happy he'd come home...happy for Gabi and for Mrs. Brantenberg. He was family, and they needed a man around the farm. Especially today. Even though he was still protecting his injured shoulder, Woolly's help would make the work shorter.

Maren smiled, remembering Mrs. Brantenberg coming down the stairs with Woolly's zither, handmade by his father-in-law. Then, the sweet gathering around the piano. She couldn't recall when she'd had so much fun. Certainly not since her childhood in Denmark. If she were being truthful to herself, she'd admit that she was also happy Woolly had returned to the farm. And thankful. She liked Gabi's PaPa, and why wouldn't she? He'd made mistakes that hurt his family—mistakes he regretted—but he was a good man. She knew Mrs. Brantenberg didn't have the money for the supplies he'd brought home. Nor the credit. But Woolly had seen to it. He was a generous man who was doing his best to make things right. She'd miss her brief morning chats with him at Bootsie's stall. She would miss him and all of the family when she found work and moved to town.

❧

At the only tree on the hilltop along the north edge of the wheat field, Woolly added several sheaves to the growing stack in the wagon, then reached under the seat for the food sack and quilt. The sun had risen to high noon, time for a break. He carried the sack around to the shady side of the tree and knelt on the drying bed of wildflowers. After he spread the quilt on the ground, he pulled a loaf of crusty bread and dry sausage from the sack and set them on quilted napkins. He chuckled. It seemed everything in Mother Brantenberg's life had become fodder for quilting.

He stood and looked over the field as Gabi picked up sheaves from where Miss Jensen was reaping. The young woman hadn't slowed down all morning, the rhythm of her sickle so steady you could set a clock by it. He should've brought the scythe out. His shoulder couldn't hurt any more than his pride did watching Mother Brantenberg and Miss Jensen bent over, taking the brunt of the physical work in the harvest.

Gabi toddled toward him, her eyes barely visible over the tops of the bundles she held in front of her like a giant ragdoll. "PaPa, Miss Maren said I am a good helper."

"You are indeed!" He took the sheaf from Gabi and added it to the stack.

"Oma said it's time to break for water."

"Yes. And something to eat." He looked across the field past Miss Maren. About ten paces down the slope, Mother Brantenberg was straightening herself. She looked like a tree growing up from the field, its branches unfolding and stretching. A sickle hung at her side, looking as tired as she did.

Pulling a tin cup from its hook on the water barrel, he held it and the loaf up. If he didn't get his shoulder working right soon, he might just have to start wearing an apron. The role reversal wasn't something he would be able to live with long, although he was able to at least be of some help.

Waving, Mother Brantenberg walked across the stubble to where

Miss Jensen gathered cut stalks into a sheaf. When the older woman placed her hand on Miss Jensen's back, she stood and wiped her brow with her sleeve.

Woolly scooped the cups into the barrel and had the makeshift dinner table set by the time they got to the tree.

It was hard to tell which of the women was helping which up the rise, but it wasn't hard to tell that they were close. He heard laughter from them both as they approached, and his heart was warmed that Gretchen's mother had found a surrogate daughter to share those bonds with.

He was truly blessed with the women in his life.

Women. Of course he'd include Miss Jensen. If he was still a part of the family, she certainly was. A most important member. She knew his daughter better than he did and had been the one helping Mother Brantenberg on the farm all these past months. Despite her own hardships, she did the farm chores, was a playmate and teacher for Gabi, and did it all for room and board, as there was apparently no money to pay her.

"Miss Jensen." He gestured to a position on the quilt as if a waiter at a fancy restaurant.

"I've been thinking." Maren retrieved her cup of water. "Seeing as how we're working together, I think it's time you felt comfortable calling me Maren."

"Sounds fair to me, ma'am, and I'm Woolly." He brushed the brim of his cap. "Rutherford, if you'd prefer that."

She nodded, then downed the cup of water and retrieved another.

While he helped Mother Brantenberg to sit on the quilt, Woolly stole a look at Maren as she drained the second cup of water. Her bonnet askew, wisps of corn silk blond hair had escaped the braid wound atop her head.

Maren lowered her cup and looked straight at him. She blinked, but neither of them looked away. Suddenly growing weak in the knees, Woolly leaned against the wagon wheel.

High cheekbones covered with faint freckles flowed into smooth cheeks, narrowing to her charming pointed chin, no longer scuffed from her fall off the ladder. "I'd say we are making good progress."

"Amazing." Had he meant it as a response to her or to himself?

"Are you all right?" Mother Brantenberg looked up at him, an eyebrow arched above a smile.

"Yes ma'am." He knelt and busied himself, slicing more of the sausage. "You've filled the wagon." He chucked Gabi under the chin, making her giggle. "When we've finished eating, I'll empty it at the granary." He looked at Mother Brantenberg. "You plan on taking Thursday off for the quilting circle, don't you?"

"Yes. If we can keep this pace, we'll finish Saturday, even taking that time out."

"I'll figure on doing some threshing while the ladies are here. And since we don't have as many animals to feed, I can take a third or so of the grain to town to sell. Maybe winnow some out and take it to the mill to barter for some flour. There should be plenty to get us through."

"Hadn't thought yet how we were going to get the threshing done. Thank you. You may need to fix the winnower, though. Last I heard, the handle kept falling off."

"That's the least I can do. I hate it that I can't do more in the field."

Mother Brantenberg gave him a look that brought back the old days. Softer, with no hint of the scowl he'd earned. "Don't you worry.

You're doing more than your share hauling sheaves and keeping us watered. Besides, from the looks of all the new wood and supplies at the barn, you're going to be doing plenty more around here."

He may have been the only one who felt it, but he'd definitely experienced a refreshing breeze.

T he sun had given way to darkness, and an oil lamp flickered on the bedside table. Wednesday night already. Seems it was just Sunday, and they were all gathered around the piano. Where had the days gone? Maren sighed. The deep breath caused her aching arms to remind her. She'd given most of her time and all of her energy to the wheat harvest.

Sound asleep on her bed, Gabi purred like a kitten. Maren pulled her dressing gown tight and focused her gaze to follow the light that bounced along the path toward the barn. The candle lantern's glow was just strong enough to illuminate Rutherford's silhouette. At the barn doors, the light stopped moving forward and swung around, toward the house. Could he see her standing at the window?

Her sight couldn't confirm the notion, and it wouldn't be proper for her to wave. The lantern raised and swung right then left. He had seen her.

"Sweet dreams, Rutherford." He deserved to sleep well. And comfortably. Despite a sore shoulder, he had worked alongside them every day, today swinging the scythe. She hadn't seen him wince, but she knew he had to be hurting.

When the lantern disappeared through the barn doors, Maren closed the curtain and blew out the lamp, then knelt at her bedside. Her prayers were full of thanksgiving, as they should be. But tonight, between her praises she stacked petitions for Caroline Milburn, Hattie and her family, and for herself—for a job. Because of Rutherford's help in the fields and with the chores this week, they'd take all day tomorrow for the quilting circle and finish the wheat harvest Friday.

At the close of her prayer, she hung her dressing gown on the bedpost and laid her head on the pillow. Poor Rutherford had been through enough, losing his wife, fighting in two wars, separated from his daughter and the mother-in-law who still loved him deeply. He deserved to sleep in a bed…in the house with his family.

After the wheat harvest, she'd do some deep cleaning for Mrs. Brantenberg, but the next time they went into town, she'd see about a new job.

❧

His strength buoyed, Rutherford pulled the barn door closed behind him. Trudging the path from the house, he'd barely had the energy to place one foot in front of the other. But then he'd looked up at the window on the second floor. Lamplight glowed behind the young woman, creating the image of a guardian angel. Maren hadn't waved, but he knew she was watching for him, watching over him. He hoped she'd been able to see the lantern swinging to and fro, his *good-night*.

A rooster protested the disturbance with a cackle and fluttered across the rafter. "Clearly, Orvie Christensen is a fool. What kind of man would walk away from the gift of Miss Maren? She is a treasure more valuable than a boatload of pure gold."

So were his daughter and Mother Brantenberg. "Turns out me and Orvie aren't all that different." Orvie had run from Miss Jensen, and Rutherford had run from a newborn and Mother Brantenberg.

Rutherford shook his head. Partly because of the mistakes he and Orvie had shared, but mostly because he was in a barn talking to a rooster as if the bird were a confidant.

As he climbed the ladder to the loft, new memories swirled about him. Maren on the ladder that first day of his return, her wielding the shovel like a weapon when she thought him a threat, her cradling and comforting his daughter like a mother would. Her quiet faith ran deep and her wisdom wide.

After Maren and Gabi had retired for the night, he'd lingered in the kitchen with Mother Brantenberg. She'd taken his hands in hers and shared with him what Maren had said to her on Sunday that had awakened her heart and pushed her up the stairs to retrieve his zither.

Grace cannot be earned, only given.

She pulled him into an embrace and kissed his cheek.

His soul feeling quenched, Rutherford sank onto his cot and unbuttoned his shirt. Suddenly, he couldn't help but think how good it would feel to have Maren rubbing mint poultice on his aching shoulder.

Like a wife would.

11

On the last day of August, the wheat harvest completed, Rutherford couldn't help but smile walking hand in hand with Gabi from the livery up to Main Street, then north to Gut's Saddlery and Harness shop. Two old harnesses draped his shoulder and slapped his back with every step while Gabi hummed a happy song. His daughter's warm love was more than he'd dared dream of when he'd made the long trek back to Missouri from Arizona Territory. Yet, Gabi and Mother Brantenberg had given him a far warmer reception than he deserved. And Maren, well, she was a true marvel. Her music. Her hard work. Her heart and soul. The way her mouth curved into a captivating smile that made him want to say yes to the spark of hope burning inside him.

Could Maren ever trust him with her heart? Was he a fool to daydream that the four of them could one day become a real family? That he and Maren could ever live as man and wife?

"PaPa, do you see the horse?"

His gaze followed Gabi's pointed finger to the shop across the street. A mounted white horse stood in full harness on the sidewalk in front of the saddlery.

"It isn't a real horse, Gabi."

Letting go of his hand, she looked up at him. "It is real. Oma told me the old horse died and they stuffed it."

"Oma is right, little one." Only four years old, his daughter had already learned so much, and he'd forfeited the joy of teaching her. Rutherford tamped down the regret threatening to topple him, remembering that grace was a gift...one he was still having trouble accepting. "It is a real horse, but not a live one."

Nodding, Gabi bounced the brown curls framing her blue eyes. "It was big like Boone and Duden. Too big for me. I need a pony."

His daughter's matter-of-fact statement tickled him, and he couldn't help but chuckle as he reached for the door. The shop smelled of freshly tanned leather and he paused to breathe it in. Gabi darted to the displayed saddles in the front window.

"I like this one, PaPa." She brushed the saddle seat as if it were a horse's back.

Rutherford studied the finely tooled leather. "It's a fine saddle, for certain." He was a long way from affording a saddle, let alone a pony.

"Those harnesses a decoration, or you need help with 'em?"

Rutherford turned to face the deeply creased features of the owner, a man known by most folks as Old Man Gut.

Bushy white eyebrows waggled in recognition. "Woolly Wainwright, if you ain't a sight for weary eyes." Edward Gut slapped him on the shoulder. "When'd you get back, son?"

"Last Wednesday. Finished out my enlistment in Arizona Territory."

"The Indian troubles." Edward shook his head, causing his bowler to shift. "With you survivin' not one, but two wars, the good Lord must have somethin' more for you to do."

He knew what he wanted to do—take care of Gabi, Maren, and Mother Brantenberg—but he wouldn't guess why God had spared him while hundreds of thousands of other men and women serving in the wars perished.

Edward pulled a peppermint stick from a pocket on his leather apron and smiled at Gabi.

"This can't be the toddling baby I seen with your mother-in-law. Has it been that long?"

Rutherford patted Gabi's soft curls. "Yes, this is Gabrielle…Gabi. She took to being four in April." He wouldn't believe his daughter could be that old either if he hadn't been marking off the months on the butt of his rifle since May of '61 when he'd left home.

"Gabi, this is my friend Mr. Gut. Your grandfather and I bought our saddles here."

Edward bent to her level and held the candy stick out to her.

When Rutherford nodded, Gabi reached for the treat. "Danke," she said.

"*Bitte Schön.* You're welcome, little lady." Edward looked at him and scrubbed his fuzzy cheek. "You're a lucky man. My daughter is all grown up—has the Queensware shop next door." He nodded then grabbed the straps of the harnesses Rutherford carried. "Now about these."

"These are the ones me and Christoph bought from you years ago. They're both in bad need of stitching."

"She brought 'em in last year. I could not do the work." His lack of eye contact told the same story Rutherford had heard at the lumber mill.

Rutherford reached into his pocket and pulled out some of the bills he just got from selling the sacks of grain at the mill. "I can settle the account."

Meeting his gaze, Edward took the harnesses from him. "I didn't want to turn her away, but I had to—"

"I understand." Rutherford glanced at Gabi, who was busy stroking the saddle and licking her candy stick. "The war was hard on everyone."

The man nodded, his shoulders lifting a little bit. "Real good to see you made it through, and that things are getting better for Mrs. Brantenberg."

"Thank you. Good to be back." Doing something worthwhile for his family.

"If you're in town for a while, I can have Peter stitch these and have 'em ready for you by noon."

"Hadn't expected to get 'em back today. But thank you. We'll see you this afternoon." He waved and led Gabi out the door.

"He was a nice man." Gabi quickly returned her attention to the peppermint stick.

Up past the candlemaker's house, he guided his daughter across the mismatched stones in front of the Old Capitol Building and Heinrich's Dry Goods and Grocery.

Maren had been waiting for the day when she could act upon her decision. It came on Wednesday, after the completion of the week of harvest, when Mrs. Brantenberg chose to take the wagon into town for supplies. Rutherford sat at the reins and stopped to let her and Mrs. Brantenberg out of the wagon on Main Street. Gabi stayed behind with her father while Mrs. Brantenberg went to visit her friend. Using an umbrella as a walking stick, Maren carefully maneuvered the uneven limestone walk in front of the Old Capitol Building. The bottom floor housed Heinrich's Dry Goods and Grocery.

Maren breathed a prayer for God's provision and opened the door, jangling the bell overhead.

"Good morning, Miss Maren."

Blinking against the dim lighting, Maren turned toward the wooden counter where Mr. Heinrich folded and stacked men's blouses, his spectacles low on his nose. "Good morning to you too, Mr. Heinrich."

"Emilie will be sorry she missed you. She went to Lindenwood for her examinations today."

She nodded.

He looked past her. "You came into town alone?"

"No sir. Mrs. Brantenberg will be along shortly."

He pushed the spectacles higher on his nose. "I have new cloth to show her," he said. "And the little one?"

"Gabi is with her PaPa."

"Ah yes. Woolly was in last week. A joyous sight!" He studied Maren. "And you, are you well?"

"Yes. Thank you." Maren glanced toward the door, then at the various people milling about the store.

"Can I help you find something?"

Satisfied that no one she knew was within earshot, she stepped up to the counter. "You were so kind to recommend me to help Mrs. Brantenberg out at the farm, and I—"

"You need a different job?"

"Yes sir. And a place to live."

Leaning forward, Mr. Heinrich removed his spectacles. "It is because Rutherford is back on the farm?"

She nodded, her cheeks growing warm at the mention of his name. "Yes. Now that he is home, I can think about returning home...to my own family." Her hand rested on the chain lying just below her lace collar. She drew in a fortifying breath. "I wondered if perhaps you and Emilie could use my help."

He returned the spectacles to his nose and lifted the stack of men's blouses off the counter. "The good Lord works in mysterious ways. And even secretive ways. Why, just the other day, I mentioned to Emilie that I wanted to hire someone to help out here."

"I cannot see well enough to do bookwork, but I could stock shelves and help customers."

"Yes. We could most certainly use your help with the customer orders and stocking." Mr. Heinrich tugged on the points of his vest. "We'll need to fix up the basement some. You can move in next Saturday and start work that next Monday...a week and a half from now?"

"Next Saturday." Maren moved her hand to her skirt pocket. "Yes. Thank you."

"Does Mrs. Brantenberg know you're planning to leave the farm?"

"I wanted to talk to you first."

He rested his hand on hers. "Dear, Saint Charles has become your home. Are you sure you want to leave?"

"It is the right thing."

She had been sure of it, and not all that long ago. Before Woolly startled her in the barn a mere three weeks ago. Before she'd begun to see the four of them as a family.

CRG

The bell on the door was still jangling when Gabi darted toward the counter, holding up a peppermint stick. "Miss Maren!"

Maren turned toward Gabi and her father, her expression more serious than usual. Gabi fairly jumped into Maren's arms—the way Rutherford would picture her doing with her mother.

Maren stroked Gabi's cheek. "You have candy?"

"The fuzzy man in the horse shop gave it to me."

Maren's eyebrows arched. "The horse shop?"

"The saddler," he said, drawing her attention momentarily.

"Ah yes, the one with the horse out front."

Gabi nodded, bobbing her curls. "This time I got to go in there, and I found a saddle for my pony."

Maren's solemn blue eyes widened. "Her pony?"

"The one she dreams of someday owning."

"Oh." Maren's mouth formed the word perfectly.

Johann cleared his throat, looking rather serious himself. "Woolly, you're already lookin' better than the hungry fox you were the last time you were in."

"Feelin' much better too. Thank you."

"Nothin' like good home cooking to add meat to a man's weary bones."

"True enough. Between Mother Brantenberg's German onion cake and Maren's Danish meatballs, I'm surely enjoying some fine cooking." He looked at the list in Maren's hand.

"I have yet to start on the list."

Rutherford reached for the list. "I can help."

"Why don't you two work on it together while Gabi and I see

what trouble we can find." A wily grin didn't quite reach the corners of Johann's gray eyes.

While the shopkeeper entertained Gabi with a woolen sheep puppet, Rutherford seized the opportunity to spend a little time with Maren. He added a pair of sheepskin gloves to a stack on the end of the counter, then looked into her eyes. If not for the sack of salt she held between them, he would've been tempted to reach for her hand. "Maren—"

Her eyes widening, she glanced toward Gabi, then looked up at him. "I asked Mr. Heinrich for a job, and he hired me."

Feeling gut-punched, Rutherford stepped backward. "You what? Why?"

He followed her to the far end of the store, where she stopped in front of a dangle of beaver traps. Drawing a deep breath, she looked at him. "I need to work in town, Rutherford."

"I thought the farm was your home." He'd looked up at her bedchamber that night outside the barn. She'd noticed his attentions. Did she have feelings for him too? Is that why she couldn't stay? "You were comfortable on the farm before I arrived. It's because I'm there, isn't it?" Leaning forward, he lowered his voice. "But I'm not living in the house."

Her face pinked, and she studied the traps, as if they were something she had use for.

If they married, he could live in the house…they all could. And Maren could remain there without feeling she was doing something improper. So, why couldn't he say as much?

"Working here, I can earn the money I need to go home."

"To Denmark?" He hadn't meant to blurt out the question, but it seemed an absurd idea.

She flinched. "Yes. Denmark. I want to be with my family."

Another gut punch.

"You're back on the farm now...working. Mrs. Brantenberg doesn't need my help."

He shrugged. "It's not about that." *Tell her why you don't want her to leave.*

But she didn't want to stay.

"Miss Maren!" Gabi skipped toward them, her face beaming with a smile that, as soon as she knew what was happening, would quickly fade. "Mr. Johann has a dollhouse. Come see."

Maren looked at Rutherford, her brow creased.

Against his will, he nodded. After a quick glance at the list in his hand, Rutherford turned toward the barrels at the front window while the hope he'd entertained earlier sank like dead weight.

12

Her entrance examination complete, Emilie Heinrich rushed past a gaggle of chattering girls and out the door of Sibley Hall. She pulled her shawl tight against a bothersome wind. Most of the students at Lindenwood Female College planned to take their boarding on the campus, but she wasn't one of them. Not with a father who needed her.

Her unladylike dash up the path and out of the iron gate would surely earn her at least a frown from the faculty and possibly a denial of her application. It seemed most young women in the city had nothing better to do than to fuss over deportment and elocution. She was probably the only one who had a dry goods and grocery store to manage. And now, thanks to some wild notion that had settled on her PaPa, she'd been forced to concern herself with higher education *and* the family business. All for the sake of a future she wasn't sure she wanted.

At the tree-lined road, Emilie turned toward Main Street, setting her gait at just below a run. Her PaPa had plans to place a big order this week. Lest she find herself storing an overabundance of tools and gadgets in her bedroom, she'd best have a say on the list. She wished to join the quilting circle tomorrow. That left the remainder of her afternoon and evening to review his order, tend to the record books, fix dinner, and look over the Course of Study to decide if she wanted to earn the Mistress of English Literature or the Mistress of Arts Degree. Since this was all her PaPa's idea, she had a mind to ask him which degree he preferred.

On days like today, she envied Maren Jensen's life on Mrs. Brantenberg's farm. Wide open spaces and the song of God's animals.

At the corner, she stopped and blew out a long breath—another act unbefitting a lady—then stepped onto the cobblestone walkway in front of the Old Capitol Building. She glanced in at the display windows on either side of the door into Heinrich's Dry Goods and Grocery before entering. Hardware items for men on one side and household items for women on the other. Deciding she would wait for the new freight to arrive before refreshing the displays, she shifted her reticule up her arm and pushed the door open.

"Meine Tochter." Her father stood beside the checkerboard at the center of the store. Two local men bent over the crock that held the game board. He waved her over.

She drew in a deep breath and joined the men as if she had nothing better to do. The Rengler brothers were fierce competitors and didn't look up immediately. "Gentlemen."

"Miss Emilie." Owen, dressed like a dapper businessman, doffed his bowler while Oliver greeted her with a nod, bobbing his bearded chin, no hat or jacket in sight. The brothers owned one of the steamboats on the Missouri.

Her PaPa smiled, pushing his spectacles higher on his nose. "You've arrived in time to toss your answer into the circle."

"I suppose that depends upon the question."

Oliver chuckled. "Your father thinks it's still mostly men that entertain dreams of goin' all the way west."

She sighed. "I have work to do, Oliver, and no time for tomfoolery."

"Ah, Miss Emilie, this ain't tomfoolery. Folks are really gonna do it." He sat back on the stool, resting his hand on a knee. "Come on… you never think about goin' west?"

If it meant getting out of going to college or looking over the store record books or answering silly questions, then maybe she should consider it. But right now, if she had to think about moving too, she might crumple under the weight of it all.

Some folks called Oliver *touched,* but mostly he was just sweet and kind. The least she could do was answer his question.

"I never have thought about it." But that didn't mean it was a bad idea. Perhaps if PaPa changed the plans for his future, hers could change too. "Are you fellows thinking about leaving Saint Charles to chase after gold?"

"There's lots more reasons to go to California than that." Oliver pinched his wiry beard. "Ranching. Farming. Me and Owen heard there's fertile land that stretches past the horizon. And plenty of water. Shopkeepers are needed there too. Especially with all those people that made money in the goldfields."

Probably most accurate to say that more money was made selling gold pans than using them. Emilie looked at her father. "Are you thinking about chasing that rainbow?"

PaPa swatted the air, then cupped her elbow. "Enough with all our silly talk. I have something important to discuss with you."

"Oh?" She walked with him to the glass display cases, hoping whatever the topic, it was good news.

He scrubbed his cheek. "Miss Maren was in the store today and asked if we might have work for her here."

Emilie's heart raced with the possibility. "Here at the store? That's wonderful news!"

PaPa pushed his spectacles to the bridge of his nose. "With Elsa's son-in-law back to help with the workload, Maren is ready to start earning money for her passage back to Denmark."

"No. I don't want her to go."

"Plans can change, my dear."

"You think she'll decide not to leave after all?"

PaPa shrugged, the coy smile on his face saying he knew more than he was willing to tell her. "I'm just saying there's a lot to keep her here."

Emilie nodded. When it came time to actually leave town, Maren would be hard-pressed to say good-bye to little Gabi. Everyone could see she'd grown fond of the little one.

"Of course, you told her yes. When does she start?" Emilie brushed a line of dust from the display glass.

"Next Monday. But I don't want you to think you'll be out of a job." A twinkle in his blue eyes, he gave her a wink.

She awarded him with a giggle. "Harvest season is upon us, which leads to buying season for those who sell their crops. If I'm accepted at the college—"

"When."

"Very well. *When* I'm accepted and I begin my classes, I will be too busy to both clerk and keep the books. Maren will be perfect for the job as clerk!" Emilie clasped her hands at her chest. "But she can't drive back and forth from the farm. Where will she live?"

"We can tidy the basement for her."

"A wonderful idea." Emilie felt the weight on her shoulders lighten. Now if she could only empty her mind of thoughts about moving to the Wild West. Could PaPa be thinking about it?

The afternoon ride back to the farm was quiet. Gabi lay sleeping, her head cradled on Maren's lap and her shoulder tucked at Maren's side. The child had fallen asleep before they'd even crossed Blanchette Creek.

As Maren contemplated telling Gabi of her plans to move out of the room they shared and live in town, tears pooled her eyes. It wasn't a mere fondness or even a big sister's love she felt for Gabi. Something much deeper welled inside her, and she wiped a tear from her cheek. It was a maternal love causing her heart to ache so. She could never replace Gabi's mother or love her as Gretchen would have, but before Rutherford had come home, she'd allowed herself to slip into the role of the child's mother. Saying prayers with her each night. Tucking her in. Darning her socks. Mending her dressing gowns. Teaching her to play the recorder.

Maren wiped her wet face. Perhaps she was foolish to think she could actually leave the farm…these people.

Mrs. Brantenberg twisted in the wagon seat. "Is everything all right, dear?"

She must have sniffled and not realized it. Her first attempt at a response came out silent, so she cleared her throat. "Yes ma'am." Everything but her heart. The way it ached, she thought it would break before she could tell Mrs. Brantenberg of her plans. And right now her resolve to leave the farm, let alone Saint Charles, had shrunk to the size of a proverbial mustard seed.

◦∞◦

Straightaway after supper, Rutherford excused himself to the barn. Maren had tucked Gabi into bed and helped Mrs. Brantenberg clean the kitchen. Now, her dear host sat quietly on the cane rocker with her German Family Bible on her lap, apparently in prayer, while Maren positioned herself on the settee, her mind held captive by her secret. The oil lamp filled the room with a soft glow while they sat in quiet for what seemed hours.

Mrs. Brantenberg cleared her throat, drawing Maren's attention to the woman, whose gaze was fixed directly on her.

"Are you ready to tell me what went on today? You and Rutherford have been uncommonly quiet. What is it?"

Maren moistened her lips. "I made a decision your son-in-law doesn't like."

"And me, will I agree with your decision?"

"I have given it much thought."

Mrs. Brantenberg stacked her hands on the open Bible. "You're leaving the farm, aren't you?"

Maren worried the seam on her skirt. "Yes. I have found a job in town."

"In the store with Johann and Emilie?"

Maren nodded. "Yes ma'am. I start work there next Monday." She swallowed hard against the lump forming in her throat. "It's not that I don't appreciate all you've done for me." Her voice quivered. "I do. And I will miss—"

"But if you are to return to your family in Denmark, you need a job that pays."

Tears stung the backs of Maren's eyes. She didn't want to seem ungrateful. The woman had done more for her than just give her a bed and food. She had welcomed her into her home and her heart.

"I don't want to leave, but I didn't expect to be apart from them all these years."

"I know. And I trust your judgment, dear."

Maren was nowhere near having that much faith in her own reasoning. Time would tell. It would take her at least a year to earn enough for passage home.

13

After very little sleep, Rutherford forced himself up from his bedding. Maren would soon move into town. Gone, but for an occasional visit when he went into town for supplies or she came to the farm for the quilting circle. Until faced with her leaving the farm, he hadn't realized how much he depended on seeing her every morning when she'd come in to milk the cow, and at every meal. Sitting across the supper table from her after a long day of mending fences and slopping whitewash felt like an extra helping of dessert.

He moved along the edge of the loft, dropping feed into the swinging mangers. He'd handled Maren's proclamation of her departure from the farm poorly. He understood loss and needing the comfort of family. It's just that he had assumed…too much. He grabbed his kepi from atop the empty apple vinegar barrel at his bedside and climbed down the ladder.

He'd never been a man of many words, and now whenever he found himself on the edge of emotions, he would have to stop talking for fear of breaking down. It seemed easier to walk away than try to express his true feelings. But he'd been married to Gretchen long enough to know that he liked having someone at his side, all times of the day and night. He'd already spent enough time with Maren now to know that he didn't want to let her go.

At the barn door, Rutherford grabbed the egg basket off a peg and headed for the chicken coop. He adjusted his cap to shade his eyes from the rising sun and glanced toward the house. The quilting circle would soon be here, and Maren was no doubt busy with preparations. If they had any time to talk, it wouldn't be much. So he'd better figure out what he wanted to say to her. Better yet, how he would force the words in his heart out into the open.

Maren stepped off the back porch and strolled the path toward the barn. She and Rutherford needed to talk before the quilting circle began arriving. She was determined to resolve the tension between them. It wasn't about her abandoning Gabi. Or Mrs. Brantenberg. It was about not being able to keep her promise to Moder, Erik, and Brigitte, and if she couldn't bring them to America, she had to go home.

"Maren."

Following the familiar baritone voice, she turned toward the chicken coop and blinked to focus her vision. Rutherford pushed open the slat door and stepped out of the coop, egg basket in hand.

She brushed the cape covering her arm. "It is a bit cool this morning, but it feels like we may have a temperate day for the quilting circle."

"Yes." He raised the basket. "The hens have given us fifteen eggs this morning."

"Good." She reached for the basket and he held on to it, momentarily suspending it between them.

She would sorely miss seeing this man every day. She set the egg basket on the new fence post and met his gaze.

He rested his hand on her arm. Despite the barrier her cape and dress sleeve created, his touch sent a shiver up her spine.

"At the store...when I said you were back working on the farm, that Mrs. Brantenberg didn't need my help, you said my leaving wasn't about that."

He nodded, his brow creased.

"What did you mean?"

"I want to court you."

She glanced at his hand. "You do?"

"I do." He removed his hand from her arm and slid his hand into his trouser pocket, leaving her arm chilled.

"How do afternoon walks, listening to steamboats as they sidle up to docks along the Missouri, sound?"

Perfect, as long as he was at her side. "But what about Denmark? I don't plan to stay."

"I'm willing to take it one day at a time. Are you?"

She nodded.

Bootsie's low moan drew her attention to the barn.

"It's not easy to admit," he said, "but it's probably best that you not live here on the farm."

"Oh?"

"You're a very distracting single woman. I'd choose spending time with you over work any hour of the day." His wide grin weakened her knees.

"I had best return to my work before we both miss breakfast."

"I'll see you at the table then."

She sighed and took a first step toward the barn. She'd miss their daily talks, but the prospect of courtship quickened her steps.

⟨✕⟩

The sun had begun to wane before Maren and Rutherford returned from a walk in the apple orchard. Harvest was fast approaching. A crowd would gather at the farm to help with the picking, and she wanted to be a part of it. She didn't want to miss anything here, least of all any walks with Rutherford, her talks in the kitchen with Mrs. Brantenberg, and Gabi's joy during their Sunday music time.

Rutherford slowed his pace. "Do you want me to stay with you when you tell her?" His voice echoed the emotion welling inside her.

"Yes. I want Gabi to focus on what she's gained—her PaPa."

As Rutherford guided her up the porch steps, his firm hand cupping her elbow, she prayed for the right words. She had shared the news of a job at the grocery with Mrs. Brantenberg. Rutherford had agreed to move her into the basement at Heinrich's store on Saturday. Now it was time she told Gabi of her move.

Rutherford held the front door open for her, a gesture she'd come to appreciate...and expect. The door clicked shut and Rutherford joined her, his hand resting across her upper back.

Mrs. Brantenberg's and Gabi's voices sounded from the sitting room.

"Gleich und gleich gesellt sich gern," Mrs. Brantenberg said in her German tongue.

Gabi translated the proverb into English. "Birds of a feather flock together."

Maren looked at Rutherford. "I will miss you all so."

"PaPa! Miss Maren!" Gabi skidded to a stop in front of them, waving her cloth doll. "Did you hear us?" The child's whole body wiggled like a ribbon on a breeze. "I will say the German and English sayings at the apple picking party and Oma will say a poem."

Rutherford lifted Gabi into his arms. "That will be a special time."

Maren followed them into the sitting room. A fire glowed at the hearth and oil lamps flickered from the wall and a side table.

Mrs. Brantenberg looked at Maren and rose from her armchair. "I will make coffee."

Maren seated herself on the rocker. "Come sit with me, Gabi. I have something to tell you."

"I know." A smile filling her face, Gabi climbed onto Maren's lap and settled against her arm. Rutherford sat across from them on the sofa. "You and PaPa are going to marry."

Maren's pulse quickened. She dare not look at the man. She knew what courtship generally implied, but they hadn't discussed marriage. They both still had too much to work through for marriage to be a possibility. When she had regained her composure, she hooked her finger under Gabi's chin and looked into her blue eyes. "No. Your PaPa and I do not have plans to marry. I need to live in town, and your PaPa needs to live in the house with you and Oma."

"I want you, too."

Maren pressed her lips against the emotion threatening to undo her. "I know, little one. But I have to do what is best for all of us."

"That is you. The best."

Tears stung Maren's eyes. Oh, how she loved this little girl. But she couldn't stay. She wrapped her hands around Gabi's. "Saturday I will move into town and work in Mr. Heinrich's store."

Gabi's bottom lip quivered.

"I will come see you, and you will come see me. I will see you at church, and I will be here for the apple picking party." Maren blinked and finally made herself look at Rutherford—a mistake.

A pleading frown dulled his eyes.

14

Saturday had come too soon, and Maren was not ready to leave the farm. The cow had been milked, but she had skipped her morning chitchat with Rutherford. Instead she had enjoyed a music time with Gabi and helped Mrs. Brantenberg clean up after breakfast. Now she was upstairs packing the flute box into her trunk.

Gabi stood beside the trunk, her face long. "Thursday you will come with Miss Hattie to quilting." A statement rather than a question.

Maren brushed a curl from Gabi's sweet face. "I may be working and not able to come every week, but I will see you often. Your PaPa will bring you into town, and I will come to the farm when I can." Her voice cracked, and her resolve to leave threatened to do the same.

Mrs. Brantenberg rushed into the room, a sack cradled in her hands. "I brought you some food."

Maren smiled. "I will be working at a grocery store."

"For a man." Mrs. Brantenberg seated herself on the bed. "Johann Heinrich is a good man, mind you, but he will not watch that you are eating well."

Maren sat beside Mrs. Brantenberg on the bed and looked at the red needlework on the sack, too tiny for her to read.

"Geteiltes Leid ist halbes Leid," Mrs. Brantenberg read. "Trouble shared is trouble halved."

Nodding, she ran her finger over the lettering. No one could match Mrs. Brantenberg's generous cooking or her warmth of heart. She had given Maren a job, a home, a family, hope—her German friend had more than halved her troubles.

Mrs. Brantenberg pulled a smoked sausage from the sack. "I only packed a few of your favorites—ones that would travel and store well."

Maren pulled each item from the bag and showed them to Gabi. A loaf of rye-wheat bread, a tin of cranberry pemmican, four bacon popovers, a small wheel of white cheese, and a jar of Mrs. Brantenberg's German mustard. Fighting the emotion clogging her throat, she rested her hand on Mrs. Brantenberg's arm. *"Takke.* Thank you. For everything."

Mrs. Brantenberg nodded, her lips pressed together.

Footsteps on the staircase drew their attention to the doorway. Rutherford stopped in the open doorway, looking first at the plentiful array of foods, then at Maren. "It looks as though Johann could depend on you to stock the grocery." He chuckled.

Oh, how she would miss that baritone laugh.

"Johann is too occupied to cook," Mrs. Brantenberg said. "And Emilie will soon be engaged in her studies at Lindenwood. That basement won't have any kind of real kitchen. It's but a few things to give her a solid start."

Rutherford raised his hand as if to surrender, and Maren bit back a giggle, wondering if he had staged this bit of lightheartedness to soften her departure.

He peered at the bag. "I still have the sack you sent with me."

Mrs. Brantenberg lifted her hand to her collar. "You kept it?"

"I did."

"Der Apfel fällt nicht weit vom Stamm." Mrs. Brantenberg wagged her finger at him. "Thankfully, it's true—the apple doesn't fall far from the tree. You came back."

He nodded. "I moped all about camp the day the bag emptied, and for several days more."

"I, too, will treasure the sack you have given me, and the food will surely keep me fed until I can settle in." Maren looked long into Mrs. Brantenberg's eyes. "Thank you."

Rutherford glanced toward the window. "Boone and Duden are waiting at the rail."

Maren tucked the sack into her trunk. There was no place like home, but this farm had been the closest she could hope to come to it.

∞

Maren and Rutherford were nearly to the dry goods store when she shifted on the wagon seat. They'd not spoken more than a handful of sentences to each other on the ride in, and those were limited to the turkey they had seen bustle across the road and the clouds Rutherford saw gathering on the horizon.

He cleared his throat. "The store is closed on Sundays. Will we see you at church tomorrow?"

She glanced at the darkening sky. "If the weather permits it, you will."

"Then I'll pray for good weather." He reined the horses to a stop at the back of the store and looked at her. "You're sure about this?"

"I am." But was it too much to hope that her stay here—away—would be short-lived?

"As you wish, then." Rutherford jumped from the wagon and was at her side in an instant.

She accepted his hand, allowing him to help her to the ground. If she had her way, he would never have let her go. But he did, and he slid his hand into his trouser pocket. Had he, too, felt the chill in the letting go?

༄

By the time Rutherford reached the lane to the farmhouse, rain had begun to form mud puddles.

Mother Brantenberg greeted him at the kitchen door, a frown dulling her eyes. The kitchen smelled of sauerkraut and sausage.

"You left her there?"

He set his rucksack on the bench. "It's what she wanted." He sighed. "And probably best, for now." Believing that may make the separation more tolerable.

Mother Brantenberg nodded and pulled three dinner bowls from the shelf. "You are a wise man."

"I don't feel very wise." A lonely man, yes. An impatient man.

A warm smile deepened the creases at her eyes. "I could ask the Becks to bring me and Gabi home from church tomorrow."

"And I could take Maren on a picnic." He looked out the window at the soggy sky. "Or bring her back here for lunch and music."

"That would be nice. Gabi and I moved her things into my bedchamber."

He kissed Mother Brantenberg's forehead and glanced at his bag. "I'll take mine to the room and tell Gabi dinner is ready."

To the room where he'd seen Maren's dressing gown hanging on the bedpost.

Maren sat on the narrow rope bed and glanced around her new home. An oil lantern flickered atop a small table. A pot-bellied stove popped and crackled at the far wall. Still, the room was too quiet without Gabi's slumber-purr. Blue gingham curtains hung at the window above her trunk. She already missed looking down from her bedroom window at the farm to watch Rutherford walk to the barn and stop to wave at her. Her fingers slid down the chain about her neck and grasped the whistle, tempted to sound it.

Just in case... I would come running.

No. This was something she needed to do on her own—with God's help.

Maren pulled her Bible and reading glass from her trunk. While a hardy rain splashed the cobblestone street outside and thunder boomed overhead, she reread the third chapter of Ecclesiastes.

To every thing there is a season…. A time to cast away
stones, and a time to gather stones together; a time to
embrace, and a time to refrain from embracing…. A
time to love.

She crossed her arms, hugging herself. This was her time to refrain
from embracing life on Mrs. Brantenberg's farm. She would trust God
with her present and her future. Even if it meant she would sleep very
little tonight, if at all.

15

Mary Alice Brenner's toddling twins joined Mr. Heinrich at the candy counter while her two-week-old daughter lay in the crook of her arm. And Maren couldn't seem to tear her gaze away from baby Evie's sweet face.

Rutherford had moved her into town two weeks ago. Since then he had driven her to the farm twice for Sunday dinner and music, and they had walked in the orchard the past two Thursday afternoons. Last Saturday, he'd bought two sodas and they'd enjoyed a sack lunch on the banks of the river. She counted all that as courting. But Rutherford had loved and lost, and she had family in Denmark she was desperate to see.

Past dreams of being married and having children of her own followed her to the yard goods. "Mary Alice, are you looking for a practical fabric like cotton or denim, or something with flair like taffeta or silk for a special occasion?"

"I need a heavy, durable fabric for the trail."

Maren ran her hand across a green-print cotton duck, which seemed most practical for the mother of three.

Mary Alice hooked a wily strand of dark brown hair behind her ear and reached for the bolt of green cloth. "I'll also take ten yards of those two cottons." She pointed to a red calico and a brown floral.

"The trail?" Maren shouldered the other two bolts and carried them to the cutting table.

"My husband heard talk of wagons headed west this next spring, and he's all aflutter to go."

Maren looked at the tiny hand curled at the baby's pursed mouth. Mary Alice had lived here a dozen or more years. She and Mrs. Brantenberg had both shared stories with Maren of her and Gretchen's friendship. "You're planning to leave Saint Charles?"

"Evie will be near seven months by then…plenty big enough to travel. Women have babies in wagons, you know."

Nodding, Maren unfurled the first bolt to measure ten yards. That wouldn't be her choice. She wasn't even sure if she'd want Gabi making a trip like that.

While picturing Mary Alice and her two daughters in the same fabric, the image of her and Gabi in matching dresses flitted across Maren's mind. Gabi would pick the red cloth. She set the scissors to the fabric and began cutting, wondering how long her failing eyesight would allow such tasks.

"I figure I best prepare for the journey. Men get a notion, and well, I don't want to get caught with nothing fresh to wear at our new home in California. And speaking of men…" Mary Alice sighed. "I saw Woolly Wainwright in town. Was that two or three weeks ago?"

"I know it's been longer than that since you've been to quilting circle."

"It was a few days before the baby came." The young mother shrugged. "Well, I hadn't seen him since Gretchen died. He left town so suddenly, and I had my twins." She pulled the first cut fabric to her and began folding. "The man looked positively dreadful. Too thin. And so sad."

Nodding, Maren laid her scissors down. She remembered that man...just returned from the ravages of war. Dejected, and rejected. But determined and persistent.

"Got me to thinking, Maren."

Thinking about Rutherford? Maren unrolled the calico, her thoughts rolling with it.

"I know both stories—yours and Woolly's, and I think you two would be a good match."

Maren's neck warmed and she swallowed hard. "Did you tell him that?"

"No. I said no such thing." Mary Alice raised a thin eyebrow. "But if you'd like me to—"

Maren shook her head. "No need."

Mary Alice trailed her finger down baby Evie's cheek. "One can't mourn forever what could've been, should've been, or was. Life is far too short for that."

Smiling, Maren met her friend's gaze. "He's courting me."

"That's wonderful news!" Mary Alice's eyes widened.

"Thank you. This evening, we're having formal supper together for the first time."

Her friend's smile grew. "Sounds like I've missed out on far too much not going to the quilting circle. I'll be there Thursday, but right now I've got to get my goods and go home." With her free arm, Mary Alice pulled Maren into a warm embrace. "Oh, I feel so much better. He's a good man, and deserves to have love again."

Maren nodded. Did she love Rutherford? Is that what she felt for him?

☙❧

The air carried a chill, but sunshine warmed Maren's back as she and Rutherford walked down Main Street toward The Western House Inn for supper.

"How are things looking for apple picking?" She shifted her reticule to her other arm so she could hold his hand.

"I readied the cider press this week—gave it a good scrubbing. Mother Brantenberg and Gabi are weaving apple baskets."

"Johann said he'll close the store so he and Emilie can help. Hattie plans to join us too."

"Several neighbors have offered to come pick. We'll make short work of it, for sure."

"I am looking forward to the harvest and celebration—one more opportunity to spend a day at the farm."

He nodded. "And I'm anxious for you to be there."

The Western House Inn sat on the corner of South Main Street and Boone's Lick Road, and marked the beginning of the trail west. Wagons and tent cabins dotted the area while men buzzed about like bees to a rose garden, and she suspected Mr. Brenner may be among them. "Mary Alice Brenner was in the store this morning."

"I saw her just a few weeks ago, and she hadn't yet had her baby. Is she well?"

"Yes. A baby girl."

His silence told her he was battling old regrets.

"You're here now." She squeezed his hand.

He nodded and gave her one of his knee-weakening smiles.

"She said they plan to take a wagon to California in the spring."

"That's curious." He cocked his head. "I received an interesting letter from a childhood friend today who talked about going west." After stuffing his cap in his pocket, he cupped her elbow and guided her over the threshold toward the dining room. "I'll tell you about his writings when we've settled at our table."

Seated across from her, Rutherford glanced at the menu board on the wall behind her. "I think I'll have the venison stew."

"And one for me as well."

A woman with a thick braid over one shoulder returned with two coffee mugs, and Rutherford placed their order. When she walked away, he pulled an envelope from his pocket. "Garrett Cowlishaw and I were in school together in Virginia. Swam. Fished. Hunted. His mother called us inseparable. That is, until I left at sixteen to make a fresh start in Missouri."

"That would've been right after your parents died."

He nodded. "Within the month. My uncle soon turned to the flask."

"You seem to have received more than your share of sorrow."

"I've seen many who have suffered far worse."

Maren remembered the little Indian girl he spoke of who had lost her entire family.

Rutherford unfurled the piece of stationery like a flag and, leaning forward, began to read.

My dear loyal friend,

*I truly regret the unforgivable length of time that has passed
since my last word to you. We have but the war to blame.
And as your new home, Missouri, was confounded in her
loyalties to the Confederacy, I am most grateful not to have
met up with you in the fields.*

   I hope these pen strokes find you and your family well.

Rutherford lowered the letter and reached for his cup. After a long
gulp, he continued reading.

*In the spirit of our lasting friendship, I feel bound to inform
you of my impending visit to your fair city. I received communication from Mr. John Joseph Mathews with an invitation
to command a caravan of wagons to California.*

"Garrett was a scout on two caravans west before the war."
"He sounds like an independent fellow."
Rutherford nodded, bobbing the brown curls at his ears. "He is
without a wife or other encumbrance."

*My old friend, you will soon have the pleasure to look upon
my face again.*

In all sincerity,
Garrett Cowlishaw

Maren's stomach knotted. Now that Rutherford had heard from
his dear friend of the expedition headed west, would he too sense a call
to adventure? She knew what it was like to set off for the unknown,
albeit on a ship rather than in a covered wagon, and the feeling was no
doubt the same—that of a dandelion on the wind.

16

Thursday morning, Rutherford lay awake the last two or three hours before dawn sorting through various memories of his times with Maren. Their conversation at The Western House Inn occupied his thoughts. Specifically, Garrett's letter and Mary Alice Brenner's talk of going west. Thus far, the idea of moving to Oregon or California had been a phantom impulse that he'd refused to entertain. But now that a caravan would be leaving from Saint Charles in a matter of months, the thought swirled in discord with his affection for Maren and the promise of settling down. What if he wanted to go and Maren didn't want to?

After he dressed, he took his Bible from the bedside table on his way out the door. The brisk morning air soon chased away any remnants of sleepiness. The sun streaked the sky with stripes of reds and oranges, stretching its light across the top of the orchard like a crown.

At the creek bank, Rutherford settled on the log he'd first come to with Gretchen more than six years ago. That was when the thought of leaving the farm or Missouri hadn't yet crossed his mind. That was before the Union and the Confederacy declared war. Long before his future wife drew her last breath. He glanced at the Bible in his hands and flipped it open to the book of Psalms. He'd spent a lot of time there during the war, commiserating with King David and learning that he wasn't in charge.

How sweet are thy words unto my taste! Yea, sweeter than honey to my mouth!... Thy word is a lamp unto my feet, and a light unto my path.

Maren didn't depend upon sight to guide her. The day would come, perhaps soon, when her eyes would fail her completely. And yet Maren trusted God to light her path, to show her the way and guide her. One step leading to the next, despite the path's hazy unevenness.

Rutherford heaved a sigh. He'd mapped his own course and placed his faith in it, until his life took a fork in the road he wasn't prepared to navigate.

Lord, forgive me. I want to have the kind of faith Maren has. I want to walk this earth by faith, not in dependence upon my sight or on my own strength.

Wiping his eyes dry, he turned to the book of Proverbs.

Trust in the LORD with all thine heart; and lean not unto thine own understanding. In all thy ways acknowledge him, and he shall direct thy paths. Be not wise in thine own eyes.

Rutherford set his Bible on the log and picked up a twig. His own understanding certainly couldn't be trusted. He needed to trust his past, his present, and his future to what PaPa Christoph referred to as "God's supreme knowing."

He studied the shimmers on the rippling waters and rolled the twig between his hands. "I loved you, Gretchen. I always will, but—"

But what? His insides quivering, he fought to draw in a deep breath.

"You're gone. Not coming back to me. And I trust God's plan— His future for me."

Rutherford watched a squirrel scamper up a nearby linden tree. Then he stood and walked to the shore.

"You'd like Maren." He twirled the twig in his fingers. "She plays the flute. She is kind and cheerful. She loves your mother and our little girl. And she sees more in people than most folks with full sight. I love Maren." There, he'd admitted it.

God had shined His light on the path. He'd led him back to Mother Brantenberg and to his precious daughter, Gabi, to Maren Jensen, and to a future he hadn't dreamed of. He was ready to follow, wherever the path may lead.

Maren would be at the house this morning. She and Hattie Pemberton had been coming early on Thursdays to help Mother Brantenberg prepare the food for the quilting circle. It would be a good time to let Maren know his intentions.

After completing the chores and apologizing to Bootsie once again, he carried the egg basket and milk bucket toward the house. Stepping onto the brick walkway, he caught sight of the Pembertons' wagon turning onto the lane. He set his load on the step and headed out front.

His pulse raced as he quickened his steps to meet them. Instead of Maren and Hattie sitting on the backseat, Hattie was seated in the front beside her mother.

He waved and the wagon pulled to a stop beside him.

"Ladies." He stared at the back of the wagon as if he could will Maren to be there.

"Good day, Woolly."

Hattie lifted the generous brim of her pumpkin-colored hat. "I'm sorry to inform you that Maren is unable to join us today. Mr. Heinrich took sick in the night and needed Maren and Emilie to work in the store."

"I'm sorry to hear that." Both that Johann was ill, and that Maren wasn't here. "Does he require a doctor?"

"Emilie said he was suffering from exhaustion and needed bed-rest." Hattie pulled a folded sheet of paper from her skirt pocket. "Maren sent a note for you."

"Thank you." He unfolded the note.

Dearest Rutherford,

I regret not being able to see you today, to walk beside you in the orchard. I am needed here at the store and must remain. I will look forward to seeing you in town Saturday. Until then.

Sincerely,
Maren

Now that he'd accepted the depth of his feelings for Maren, he couldn't possibly wait until Saturday to speak with her.

Harvest season had begun, and it seemed most farmers had chosen today to bring in their goods, both raw and canned, carried in baskets, sacks, or crocks. Emilie served as the clerk for the dry goods while Maren managed the grocery side. She had filled five barrels with green beans, onions, carrots, eggplant, winter squash, figs, and beets.

She gathered the strips of butcher paper used to list out the credit vouchers, then looked up. Rutherford walked toward her, waving in broad strokes. He knew of her failing sight, and had adapted to it quickly and graciously.

As he approached the worktable, he removed his cap and tucked it into his pocket.

"You read my note?"

"Yes, Miss Hattie delivered it with finesse." He raised his hands, forming a wide bonnet brim, and bounced his head.

Maren giggled.

Rutherford glanced toward Emilie, who stood at the yard goods table with a customer. "How is Johann feeling?"

"Better, I believe. About an hour ago Emilie went upstairs to check on him and said he was sitting in his chair, reading."

"Good. Can't keep a good man down."

She was looking at one now. "You're a good man."

"Why, thank you, ma'am." He leaned over the table slightly, close enough for her to see the shine in his brown eyes. "It's the company I keep."

She drew in a deep breath to still the flutters in her stomach.

"Can we talk for just a moment? Privately?" He nodded toward the back door.

Her mouth suddenly dry, Maren moistened her lips and glanced at the customers milling about. "Let me ask Emilie." She carried the papers to the dry goods counter, then received Emilie's blessing for a short break.

❧

Standing on the lawn at the bottom of the back steps, Rutherford looked out toward the Missouri then back at her. "The Lord has been so good to me. I've only been back for six weeks, and I've already been so blessed with sweet times with family and friends."

He reached for her hand, sending the familiar shiver up her spine.

"That first night after you had returned home, in her bedtime prayers, Gabi thanked God for you. She adores you." *And I love you.*

After Orvie's rejection, Maren never expected to give her heart away, but Rutherford Wainwright had surely captured it.

He held her hand up between them. "Gabi loves you, Maren. And so do I."

Tears welled in her eyes. Had she heard him right, or was her hearing playing tricks on her too?

He drew in a deep breath, and, dropping to one knee in the grass, he enfolded her hands in his. "Until I got to know you, I never would've believed it possible that I could love again. But I love you, Maren."

And, oh, how she loved this man! Tears of joy spilled onto her cheeks. "I love you too, Rutherford."

"I know you've had plans to return to your family in Denmark. Would you consider a plan that would bring them to America instead?"

"Gladly."

"Maren, my beloved, will you honor me by becoming my wife?"

"Yes!"

Rutherford's smile promised forever as he stood close enough for her to feel his warm breath on her face. He rested his hand on her cheek, then brushed her lips with his.

The kiss sent shivers down her arms.

After a moment, he looked into her eyes, his own brimming with tears. "God has surely shed light on my path."

"And on mine." Maren smiled at the man who would become her husband. "I don't want this moment to end, but—"

"It must for now. Emilie needs your help."

She nodded.

"I'll return this afternoon. A walk along the river?"

"Yes." As she opened the door, she turned for another glimpse of the man with the brown woolly hair and thanked God for a time to love.

1. Maren Jensen would've preferred to remain in her homeland, Denmark, where things such as landscape, language, and customs were familiar to her. Due to circumstances beyond her control, the young woman is forced into one change of plans after another. In Psalm 20:6, the psalmist says the Lord saves His anointed; that He will hear them from His holy heaven with the saving strength of His right hand. In what ways did you see Him at work in Maren's circumstances? Have you ever found yourself floundering in an unfamiliar setting or facing an unexpected circumstance? Did you see God at work in your situation? At the time or in hindsight?

2. Maren was growing into a young woman when an unexpected health challenge stepped squarely into her path. What the medical community now calls Retinitis Pigmentosa (RP) began taking Maren's eyesight, further limiting the possibilities for a single woman with a disability. How did this reality affect Maren? What guided her?

3. While the Civil War represented an act of patriotism to many men who joined the fight, for Rutherford "Woolly" Wainwright, the Conflict Between the States offered him an excuse to run from his grief after losing his beloved wife in childbirth. What were the results of Rutherford's strategy?

4. Elsa Brantenberg buried her daughter, watched her son-in-law walk away, and was left to care for her newborn granddaughter. When her prodigal son-in-law returns after leaving her alone for four years, Mrs. Brantenberg struggles with regret and anger while Rutherford prays for reconciliation. How would harbored bitterness and withheld forgiveness have affected Mrs. Brantenberg? Her family? Did you find yourself identifying with Mrs. Brantenberg or with Woolly? Why?

5. Do you see meaning in the title *Dandelions on the Wind* for Maren and for Rutherford? Explain. Have you ever felt tossed about on someone else's whim?

6. Elsa Brantenberg hosted the Saint Charles Quilting Circle on her farm for women of all ages. In the story, she said, "Here, in this quilting circle, none of us are alone. Not in our sorrows, nor in our triumphs." What role did the quilting circle play in Maren's life? Are you part of a group of women that is mutually nurturing? In what ways?

7. Even as her world was growing dark, Maren claimed that God's Word was a lamp to her feet and a light to her path (see Psalm 119:105). Do you look to God's Word to light your path? In what ways does His Word guide you?

Mona is available for conference calls where she joins your book club or reading group for a prescheduled conversation via Skype. When possible, Mona is happy to add an "in person" visit to a book club in a city she's visiting. Visit www.monahodgson.com for more information.

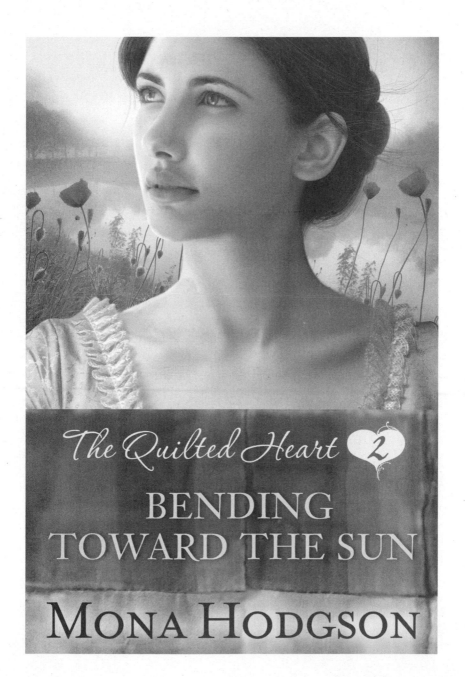

The Quilted Heart 2

BENDING TOWARD THE SUN

MONA HODGSON

To my hubby, Bob Hodgson
The man whose heroic qualities inform and
inspire all of the leading men in my stories

Keep thy heart with all diligence;
for out of it are the issues of life.

—PROVERBS 4:23

September 30, 1865

Emilie stood in one of her favorite places—Mrs. Brantenberg's kitchen. Anywhere on the farm was, really. But this airy room, with the big window looking out on the back acres, plenty of cupboards and workspace, and two well-stocked sideboards, made cooking and baking a delight. Even better, today was the day she and *PaPa* came to the farm to help with the apple harvest. She and her friend Maren were hard at work preparing the feast for those picking in the orchard.

Emilie sprinkled the cinnamon-perfumed topping on the soft apple wedges, then slid her skillet apple crisp into the oven. Brushing a strand of brown hair behind her ear, she looked at Maren, who stood with her hands in the dish tub. "Have you set a date for the wedding?"

"Rutherford and I have spoken with Mrs. Brantenberg about February." Maren's blue eyes sparkling at the mere mention of Rutherford's name, she pulled a cook pot into the dishwater.

"That's only four months away. Will you be ready?"

"I'm ready now."

"You are?" Surprised by her friend's tranquil response, Emilie slid a cooled loaf of Mrs. Brantenberg's honey-wheat bread into a sack. "You don't want a special dress or cake or feast? Where will you have the ceremony? How many guests? It seems there would be myriad details to look after."

"I didn't say everything *else* was ready." Pink tinged Maren's cheeks. "I meant that I'm ready to be Rutherford's wife."

"Oh." A different set of details altogether occupied Maren's thoughts. Warmth rushed up Emilie's neck. She obviously had much to learn about that kind of love.

"Now that I'm living in town, I miss seeing him every day. Before I met Rutherford, I wouldn't have believed it possible to love so deeply." Drying her hands on her apron, Maren met Emilie's gaze. "What about you?"

"Me?"

"Yes." Maren sighed. "You don't want love in your life?"

"I have love in my life." Emilie tucked a second loaf of bread into the sack and carried it to the crate. "My father loves me and I love him."

"A father's love is not at all the same."

Emilie didn't doubt that. But as full as her life was with PaPa, the store, and now college, there was no time or energy left to even entertain the thought of such foolishness. One man in her life was enough to keep her busy. "Maren Jensen, you have become a hopeless romantic."

"Perhaps. But don't be too surprised if you discover that romance can be contagious."

Not for her. Having her father and the store to take care of had made her immune to romantic notions. And that was best.

Maren glanced out the window, and Emilie followed her gaze. Mrs. Brantenberg's wagon bumped up the road from the orchard.

"I know you're extra busy with your college classes these days." Maren added a butter crock to one of the crates. "Is there more I can do for you at the store?"

"It's been wonderful having you there the past few weeks, almost like having a sister. But soon you and Rutherford will marry, and he'll want you here on the farm. Not working in town."

A shadow crossed Maren's face. "If he decides to stay in Saint Charles."

"If? I thought—"

"He received a letter from a childhood friend, a Mr. Garrett Cowlishaw, who is coming to lead the caravan of wagons west in the spring."

"Oh." Emilie had heard about the caravan, of course, but... "You think Rutherford will want to join him? Take you and Gabi and Mrs. Brantenberg on the trail?"

"He has not said as much, but I would not be surprised."

"My father and the Rengler brothers were talking about the caravan." Emilie pulled the cast-iron skillet from the oven, inhaling the sweet scent of baked apples. "He seemed drawn to the idea and asked me what I thought."

Maren tucked a strand of blond hair into her coiled braid. "I had my fill of traveling, coming from Denmark only four years ago. I'm content in Saint Charles. On the farm. How do you feel about leaving town and the store?"

"Leaving my classes behind is a temptation, but I feel no compulsion to go west."

"I agree. Unless the man I love decides to go."

Emilie pulled tin cups from the shelf. PaPa wouldn't insist on going, would he?

They had the three crates loaded when Mrs. Brantenberg walked through the kitchen door and stopped at the worktable.

Maren smiled at the older woman. "Emilie and I have all the food prepared and ready to go."

"Good. Many hands make the work short." Mrs. Brantenberg lifted a crate off the worktable and walked to the door. "Our pickers are hungry enough to eat tree bark if we don't feed them right quick."

The two young women set the remaining crates in the back of the wagon and climbed onto the seat behind Mrs. Brantenberg.

"Rutherford is already working the press." Mrs. Brantenberg lifted the reins from the floorboard.

"We'll have fresh apple cider with our meal." As the wagon jerked forward, Emilie looked ahead to the tables set up left of the orchard. It appeared that her father was seated there. Hopefully he hadn't done too much and worn himself out.

"Emilie and I were discussing the wedding," Maren said. "She thinks the notion of love and romance is all a bit silly."

"The wedding plans, or the way you and Rutherford are distracted beyond all reason?"

Emilie giggled. "Both." As the wagon rolled to a stop, she watched neighbors and friends fill a constellation of baskets with apples.

"Who will haul the baskets to the dock?" Maren said. "Will Rutherford do that?"

"He arranged for McFarland Freight to do the hauling again this year."

No doubt it would be the elder Mr. McFarland, or Brady, his oldest son, doing the pickup. They'd been delivering freight from the steamboats and barges to the store.

But it was the youngest McFarland boy Emilie was curious about. From all the talk at the checkerboard, she knew Quaid had returned, but she hadn't so much as caught a glimpse of him in town. The last time they'd seen each other was Christmas in '61. The memory of Quaid slipping several of Mrs. Brantenberg's *Zimtsterne* into his coat pocket made her smile. That was after he'd already enjoyed a few of the cinnamon stars. Not long afterward, he joined the Union Army and marched off to war.

The reins lay slack in Quaid's hand as he guided the freight wagon up Salt River Road. Red and golden leaves fluttered on the tangle of trees that characterized the river valley. If there were words strong enough to describe how right it felt to be away from the city, they'd escaped him.

Ever since he'd returned from the war, he'd been cooped up under his mother's watchful eye. He knew why she'd clung to him. Scores of mothers didn't have the opportunity to welcome their sons home. But when his father mentioned this job, Quaid pled his case until he broke free.

Smoke curled above one of several chimneys on the plantation house. He pulled up on the reins and slowed the two horses, guiding them beyond the rose bushes that lined the long path to the columned front porch. The freight wagon rumbled up Brantenberg Lane past the cluster of brick and wood buildings. Widow Brantenberg's palatial house was set in the center with its milk cellar, granary, and the smokehouse. All German farmers here had one.

Quaid's Irish ancestors, however, could do without a smokehouse, but wouldn't own land without a hops garden for the making of a little stout.

He passed the hog pens, grazing cows, and wheat and oat fields. The orchard came into view, and so did about two dozen people, including a few scampering children. A couple of buckboards were parked in front of the rows of trees.

Rutherford Wainwright waved his kepi from the cider press and pointed Quaid toward an assembly of baskets—the freight he'd come to haul into town. Quaid returned his friend's wave, then stopped beside the baskets and hopped down from the wagon. Apple cider scented the cool air.

"Quaid." Rutherford shook his hand. "Good to see you."

"Thanks, me friend. It's by the grace of God that I'm able to be seen by anyone."

"You finished the new cupboard?"

"I did." Quaid wrapped the reins over a low branch. "Then me mother said the family had outgrown the meager number of porch chairs and wanted two more."

"No wonder I haven't seen your hide but once since you come home."

"Plenty of rockers now for you and your intended to come and sit in the shade of our roof for a spell."

"We might just do that. Especially if I catch wind there's a pot of your mother's stew on the stove." Rutherford pressed his cap over his brown woolly hair. "You and I were two fortunate ones to be able to return."

"We were." They'd fought in the war together and seen hundreds of men face to the sky.

A young woman waved from one of the tables.

Rutherford returned her wave, his smile as wide as the Missouri. "There's my intended now." He motioned for her to join them.

But it was the young woman walking beside her that captured Quaid's attention. Emilie Heinrich?

Couldn't be her. Since when was she so tall and…shapely?

"Mr. McFarland, permit me to present to you Miss Maren Jensen." Rutherford turned to Miss Jensen. "Corporal Quaid McFarland and I served in the same regiment." His glance came back to Quaid. "Miss Jensen and I will wed in February."

Miss Jensen bowed with measured dignity. "I am pleased to make your acquaintance, Corporal McFarland."

Quaid offered a proper nod. "The pleasure is mine, Miss Jensen." He turned his attention to the woman standing next to her, whose cocoa-brown eyes shined like polished stones.

"I trust you remember Miss Heinrich from the—"

"Yes. I do." As a girl with pigtails. "It's a pleasure to see you again."

"And you." Emilie held his gaze with a confidence he didn't recall. "The last time I saw you, you were…skinny as a pole."

Her face suddenly flushed pink. Had she just realized she'd been staring?

"The man has done some growin' up since then. Saved my hide at least once." Rutherford glanced toward the food-laden tables, then at

Quaid. "We smoked a pig and we're fixin' to sit down to a feast. Please join us."

Quaid was hungry, but it was his curiosity about Emilie Heinrich that compelled him to say yes.

Emilie had satisfied her hunger with generous helpings of pork and potato salad, red cabbage slaw, and apple crisp. Rutherford had read from the Scriptures and thanked God for the bounty of the harvest. Mrs. Brantenberg recited a poem, and then she and her granddaughter, Gabi, delivered three proverbs in German and English.

Emilie always enjoyed harvest days and the feast that followed. But today's celebration... She couldn't remember when she'd sung loud enough to hear herself and laughed hard enough to have tears stream her face. And it was all thanks to Mr. Quaid McFarland.

She remembered him as an ornery kid full of vinegar around his friends. But he'd changed.

After the meal, Rutherford seated himself with his zither on a bench at one end of the tables, next to a balding neighbor who had brought his mandolin. With very little coaxing from Rutherford, Quaid had pulled a harmonica from his coat pocket and joined them for a stirring round of patriotic songs and a few hymns.

Judging from the fervor with which Quaid played his harmonica, she'd say he, too, was enjoying himself. On the last note, Maren started stacking plates, and Emilie reached under the table for a crate.

"Been too long since I've had that much fun." The familiar Irish lilt drew her gaze to the bronzed face of the man now standing beside her.

Emilie moistened her suddenly dry lips. "Yes." She didn't remember his eyes being such an intense shade of green. Bright like emeralds. "When did you take up the harmonica? You're quite accomplished."

His smile having faded, he lifted the stack of plates into the crate. "It belonged to a buddy o' mine. In the war. Didn't have need of it anymore."

Breathing a prayer of thanksgiving for Quaid's safe return, Emilie added empty bowls to the crate. "You haven't been in the store, and since I hadn't seen you, I worried—"

"I'm fine. Thank you." Quaid reached across the table for the empty steins and goblets. "'Twas me mother."

"Was she ill?"

"Some folks may call it an illness." He glanced at his tatty boots. "With all the desperate reports coming from the battlefields, she feared the worst for me. Feared she'd never see me again. When she did, she wailed like a steamboat coming into dock and hasn't wanted to let me from her sight."

"And today? Your mother was ready to let you go?"

He darted a glance toward the road as if she may have followed him. "Me mother ran out of room to place any more furniture. She had to let me put me saw and hammer down."

"You build furniture?"

"Of sorts. I like to work with wood. As a boy, I made a box for me sisters' dolls and a footstool for me mother. Right before I left for the war, I made a desk for me father's office and promised me mother I'd make her a cupboard when I returned."

A man of his word. "I had no idea you were so talented."

"You've changed some yourself. No longer the girl whose pigtails I used to tug." He smiled. "Grown up and become a handsome lass."

Heat rushed into her ears. "I'm attending college."

His eyes widened. He looked as surprised by her odd response as she was.

"Lindenwood, not far from the store."

"At fourteen you were already smarter than most of us in town. Going for more sophistication, are you?"

"I gave up on sophistication the day I tripped in those fancy heeled shoes and spilled the sack of dried beans. We still find those beans." She smiled.

A grin widened Quaid's eyes. "I was in the store that day. Your father paid me fifteen cents to help clean up. They'd scattered clear to the back door."

Emilie set a folded tablecloth on top of the crate. "I'm taking college classes because it's what my father wants."

"Ah. What we won't do for our parents."

She nodded, unable to keep from smiling around this new Quaid McFarland.

"You're not working at the store anymore?"

"I am. On Tuesdays, Fridays, and Saturdays. That allows for my classwork. I try to come here on Thursdays for Mrs. Brantenberg's quilting circle."

They quieted, watching Rutherford walk toward them.

"I apologize for the interruption, Miss Emilie, but the sun is starting its descent." He turned toward Quaid, an eyebrow cocked. "You about ready to load your wagon?"

"Yes, of course." When Rutherford started toward the baskets, Quaid faced her, his green eyes commanding her attention. "It was indeed a pleasure to see you again, Miss Emilie."

"And you." She moistened her lips.

"Perhaps I'll see you at the store. Or at Lindenwood on a Monday or Wednesday. We make deliveries there too."

"I'd like that." Emilie felt herself blushing. But it didn't stop her from watching Quaid heave the baskets of apples onto the wagon as if they were feather pillows. He'd become a broad-shouldered man. An intriguing man.

"Emilie."

She turned to see her father walking toward her, looking as if he'd downed a glass of vinegar.

2

Her father sat taller than usual in the wagon seat, his back stiff and his jaw tight. He hadn't spoken a word since they'd pulled away from the harvest feast.

Emilie pressed her hand to his arm. "Are you not feeling well?"

"Mir geht es gut." His tone wasn't necessarily gruff, but definitely flat.

She knew better; he wasn't fine. "Did you do too much picking? Overfill your—"

"I'm not a child, Em. I don't need you fussing over me."

Her shoulders tensed. "You haven't felt your best of late. And it's not like you to be so quiet. If it's not because you don't feel well, then what's bothering you? Are you upset with me?"

"I'm thinking you and Quaid McFarland were looking at each other like you'd never seen the other before."

They hadn't—not as adults.

"The two of you were talking as if no one else existed."

He was upset because she had talked to Quaid? Was he jealous, or accusing her of being rude? Swallowing her frustration, Emilie folded her hands in her lap. "PaPa, I've known Quaid McFarland and his family since I was a little girl. He and I hadn't seen each other for several years...since he left for the war."

"You have your status to think about."

Her stomach knotted. "My status?"

"The McFarlands are—"

"You're upset because I was speaking to an Irishman?"

PaPa looked everywhere but at her. "The McFarlands run freight wagons to and from the docks. They're teamsters. They're Irish."

The knots tightened. PaPa didn't seem to mind that Quaid wasn't a German farmer or shopkeeper while laughing at his stories and singing to his accompaniment on the harmonica.

Out of respect for her father, she swallowed her impudent retort. "What does that have to do with two friends catching up during a harvest celebration?"

"I didn't say he was a bad man." PaPa met her gaze. "Just not suitable for you to waste your time, is my point."

"To talk to?"

"To marry."

"Then perhaps it's wise that you keep me too busy to think about such things." Turning away, she stared at the fluttering sycamore leaves. Quaid had it easy...all he had to do was fill his mother's kitchen and porch with furniture before she'd let him go.

∞

The bank of the Missouri teemed with activity. Wagons and carts vied for position at the freight docks, and Quaid's was one of them. But he felt like he was floating high above the road...above the tree line on the riverbank. Getting away from the city today had proven to be his best decision in longer than he could remember. Certainly an Irishman loves a party with rich food and lively music, but it was Emilie Heinrich who had him floating on the clouds. Emilie's winsome smile. Her melodic laugh. Her puckered brow when he'd mentioned her going to college to gain more sophistication.

He chuckled, remembering her mock indignation.

Emilie and her father had left the farm before he'd loaded the wagon. She was no doubt already tucked away above her father's store, just up the hill from the river. First thing Monday morning, he'd make it known at the freight company that he had first dibs on any Tuesday, Friday, or Saturday deliveries to Heinrich's Dry Goods. Those were the days Emilie didn't have classes. He'd also throw his hat into the ring for any deliveries to Lindenwood Female College on Mondays and Wednesdays.

"Hey, you. The Irish bloke."

That's what Owen Rengler called him, but it wasn't Owen's voice. Quaid looked up. Oliver, the youngest of the two Rengler brothers, stood at the stage of the Rengler River Freight steamboat, waving him forward, his other hand clutching the strap of his overalls. Quaid reined the horses to a stop in front of his friend.

"You had me thinkin' you weren't gonna make it in time for tonight's shipments."

Quaid hopped from the wagon and shook Oliver's bear-sized hand. "What, and miss doing business with a river rat the likes of you?"

A generous grin revealed the gap between Oliver's front teeth. "Finally saw fit to leave the house and visit the slums, did ya?"

"Forced to, with the war ended and the freight business picking up."

"Owen says we're to thank the good Lord for that."

Townfolk called Oliver a simpleton, but it was the young man's simple faith that had always impressed Quaid.

Oliver pulled a handcart to the side of the wagon. "You got the widow Brantenberg's paperwork?"

Quaid patted his coat pocket, then the pocket on his trousers. He'd had Rutherford sign for the load and remembered taking the papers from the table.

Oliver blew a low whistle. "I've seen treed bears less distracted than you." He hefted a basket of apples. "Somethin' got ahold of you?"

Just a German girl turned young woman. Quaid walked to the front of the wagon where the papers lay tucked under his hat.

He laid them on top of the basket Oliver carried.

"You meet Rutherford's intended?"

"Miss Maren Jensen. I did." Quaid pulled another basket from the wagon. "As it turns out, Miss Jensen is working at Heinrich's Dry Goods and Grocery and is good friends with Emilie."

"Miss Emilie and Johann were at the farm today?"

"They were." Quaid took off for the deck, pushing the cart up the ramp. He'd rather think about Emilie than talk about her.

His arms full, Oliver caught up to him. "Emilie Heinrich's the cause of your distracted nature, ain't she?"

He wasn't about to give Oliver any more grist for the river's gossip mill.

"Quaid McFarland. That you down there?"

He glanced at the wheelhouse next to them. Pete stood at the window. "It's me, all right. In the flesh." He'd missed coming to the river for pickups and deliveries with his father. Forgotten how much he enjoyed kidding around with some of the ship crewmen, stevedores, and teamsters. He waved at the squatty captain. "How are you faring, Pete?"

"Better than you tromping them hills in worn-out boots and carrying all that weight from here to yon." Captain Pete leaned out the open window, hanging on to his uniform hat. "You sure weren't in no hurry to let yourself be seen here."

"Look around…you blame me?" They all laughed. "I've been doing woodwork around the house. But I'm working as a teamster now. So don't be shy about sending more work me father's way."

"Happy to do it. Welcome home."

"Thanks." Quaid waved, then turned toward Oliver.

"Speaking of your woodworkin'," Oliver said, "Owen and me been talkin' about havin' the deck railin's done over. You interested?"

"Workin' on your boat? I'd have to do it on my off time, but yeah. I could build 'em while you're downriver and have 'em ready next trip."

"I'll tell Owen." Oliver heaved an apple basket. "He makes all the big decisions, you know."

Quaid nodded, then slid a basket off the back of the wagon and followed Oliver to the boat.

When they'd emptied the wagon, Quaid returned it to the McFarland Freight House on Pike's Street, then walked around the corner to his family home, which faced the river.

He stepped onto the porch. The riotous chatter and laughter on the other side of the log wall warmed his heart. Someday, he would have a lively household of his own. He opened the door and stepped inside. "I'm home."

His mother strolled out of the kitchen, drying her hands on her apron. "That has to be my favorite declaration nowadays."

"And I'm blessed to say it." Quaid bent and kissed his mother on the forehead.

"Good thing you finally decided to come home." His older brother walked in from the kitchen with his wife at his side. "Mother wasn't going to feed us until you did."

"Then I'd say you owe me first pick of the freight deliveries next week."

Brady scrubbed his whiskered jaw. "You have particular deliveries in mind, do you?"

He didn't have the patience to wait until Monday to stake his claim. "Heinrich's Dry Goods Store and Lindenwood Female College."

"You takin' up playing checkers with Johann Heinrich?" A grin lit his brother's green eyes. "Suppose it could be his daughter you're interested in seein'." Brady waggled an eyebrow. "That might be it because I heard Emilie Heinrich had signed up for a course at Lindenwood. Afraid I can't oblige you, little brother."

Couldn't or wouldn't? Quaid kept his posture steady, hoping his voice would follow the example.

Brady regarded his wife, standing at his side, swollen with their first baby. "Siobhan was afraid all them single women would steal me away from her. Father makes both them deliveries."

"I don't have a wife to worry about such things. You think Father would mind me taking those from him?"

"Taking what?" Quaid's father stepped over the threshold with the giggling, curly-headed twins in tow.

Quaid greeted his seven-year-old sisters, then looked at his father. "It felt good to get out and make deliveries today. I'd like to do the deliveries to Heinrich's Dry Goods and to Lindenwood Female College for you."

"Methinks he developed an attraction to a certain young woman?" Brady chuckled.

Quaid resisted the impulse to stick out his tongue. He'd expected Brady's ribbing, but he had to try. He wanted to see Emilie again—and often.

"Heinrich's and the female college?"

Quaid nodded. "Yes sir."

Father cocked his head. "If that *certain young woman* is Emilie Heinrich, she has a father who keeps close watch on her." His voice fell flat. "You can make the deliveries. But no dawdlin'."

"Thank you."

"Mind yourself, son. *Herr* Heinrich may not appreciate you becoming any more than friends with his daughter."

His father's exaggerated German pronunciation in a distinct brogue would be comical—if the inference wasn't so menacing.

3

Thursday, Emilie chose to sit close to the crackling fire. The ride to the farm for the quilting circle had been cold and damp, but the hugs were warm and Mrs. Brantenberg's home cozy. Emilie drew a deep breath, savoring the sweet scent of the burning applewood, and pulled a cloth appliqué from her stack on the table. Using scraps from discarded clothing, she was making a Floral Basket quilt for her bed. Today she would begin stitching the baskets on the squares. After capping her finger with a thimble, she pushed the needle through the fabric. This step in the quilting process was likely her favorite—the moment a pattern began to take shape on the quilt top.

The design for her life had become clear when her mother ran off, leaving her to care for PaPa. So why, after twelve years, was the pattern beginning to look misshapen?

Corporal Quaid McFarland was to blame.

"It's a pleasure to see you again."

The pleasure was all hers.

"You've grown up and become a handsome lass."

Emilie felt her face grow warm even in the remembering. They'd both changed and grown up in the separation. And yet their shared memories had created a bond she'd not realized until Saturday.

Emilie positioned a flower petal on the square. If she was seeing flaws in her life's pattern, it was actually Maren who was at fault. Before Maren started singing the praises of a loving companionship, Emilie had been quite content to keep her little-girl dreams at a safe distance.

"Life is much like quilting—a patchwork of scraps and remnants." Mrs. Brantenberg's voice returned Emilie to the present. "Like a quilt is made up of remnants...scraps, so is your life and mine."

Emilie stared at the basket appliqué on her quilt top, her own remnants coming to mind. Her mother leaving. Her friends in the quilting circle. Her father insisting she go to college.

Seeing Quaid again.

"We all have a long list of the scraps and squares that make up our lives."

Emilie looked around the room. Many of the women here— younger and older—faced difficult circumstances. Miss Hattie had lost her father to the war. Maren was losing her eyesight. Mrs. Brantenberg had buried her husband and her daughter. The young Mrs. Kerr's husband had lost an arm. Caroline Milburn still hadn't received word of her husband's fate.

"Every one of us has loved and lost, even recently. No doubt, we'd choose a dreary, dark piece of fabric for our losses."

Emilie followed Mrs. Brantenberg's gaze out the window, where Gabi played with the other children.

"I know I'd choose bright, cheery patterns to represent the joy my dear granddaughter brings me, for the return of Rutherford, and for his upcoming marriage." She and Maren exchanged warm smiles.

"I, for one, am thankful for the reminder." Jewell Rafferty looked at the quilting project she had laid out on the braided rug. "Thomas comin' home with only one leg hasn't been easy. Him not able to do the work he once did. Nor has waiting with my sister for word." She glanced at Caroline. "But any quilt worth a dollar offers a mix of light and dark."

"It's true in the quilted or transformed heart as well." Mrs. Brantenberg lifted the Bible from her lap. "I woke up with the third chapter of Proverbs on my mind. We may all know the fifth and sixth verses by heart, but I'd like to read them anyway.

> Trust in the LORD with all thine heart; and lean not unto thine
> own understanding. In all thy ways acknowledge him, and he
> shall direct thy paths.

"God, the Divine Quilter, has the perfect patchwork pattern for our lives. Each will be different as sunshine and snowfall." Mrs. Brantenberg returned the Bible to her lap.

Caroline sniffled.

"It's the batting that gives warmth to the quilt. Otherwise we may end up with a beautiful, but limp, blanket. We may choose wool or cotton for filling our quilts. In our quilted heart, our faith in the good Lord is the filling."

Emilie pushed the needle through the next flower petal. Quaid had said she might see him at the store or at Lindenwood. She would choose a bright colored fabric for that moment. But if her father found out about such a meeting…

The patch could quickly change to dark.

❧

Caroline sank into the sofa and wrapped her hands around her teacup, trying to absorb its warmth. The steamy fragrance of sassafras tea permeated the sitting room.

"Your quilting is improving quite readily." Seated in the rocking chair across from her, Mrs. Brantenberg stirred another pinch of sugar into her cup.

She'd only gotten as far as the top of a small block quilt in the three months she'd been coming to the circle, but she welcomed the distraction. "I'm enjoying quilting more than I expected I would. Maren was right—you're a good teacher. Mostly, it has been a tremendous help to keep me occupied." She met the widow's tender gaze. "When your husband died, did you feel like a part of you was gone?" She hated that her voice cracked. Phillip thought her strong, but he hadn't seen her put to the test.

"Yes. And that missing piece left a hole in my heart as wide as the Missouri."

Caroline's heart pounded. "For four years, I've felt that part of me has been missing. Ever since the day Phillip left me to go off to war. I've not received letters from him for quite some time." She set her cup in its saucer. This was October and his last letter arrived in January. "If Phillip were no longer living, I would know it. Wouldn't I?"

Mrs. Brantenberg closed her eyes for mere seconds. Jewell called it praying in the moment, something the woman was known to do frequently during discussions in the circle. "I knew Christoph was with the Lord because I had all but watched his spirit leave his body."

Caroline worried a button on her shirtwaist. "I don't know what to think. I don't feel that he's dead." Her voice quivered. "Neither do I have the strength to hold on to the hope that he lives."

Mrs. Brantenberg scooted to the edge of the rocker and reached for Caroline's hand, her tender touch calming.

"I want to trust God. I want to believe He is directing my path. But not knowing whether Phillip is dead or alive is a dark, dark remnant—a piece of my life that I want to rip to shreds." Tears stung her eyes. "I need to know if he's coming home to me. I need to know if I'm a widow."

Mrs. Brantenberg wasted no time getting to the sofa with her arms open wide. Caroline leaned into the woman's embrace and let the tears fall, her sobs muffled by the heartfelt prayer the woman offered on her behalf. When Caroline had spent her tears, she pulled away and accepted a handkerchief. This was one of the blessings of the quilting circle—like a careful mother hen, Mrs. Brantenberg cared for her chicks, even the newest ones.

Caroline sat in the backseat of the wagon, her two nieces on one side and her nephew on the other. Jewell, their mother, sat in the front beside Emilie Heinrich. Her situation hadn't changed in the last half hour, but she did feel better. Although the horses' hooves sloshed and the wagon wheels plowed through thick mud, the morning rains had given way to sunshine.

"I needed to hear what Mrs. Brantenberg had to say. My father and I haven't been seeing eye to eye this week." Emilie stilled and glanced back at Caroline, her eyes wide. "Please forgive me. I'm rattling on about a simple misunderstanding when you don't even know—"

"It's all right. I'm all right." She was in this moment, anyway. "Mrs. Brantenberg is a wise woman. She gave us all much to think on. She prayed for me and said her prayers would continue through the day and into the night."

Caroline couldn't help but feel God had stopped listening to her. Dare she hope He would listen to Mrs. Brantenberg?

"Auntie Caroline."

She looked at four-year-old Mary. "Yes, child."

"You're blowing lots of air again."

She'd apparently been sighing…deeply. She patted Mary's leg. "I do that when I'm blowing out sad thoughts."

"About Uncle Phillip?"

"Yes."

Little Mary's cheeks puffed, and then she blew air at her patchwork dolly. Her brother, Gilbert, and older sister, Cora, joined her, huffing and puffing, and Caroline couldn't help but laugh. Being an aunt was definitely a bright piece of fabric in the quilt of her life.

As they rounded the corner onto Salt River Road, a thunderous crack jolted the wagon. The rear wheel disassembled itself, sending spokes flying. The rim split in half and the remains settled against the trees like two rotten-toothed smiles. The wagon remained upright, but askew.

Jewell turned to check on the children.

That's when Caroline realized she'd pinned them against the seat back with her arms. "They're fine." Her voice quivered.

"Bless the good Lord. By His grace, we weren't traveling at any speed."

Tears streamed Mary's face. "We didn't mean to blow the wheel off."

Caroline lifted the child onto her lap. "Your air didn't do it."

"The wheel broke on its own." Jewell swung Mary to the ground and tousled her curls. "This isn't your fault, Sweet Pea."

Caroline joined Jewell and Emilie, standing at the rear of the wagon.

Eight-year-old Gilbert studied the damage, then straightened to his full height. "I'll walk to the farm and borrow tools and a wheel."

Emilie brushed a shock of dark brown hair under her bonnet. "Rutherford and Maren will be coming this way soon."

"Good day, ladies."

Caroline spun toward the greeting that came from behind them. The smooth voice belonged to a man riding a black stallion. The stripe on the outside seams of his gray wool trousers was missing, but they were the trousers of a Confederate soldier.

He swung down from the stirrup and removed his gray kepi. As he approached them, Caroline detected a limp in his right leg.

A shiver crept up Caroline's spine. "You were in the war."

"Yes ma'am. Most men were."

"I heard both sides would share meals, then fight one another. You ever have dinner with a Colonel Phillip Milburn in the Union Army?"

"My apologies, ma'am, but I don't know the name."

Her hand curled into a fist. "You may have even killed him, for all I know."

Her sister and Emilie both gasped.

His jaw tight, the man in gray glanced at his trousers.

Jewell took hold of Caroline's arm. "You don't know this man. He was one of hundreds of thousands who fought, as our husbands did."

Ignoring her sister's sensible rationale, Caroline stared into the man's hazel eyes, hoping to find her answer there.

He didn't look away, but neither did his eyes tell her what she wanted to know. "Ma'am, you have my sympathies."

She didn't want his sympathies. She wanted answers.

"My sister didn't mean any offense."

Neither did she want Jewell's defense.

She wanted her husband.

He gave a quick nod, then replaced his headwear. "None taken. I'm Garrett Cowlishaw."

"Mr. Cowlishaw, I'm Emilie Heinrich, and these are my friends, Mrs. Rafferty and Mrs. Phillip Milburn."

Tears stung Caroline's eyes. Not knowing her husband's fate was undoing her.

"Unless I'm mistaken," Emilie said, "you're a friend of Rutherford Wainwright."

"I am indeed."

"I was told this morning that Rutherford Wainwright received a letter from a Mr. Garrett Cowlishaw."

"That's me, one and the same." He glanced toward the lane to the plantation house. "You know Woolly? I was on my way to his farm."

Emilie stepped toward him. "I understand you've come to town to command the caravan of wagons going west in the spring."

"Yes ma'am." He glanced past them at the disabled wagon. "In the meantime, it would please me to mend your wagon."

Caroline pinched the sides of her skirt. "I'm going to the farm to get Rutherford."

Mr. Cowlishaw's eyebrows knit together in a frown.

It didn't matter if he thought her rude or deranged.

Not unless he could tell her what had happened to her husband.

4

Mother was nearly out the front door when she spun toward him.

"Quaid Patrick McFarland, God brought you back to us. You've been home nearly three months and haven't set foot in Saint Borremeo's." She raised her hand, a rosary slipped over her thumb, the beads dangling across her palm. "Folks'll surely think you heathen."

If doubt was the ruin of a godly man, he probably was a heathen.

Thankfully, before he could say as much, Father stopped him with a pointed look, then threaded Mother's arm with his.

"Missus, me son's a grown man, just come back from fightin'. It's high time you let him decide his church attendance for himself. Jesus, Mary, and Joseph will be waitin' for him when he's ready."

"Very well." Her sigh was nearly strong enough to tumble the log walls.

Father pulled her toward the door, then jerked his head, motioning for the twins to follow. Maggie and Mattie waved at Quaid, then skipped down the steps to the brick paved street.

Quaid closed the door and breathed a deep sigh of his own. Maybe his mother was right. His sergeant had told him he had a stubborn streak bigger than the horizon. Perhaps he should've gone to church with them. But if it was God who spared his life, why hadn't He done so for the hundreds of thousands of others who'd fought? What about their mothers? wives? sisters?

No. The time alone would afford him the perfect opportunity to think through the new railing for the Rengler brothers' boat. He'd had so many freight deliveries the past week, he'd had little time to do much besides work. He didn't know when he'd fit in carving a new handrail for Owen and Oliver, but he'd make the time. Working with wood is what fed his soul.

He grabbed his coat and hat from the peg, then walked to the small shed he'd turned into a wood shop. If he did attend church, it'd be for the wrong reason: to see Miss Emilie Heinrich. He'd not seen her since they'd parted at the farm, and he'd been pining for her lyrical laugh and easy smile.

Emilie teetered between looking at her professor and glancing out the window. Quaid knew where she'd be on Mondays and Wednesdays. Now that he was making freight deliveries, she'd expected to catch sight of him last week.

"Miss Heinrich."

Straightening in her seat, Emilie met her instructor's steely gaze. "Yes, Mrs. Barbour."

"Is there something outside the window that is more urgent than my instruction?"

"No ma'am. Please accept my apologies."

"I realize not everyone is as enthralled with the works of Shakespeare as I am, but if you wish to rise above the chaff in proper society, you will do well to pay attention."

Proper society? Would that be the farmers flocking around the newest plowshare? Or the folks gathered around the checkerboard? She forced down a laugh, trying anew to focus on the classic quotes listed on the blackboard.

The moment Mrs. Barbour dismissed the class, Emilie hung her book sack from her shoulder, and quickly made her way through the door and down the tree-lined path toward the road. She'd placed a merchandise order for the store. Although it was likely too soon to expect delivery this week, she held on to hope that she'd see Quaid tomorrow or Thursday. In the meantime, she had undergarments to launder before fixing supper for PaPa.

"Emilie."

Her face warmed, despite the autumn temperatures. Only one man with an Irish lilt used her given name to address her. Turning, she saw Quaid sitting atop the freight wagon, waving his slouch hat. "Emilie."

Did he enjoy saying her name as much as she liked hearing it roll off his tongue?

Giving no mind to the possibility of rumors, she walked toward the wagon, stopping beside one of the horses. "I'd hoped to see you here today."

He smiled, his emerald eyes shining. "I was in the kitchen stocking the pantry. When I didn't see you in the hallway, I was afraid I'd missed you. May I offer you a ride?"

"Yes. I'd like that." Although her father may not be so pleased...but what of it? It was only a ride, which would save her time. Before she could change her mind, Quaid took her book sack and set it in the wagon, then offered his warm, strong hand.

Settled in the seat, Emilie watched him pat the horses' muzzles on his way to his side of the wagon. With one smooth motion, he swung into the seat beside her. "To the store?"

"Yes, please." Or should she have him leave her down the block, in case her father was in a foul mood? No. She was not a child. Nor was she doing anything wrong in accepting a ride from an Irishman. A friend. She pressed her hands against her stomach, which was apparently hosting very active butterflies.

Quaid snapped the reins, setting the wagon in motion. "Is the city hosting a footrace?"

"What?"

"A footrace. With your speed covering that lane, you'd take first place."

She giggled. "I like to return home in time to tend to other things before I cook supper for my father."

"Well then, I won't dillydally getting you home."

Please. Dillydally. The flower boxes they passed on their way through town seemed especially cheery today.

"What will you cook tonight?"

"*Currywurst* and *Rotkohl.* Brats and red cabbage."

"Mmm. I might have to invite meself to dinner."

She fussed with the yellow ribbon at her waist, hoping her face wouldn't betray her. She didn't want to tell him her father wouldn't approve. "I'd like that."

He nodded.

Thankfully, there wasn't room directly in front of her father's store, so Quaid pulled to a stop at the end of the block. Again, with the speed of Mercury, he appeared at her side and helped her from the wagon.

Her hand fit perfectly into his.

"Emilie." Letting go of her hand, he looked her in the eye with knee-weakening intensity. "I suspect your father would not approve of me offering you a ride."

The sigh escaped before she could corral it. She didn't want to tell Quaid the truth. Neither did she wish to lie to him. "It's only been him and me for the past twelve years. He's not fond of sharing me."

He handed the book bag to her. "With anyone, or with someone who's an Irish teamster?"

"This is a new world from the one he escaped in Germany." Emilie met his gaze. "I value my friends. Each one of them." She gave him a warm smile, then walked toward the store, hoping, for all her brave words, that her father was none the wiser.

❧

The next morning, Emilie finished the breakfast dishes. PaPa had gone to the store, which allowed her time alone in the kitchen—her favorite thinking place. It wasn't breakfast or the cleanup that cradled her thoughts this morning.

"I might have to invite meself to dinner."

More than once since Quaid had given her a ride home, she'd found herself distracted. The intriguing image of him sitting at the kitchen table enjoying the brats and red cabbage last night was foremost in her imagination. Then she'd remember her father's hateful statements.

"You have your status to think about. The McFarlands run freight wagons. They're teamsters. They're Irish."

PaPa was a kind man who would do most anything for anyone. She didn't know this father who would slight another man for his heritage or the job he held. He'd defended the rights of all men to choose their livelihood regardless of color or race. He'd donated provisions to each of the three Union regiments that originated in Saint Charles. Had her father always been selectively prejudiced?

She meant what she'd said to Quaid. Friends were meant to be friends, regardless of status.

That very morning when her racing thoughts commandeered her sleep, she'd propped herself on her pillows and reread the sixteenth chapter of 1 Samuel by candlelight. The seventh verse still echoed in her heart.

> *The LORD seeth not as man seeth; for man looketh on the outward appearance, but the LORD looketh on the heart.*

Quaid's heart was what mattered, not his status.

At the bottom of the stairs about forty minutes later, Emilie stepped into the store, looking for PaPa. He was alone, as Maren wouldn't be in to work until this afternoon. PaPa stood at the far wall, stocking a shelf with tinware and talking to a customer. Satisfied that he didn't need her help, she headed to the grocery section. Her first duty was to pick through the vegetables to make sure none had turned. She was passing a display of dutch ovens when she overheard a conversation that slowed her steps.

"I've found the sacks of sugar, Dumpling." The woman spoke in German. "I'm too short to fetch it. Could you reach it for me?"

Dumpling. She'd heard a man at the post office refer to his wife as his *little petunia.* Whatever possessed people to assign one another the name of a food or a plant and think it complimentary?

"I beg your pardon, Miss Heinrich."

Jolted out of her musing, Emilie nearly tumbled the stack of dutch ovens. She turned to face the man who spoke with a slight Southern drawl—and who'd served her recently as a wheelwright. He pulled the white slouch hat from his dark blond hair.

"Mr. Cowlishaw." He wasn't wearing his gray trousers today. "I didn't hear you approach."

"Soldiers with any chance of survival learn how to sneak around." A shadow darkened his eyes. "Some habits stick with you, ma'am."

"I would suppose they do." She tugged her apron straight. "Thank you, again, for your help with Mrs. Rafferty's wagon."

"It was my pleasure."

Had the man forgotten the way Caroline practically accused him—a complete stranger—of killing her husband? Emilie glanced from the door to the produce. "May I help you find something?"

He reached into his coat pocket and pulled out a scrap of paper. "As you know from your quilting circle visits, I'm staying out at Mrs. Brantenberg's farm some. Yesterday, when she learned I was coming into town last night for a meeting, she presented me with a list. I'm not much good at shopping for food. Didn't have a cause for it the past four years."

"I'd be happy to help."

"I appreciate it."

Emilie glanced at the list he handed her. "These five items won't take us long. Follow me, Mr. Cowlishaw."

She stopped in front of the empty casks.

For use in pickling, he chose a kilderkin, which holds half as much liquid as a barrel, then looked at her, concern narrowing his blue eyes. "It may not be my place to ask, but I have a question. Do you mind?"

Emilie noted his serious tone. "I don't mind. However, I'll refuse the answer if the question is inappropriate."

"Fair enough, ma'am. Mrs. Milburn from the wagon the other day...did her husband perish?"

That was the very question Caroline was desperate to have answered. It wasn't Emilie's place to discuss another woman's plight, but the man *had* endured Caroline's wrath with grace. "Mrs. Milburn hasn't heard from her husband since January."

"No word of him?"

"No sir." She started toward the spice cabinet, and he followed. "As you witnessed, she is desperate to know what became of Colonel Phillip Milburn."

His shoulders broadened. "I want to help. I know someone who may be able to find the answer."

"You would do that?"

He lifted his head, his expression one of earnest concern. "I'm a man with regrets, Miss Heinrich, but I'm not a bad man."

A knot formed in her throat. Her father wasn't the only one who struggled with assumptions. She opened her mouth, but closed it and offered a nod.

"I'd rather you didn't tell your friend of my efforts. Should they fail, well, Mrs. Milburn doesn't need added disappointment."

Emilie agreed. "I'll wait to hear from you then."

She caught sight of movement and glanced to find her father walking toward them, his expression uncharacteristically somber. "Is there a problem here?"

"No." She met PaPa's brooding gaze, then turned to her customer. "Mr. Cowlishaw, I'd like to present my father, Johann Heinrich. PaPa, this is Mr. Garrett Cowlishaw. He is a childhood friend of Rutherford Wainwright's."

"It's a pleasure to meet you, sir." Garrett shook her father's hand.

"And you, Mr. Cowlishaw." Her father's face neglected to exhibit the pleasure.

"Mrs. Brantenberg gave Mr. Cowlishaw a shopping list. I'm helping him find the items for her."

"I'll finish here," PaPa said. "You're needed in yard goods."

Emilie pressed her lips against her objection, then looked at Mr. Cowlishaw. "Give my best to Mrs. Brantenberg."

"I'll do that, ma'am. Thank you."

Her shoes stamped the floor as she made her way to dry goods. Pa-Pa's insistence had nothing to do with needing help in yard goods. He could've cut fabric. Helping customers with a list was customary. Something she did every day. But she was seeing a common thread in her father's reactions.

Garrett Cowlishaw may not have been an Irish teamster, but he was a young man, and it appeared her father thought he'd captured her attention.

And she had endured about all of her father's assumptions she could take.

5

G ood day, Mr. Gut." Quaid waved at the merchant and climbed onto the wagon seat, proud of himself for remembering the German pronunciation of the man's name. Another week had passed since he'd seen Emilie. He'd delivered sugar to the soda bottler, various chemicals in gallon jugs to the photographer, and a string-tied bundle of tanned leather to Gut's Saddlery and Harness. Next stop, Heinrich's Dry Goods and Grocery for his Tuesday delivery.

With a flick of the reins, he urged the horses left, up Main Street toward the Old Capitol Building.

If he were a praying man, he'd ask that Emilie be at the store and her father be away for the time being. Last Monday, when he'd teased her about inviting himself for dinner, she'd said, "I would like that" with a fair bit of emphasis on *I*. When he'd asked if she feared her father wouldn't approve of him offering her a ride, her sigh was deep enough to have come up from her toes, telling what she wouldn't allow her words to say—Herr Heinrich didn't approve of Quaid seeing his daughter, even as a friend.

Quaid blew out a long breath as he guided the horses around a tinker's cart stopped in the road. He didn't want his father to be right about Johann Heinrich being set against his friendship with Emilie. Nor did he wish to cause tension between Emilie and her father.

At the Old Capitol Building, Quaid turned the corner and pulled the wagon to a stop behind Heinrich's store. When he knocked at the back door, it wasn't Emilie or Mr. Heinrich who answered, but Miss Jensen, Rutherford's intended.

"Miss Jensen. It's a pleasure to see you again. I hope you're well."

"I am. Thank you."

"I have a delivery. Is Miss Emilie here?"

"She is."

"Good." His shoulders relaxed. "I'll need her signature on the bill of lading." A lame excuse, seeing as Miss Jensen was an employee and could sign off on his delivery.

Smiling as if she'd seen through the ruse, Miss Jensen pointed at the floor space against the end wall. "You may set the goods there. I'll let Emilie know you're here."

Quaid watched her walk through the inside door, then wedged the back door open and started unloading the wagon. He hauled in a couple of barrels of vinegar, then returned to the wagon. He was reaching for a gunnysack when Emilie stepped over the threshold into the sunshine. His breathing faltered. Her dress was the color of spring grass, his favorite color of green. Her brown hair was swept back and pinned up, but a few strands dangled over her ear.

She fidgeted with her skirt seams as she walked toward him, her pace as smooth as a dance. "Hello. I was cutting yard goods. Maren told me you were here."

He held her gaze. "I've started unloading into the storeroom. I hope that's all right."

She nodded. "My father is at the bank." She stopped at a respectable distance from him. "Thank you, again, for the ride last week."

"My pleasure. It's nice to have a friend who doesn't smell like a week on the river." She awarded him with a soft laugh. Were those gold flecks in her brown eyes? "Much of the wagon load was yours...your father's."

"During harvest season, I order extra gadgets and the latest toys. We have many folks request special items." She glanced past him, at the wagon. "Did the dollhouse come?"

"Dollhouse?"

"Yes." Emilie rose onto her tiptoes, peeking over the sideboards. She pointed to a crate at the far side. "That there, is it from New Orleans?"

He chuckled.

She angled her head, her dark eyebrows arched. "You think I'm silly, fussing over a dollhouse?"

"Yes, ma'am, I do. But I'm enjoyin' it." Emilie was definitely a handsome and intelligent woman, but still the sweet girl he'd counted among his childhood friends. He walked around the wagon and lifted the thin plank box.

Emilie stood beside him, teasing his senses with the fragrance of lavender. "Does it feel like it could be a dollhouse?"

"Do you have a pry bar handy?"

"In the storeroom."

"Lead the way. The only way to know for sure is to open it."

Her skirts swishing, Emilie walked through the doorway to a bin on the wall. When he set the crate on top of a barrel, she handed him the bar, excitement lighting her eyes.

Quaid pressed the flat edge under the corner of the lid and pulled, causing the small nails to creak. When the lid gave way, Emilie lifted it off the crate and gasped at the sight of the dollhouse. He carefully freed the wooden dollhouse from its cage. A balcony stretched across the full width of the recessed third floor.

She trailed her finger along the gabled roofline. "Beautiful!" She faced him, her smile lighting the storeroom.

Yes, beautiful, Quaid silently agreed. But he wasn't looking at the dollhouse.

"Emilie?" Mr. Heinrich stood in the doorway, his arms rigid at his sides. "What's going on here?"

"The dollhouse I ordered, PaPa, it came in today's delivery." She stepped aside and pointed to the house, complete with sheer curtains in the many windows.

Her father fixed his stern gaze on Quaid. "Has your father taken ill, Mr. McFarland? Is that why he isn't making the deliveries?"

"My father is well, sir." Quaid didn't need to explain why he was here. The storekeeper knew he was fond of his daughter—Quaid saw that knowledge in the tightness of the man's jaw.

Emilie looked at him, the golden flecks gone from her eyes. "Thank you for opening the crate for me." Polite, but impersonal.

"You're welcome."

"I need to get back into the store."

He nodded. "And I have a wagon to unload." Turning away first, Quaid went outside with her father at his heels.

"I'll help." The man's voice was devoid of its usual cheer.

They worked in silence until they each held an end of a bale of wool. Quaid stepped off the tailgate.

"I'm not opposed to you being my Emilie's friend." Mr. Heinrich's voice had softened.

Unlike the lump stuck in Quaid's throat.

"Emilie is a handsome young woman."

"Yes. Your daughter is also kind and intelligent." And distracting.

"You're a strapping young man recently returned from war. No doubt tired of bitter loneliness and ready to start a family of your own."

"We're merely friends, sir."

"I won't see Emilie hurt." The tightness in his jaw had returned.

Quaid scuffed the heel of his boot on the threshold, feeling tripped up in more ways than one. "What are you asking of me?"

"I'm asking you not to encourage my daughter's affections. She is completing her education. She isn't available. I'm asking you to stay away from her, except when it's necessary to see her in passing."

The man was asking too much from him.

6

Emilie swept the plank floor around the barrels of oats, while Maren dusted the jugs and bottles on the shelves. With quick broom strokes, Emilie swept the trash to the back door, wishing she could manage her scattered thoughts so readily. She stopped at the side window and peeked out. "The freight wagon is still here."

"Don't you wish you could hear their conversation?" Maren said. "Then you'd know what your father is saying to him."

"Actually, PaPa usually grows quiet when he's...concerned." Like he had on their return from the farm when she first reunited with Quaid. In this case, silence could be a blessing. She leaned on the counter as Maren dusted the kettles and pots that hung on the front of it. "I told you about the dollhouse I ordered?"

Maren stilled the feather duster. "It came in today's shipment?"

"It did. I can't wait to show it to you."

"You've already seen it?"

"I was anxious, looking for it in the wagon. Quaid opened it for me."

Maren glanced toward the storeroom. "That was sweet of him."

"It was. He set the dollhouse on a barrel. We were admiring it when my father returned through the open back door."

"Oh. Not what he'd consider the activity of mere *friends*?"

Emilie offered Maren a knowing smile. No need to waste her breath declaring she only thought of Quaid as a friend when they both knew her feelings for him ran deeper. Maren had watched her come in after her classes last Monday, especially cheerful, and heard all about the wagon ride.

PaPa burst in the door and set a crate on the counter beside her. "I sure hope folks are of a mind to buy. Because we have a lot to sell."

"I may have gone a little overboard, but I think folks will appreciate the variety we have to offer."

Maren moistened her lips. "Mrs. Applegate was in here this morning asking for the set of wool cards she'd requested."

"Well, I'm sure we have them. Somewhere." Emilie studied her father for a moment. He seemed a bit chatty for the way he'd sent her away from the storage room. Made her wonder what he and Quaid had said to each other. If anything.

A bell jingled, drawing their attention toward the front door.

"I'll see to them." Maren took quick steps toward the woman with a baby on her hip.

PaPa lifted the lid off the crate of enamelware. "The merchandise is unloaded, the most critical containers opened."

"Good." What concerned her was what he *wasn't* saying. "Is everything all right?"

"As far as I know, it is." German words mingled with English. "That Quaid McFarland is a hard worker." He pulled a coffeepot from the crate and unwrapped it. "The wagon is empty. He's on his way home."

Except that she hadn't had a chance to say good-bye, and she already missed him.

"You were right about the dollhouse, Em." He pulled a bean pot from the crate. "It's lovely. I already have just the little girl in mind to enjoy it."

"You do?" Emilie knew she was a bit old for such toys but wouldn't be opposed to saving it for the little girl she hoped to have…someday. Which now seemed a waste of her time if she wasn't allowed to talk to any man she might care about.

"Little Gabi Wainwright."

"Gabi is the little girl I had in mind when I ordered the dollhouse."

"I have a mind to order another for her. After all, Christmas is coming." Were his eyes actually sparkling?

Emilie added the pot she had unpacked to the collection on the counter and headed to the storeroom.

PaPa didn't seem to be stewing over her friendship with Quaid in the least.

She wasn't sure if that was a good thing…or not.

Quaid repeatedly pushed the saw through the oak beam he was forming into a railing for the Renglers' boat. Sweat drenched the back of his cotton duck blouse. Never mind that the sun had begun its descent and the temperature outside hovered just above freezing. Or that his coat lay on the bench. He had more steam built up than the Rengler brothers' boat ever did.

He pulled the saw toward him with a rip. He had always liked Johann Heinrich. Respected him. *Rip.* Everyone in town did. *Push.* The man had personally handed him a sack of provisions the Christmas before he went off to war. *Rip.* He still wanted to like the merchant. *Push.* After all, he was Emilie's father. *Rip.*

The saw went silent. In hindsight, it was easy to see Emilie had tried to warn him about her father's bias where his daughter was concerned. Heinrich's objection shouldn't have surprised him, except he'd given more weight to hope than to predisposition.

"I'm asking you not to encourage my daughter's affections."

Before today, Quaid supposed Emilie's feelings of friendship toward him could be developing into deeper affections. Apparently her feelings hadn't been his imagination, if her father had taken notice.

"I'm asking you to stay away from her, except when it's necessary to see her in passing."

Push. Rip. Push. Rip.

Could he do what Johann Heinrich asked, when what he wanted to do was to see her every day? When what he wanted to do was build her a dollhouse?

The door to his shop screeched open and he stilled the saw. Mother stepped inside, holding her shawl tight at her neck.

"Supper's ready."

She closed the door and walked toward him, her lips pursed. "Supper's ready, but my stew can wait on yours." She stared at the saw, her frown deepening. "Did you mean to cut your workbench nearly in half?"

The bench had indeed suffered. "'Twas thinking about something else." He laid the saw on the table. "Lots of deliveries today. S'pose I worked a little too hard." And hadn't worked hard enough at not developing deeper feelings for Emilie.

"I've seen you work too hard before, Son. Something else is going on."

He brushed the sweat from his brow with his sleeve.

"You wish to tell me about it?"

"I'd rather not." This was between him and Mr. Heinrich.

"You mean you'd rather not talk about *her*."

Her father, to be more precise. He couldn't bring himself to look his mother in the eye, even though he knew his inability to do so told her she was right—that his foul mood had something to do with Emilie Heinrich.

"Very well then. But I still have three things to say before we walk to the house."

Quaid nodded.

"One, never pick up a saw when you're frustrated."

He chuckled.

"Sure way to lose a finger." She glanced at the bench. "Or worse."

"Point made."

"Two, don't chase your feelings. Make them follow you."

Could he mind his convictions when he wanted to follow his heart?

"Three, me son is a good man. You'll do the right thing."

"How will I know what that is?"

She patted his shoulder as if he were still a boy at her knee. "Don't get in a fired-up hurry, and it'll come to you." She nodded toward the door.

He grabbed his coat off the bench, then followed her outside. "Beef stew with carrots and potatoes?"

"And soda bread."

As they walked to the house, it wasn't today's menu on his mind, but Emilie's brats and red cabbage. The odds that he'd ever sit across the dinner table from her had slid from slim to none.

7

The man that hath no music in himself,
Nor is not mov'd with concord of sweet sounds,
Is fit for treasons, stratagems, and spoils;
The motions of his spirit are dull as night,
And his affections dark as Erebus:
Let no such man be trusted.

Emilie set the pages of Shakespeare's play on the kitchen table. She'd been assigned *The Merchant of Venice* for her oral presentation on Wednesday, and Mrs. Barbour had stressed the importance of capturing the emotional essence of Shakespeare's writings.

If it was emotion she wanted, Emilie had it in spades. Quaid Mc-Farland was a man with music in him. And she missed hearing him play the harmonica. She missed his easy smile and rippling laugh.

She missed Quaid.

Deliveries were the only time afforded her to see him, and he hadn't made any recently. At least not on the days she was at the college or in the store. Not since he'd lifted the dollhouse out of the crate. She knew he had taken on side work. That must be what was demanding his time.

Tired of sitting still, Emilie walked to the window. The gas lanterns on the road below cast a golden glow on the falling snow. The temperatures had dropped last night. By midday, snow had begun to fall and hadn't let up. Walking in the snow had been enough of a challenge, but driving a freight wagon in it could be treacherous. She breathed a prayer for Quaid's safety, then added a selfish request, asking God to bring him back to her soon.

Quaid had bragged on how she was no longer a girl in braids but had become a handsome lass. A lass who had behaved like a giddy schoolgirl the last time he'd seen her. It was no wonder he hadn't come around for three weeks, himself being all grown up after serving in the war.

PaPa had sold the dollhouse to the banker and ordered two more, along with another crate of cookware. Hopefully the order would arrive this week, and her wait to see Quaid would end. As it was, she was fighting the temptation to make a batch of brats and red cabbage and deliver it to the freight house for his lunch. Not childish behavior, but neither was it proper behavior.

Emilie pressed her finger to her chin. It wouldn't be unreasonable for her to visit McFarland Freight Company as a businesswoman with an inquiry about a delivery. Minus the meal, of course. She shook her head. She needed to set her thoughts of Quaid aside, finish reading, and prepare her speech. Letting the curtain fall on her own drama, she willed herself to return to the table.

PaPa stepped into the kitchen, his tailored blouse billowing above his belt. Had he dropped pounds? He'd been eating well, hadn't he?

"It seems the snow has decided to persist." At the stove, he poured steaming coffee into his favorite cup.

"Yes." She settled into her chair. "I'm thankful I don't have classes tomorrow." Especially if Quaid had a delivery for the store. She kept her favorite reason to herself.

PaPa stood at the table, looking at the pages spread before her. "Your studies look tedious, Em. I'd say you could use a cup yourself."

"I could." She started to rise.

He pressed her shoulder. "I'll get it. It's the least I can do, as hard as you're working."

"Thank you." She swallowed a twinge of guilt. She'd spent most of the evening distracted.

She knew PaPa wasn't in favor of her spending her attention on Quaid. She thought to ask him if he knew Quaid had given her a ride from the college on that day that now seemed so long ago. Or if he'd misunderstood her gaiety over the dollhouse. She could almost suspect him of keeping Quaid away from her, but that was an unfair notion. When PaPa returned to the store after helping Quaid unload the wagon, he was pleasant, even complimentary of the man.

Besides, the Irish were known for persistence. If Quaid truly valued their friendship, he wouldn't be dissuaded by an overprotective father.

Which left her with one terrible conclusion: Quaid McFarland just didn't want to see her.

CRG

"You have to draw from the boneyard." Mattie wiggled in the armed chair. "I'm going to win you like Maggie did." Her green eyes sparkling, she glanced at her twin sister.

Quaid wagged his finger in front of her. "Not so fast, fair lass. I've not given up the game yet." He studied the maze of dominoes stretched across the table, following each of its legs to the foot.

Was that what was going on with Mr. Heinrich? Was Emilie's father waiting for him to make the next move? To call his bluff? He'd much prefer to do that than what his heart told him was the right thing.

But his friendship with Emilie was not a game.

He studied the soapstone game pieces. It was bad enough that one seven-year-old sister had beat him. He couldn't let it happen again. When he found his opening, he set his piece at the end of a spotted leg and leaned against the chair.

Mattie *tsk*ed, her smile gone.

Maggie squealed. "I knew he was going to do that. That's what I'd do."

"Don't tell him how to play."

"It took me awhile," Quaid said, "but I found it on my own."

Maggie hugged his neck. "I'm glad you're home."

He patted her hand. "You're happy to have someone around you can beat at dominoes?"

Both sisters bounced red curls in boisterous nods. When he feigned a frown, their giggles filled the room.

Father ambled in with Mother close behind him. "Me son must be losing again."

"I've taught me daughters well." A sly smile tipped Mother's mouth. "'Twas what we did to pass the time while you were gone."

"You couldn't mention my disadvantage before I agreed to a tournament?"

Father laughed and wrapped his arm about Mother's shoulders, pulling her close. "I'm a blessed man, Missus McFarland."

"Indeed you are, Mister. Best you keep that memory close." She tapped him on the nose.

Quaid felt pangs of longing. He wanted a wife to hold and a houseful of children. Only one woman came to mind. One whose brown eyes sparkled with delight at the sight of a child's dollhouse.

8

Emilie awakened early to work on her Shakespeare presentation. Due to her overactive imagination, she hadn't made much progress on her speech the previous night. PaPa had suggested she take the day off from the store to attend to her studies. But she had no intention of doing so if there was a chance the merchandise order would arrive. This time she wouldn't make a fuss over the dollhouses. This time she'd not fly from her father's presence, or from Quaid's.

She'd chosen her nicer day dress—a peach colored calico with flouncing at the waist and a touch of cream lace at the neckline. She'd also given extra attention to piling her hair this morning. Now all she needed was for Quaid to arrive in time to admire it…before she left her desk to stock and sweep.

Owen Rengler set a dutch oven on the counter in front of PaPa, ushering in the memory of overhearing the woman who had referred to her husband as *Dumpling*.

My little peach? Is that what Quaid would call her?

Emilie shook her head. No. If Quaid were ever to assign her a pet name, it'd more likely be *my little bean spiller*. First, Quaid would need to see her as someone who had set aside childish enthusiasm for dollhouses and truly grown into a woman worthy of his consideration.

Time to focus on the stack of vouchers tucked in the ledger.

PaPa walked toward the desk, his thumb hooked in his storekeeper's apron. "Do you have a listing for the eggs Owen's missus brought in?"

"I do." She flipped to Owen Rengler's page in the ledger. "It was ninety-eight cents, a total of three dollars and five cents."

Owen adjusted the bowler on his head. "Figured I better take Sally something special seeing as how I've been gone the entire week, and it's her birthday."

Emilie didn't know how much the man's wife would appreciate a gift bought with her grocery money, but it wasn't her place to say so.

PaPa wrapped the dutch oven in butcher paper. "You want to use the credit then?"

"Nah. I best not touch Sally's credit, lest I find myself eating stone soup every night this week."

Smart man. Emilie alphabetized the vouchers PaPa had taken in yesterday and started recording them in the ledger.

"No time for checkers today, Johann, but I'll be back later in the week, ready for the challenge."

"I'll hold you to it." Disappointment etched PaPa's thin voice.

She looked up. PaPa was moving slowly today and seemed extra tired lately.

Mr. Rengler had barely cleared the front door when PaPa strolled to the desk and handed her the sales receipt and cash. "Those ovens are fast becoming a bestseller."

"Good thing I ordered a few more. Should be in this week."

PaPa removed his hat and ran his hand through his hair. "You think you can handle the store for a spell?"

"Sure." She glanced at the mantel clock on her desk. "Maren will come up to work in less than an hour. You going out?"

"I was going upstairs. But if you need something in town—"

"No rush. I can go to the bank this afternoon."

"Very well then." He removed his apron. "If you need me, take the broomstick to the ceiling over the pickle barrels. I'll come down."

The ceiling below his bedchamber. Was he feeling sick again? His slow steps and slumped shoulders did nothing to reassure her. "PaPa?"

He paused and looked over his shoulder at her. "I'm fine, Em. Just in need of a little peace and quiet."

She nodded, fighting the impulse to fetch Dr. Stumberg. PaPa would call it a waste of time and money. The last time the doctor said he was suffering exhaustion. She should be relieved PaPa acknowledged he was tired and was willing to rest.

An hour later, Emilie had finished her bookwork and Maren was seeing to a customer. Given the freight boats' schedules, deliveries were usually made midday. She should go check on PaPa, but if he was resting, she didn't want to disturb him. Instead she walked to Maren at the yard-goods table and whispered, "I'm going to make sure the storeroom is ready for the next delivery."

"Good idea." Maren's dimpled grin spoke volumes. Her friend

knew she was hoping to have a few minutes with Quaid before her father interfered.

Emilie had just lifted the broom to sweep when wagon wheels sloshed in the melting snow outside. She stood the broom in the corner, smoothed her skirt, and opened the door. A blast of cold air whipped her lace collar against her neck.

"Good day, Miss Heinrich." Quaid's father touched the brim of his battered derby and climbed off the seat. A smooth-faced young man, not yet of shaving age, hopped from the wagon.

Emilie wouldn't see Quaid today either. She swallowed her bitter disappointment—and a niggling feeling that her father had something to do with Quaid's absence. Working hard to muster a smile, she stepped off the stoop. "Thank you, Mr. McFarland. And a good day to you. I hope you're well."

"Yes ma'am." He met the young man at the tailgate. "Brought help today. This here's Jimmie McFarland, me nephew, come to town from Saint Louis."

"Mr. Jimmie." She gave him a polite nod, wishing he was Quaid.

"It's a pleasure, ma'am." The nephew started hauling crates inside. Real strong for a wiry fellow.

Emilie regarded the elder Mr. McFarland. "Your family, are they well?"

"They're well, yes. Thank ye for asking. Me twins have me smack in the middle of their little palms. The eldest and his wife will soon give me a grandchild. Me missus is still over-the-moon happy to have her son home." He glanced toward the door. "But you're really asking after Quaid, I suppose?"

"Yes sir."

"He said you two had renewed your friendship upon his return."

"We did." Quaid had talked to his family about her?

"He is well. Gone with his brother on deliveries to Saint Peters, and then Frenchtown on their return."

Mr. McFarland probably preferred to stay close to run the business. Disappointment still stalked her, but it eased her heart a bit that Quaid had a good reason for not making the store delivery himself—his brother needed his help with out-of-town deliveries.

At least it was business, not her father, who had kept Quaid away.

The storm had let up about midnight. Although it had dropped four inches of snow, the sun was now shining, so Quaid carried on with his plans to go out of town. But he hated not seeing Emilie, and doing the right thing had yet to make him feel any better about it.

His brother drove the delivery wagon up Salt River Road toward Saint Peters. Brady had returned from war a year earlier than Quaid and married his school sweetheart who adored him, and now he and Siobhan were starting a family of their own. That's what Quaid wanted. Instead, he was living in his father's home, forbidden to see the one lass who had stirred his heart. Shifting on the seat, he caught sight of a hawk perched on a limb looking like a king while he waited for his next meal.

If only he were so patient. It's not that he begrudged Brady the life he had; it just all seemed so easy for his brother.

Because Brady fell for an Irish girl, whose family couldn't be happier.

Quaid hadn't darkened the doors of a church in more than four years, but he still knew the teachings. Envy was a mortal sin. So now he would have at least two transgressions to confess. Right now, his primary mortal sin of anger toward Johann Heinrich topped an ever-growing list. The man was Emilie's father. His elder, and someone Emilie loved. He saw no choice but to honor Johann Heinrich's wishes. He'd found himself asking God to change Mr. Heinrich's mind toward him. At the least, cause the man to give up on trying to keep them apart.

Perhaps confession would be a better place to restart his prayer life.

"Brother."

Quaid met Brady's gaze.

"You got woman troubles?"

"That obvious, is it?"

"Like the nose on your face."

"That's pretty obvious, all right." Quaid pulled his coat tight against the cold that was raging inside and out. "It's actually father-of-the-young-woman troubles, I have."

"I figured that's why you were with me rather than making the delivery to Heinrich's Dry Goods and Grocery."

"Yes. Between you and me?"

"I've kept your secret about cutting stitches on the bean sack all these years, haven't I?"

"So ye have." Quaid rubbed his leather gloves together to warm his hands. "I like Emilie Heinrich."

A smirk brightened his brother's green eyes. "If that's the part I'm supposed to keep secret, I'm afraid you've already spilled those beans."

Quaid nodded. "I told Mr. Heinrich me and Emilie are merely friends."

"'Tis true?"

"I thought it was."

Brady's expression grew serious. "What'd he say?"

"That Emilie is trying to complete her education and I shouldn't encourage her affections. He asked me to stay away from her, to avoid her."

"And you're tryin' to oblige him."

"May be a lost cause."

"And Emilie? Does she see you as a mere friend?"

He shrugged. "I don't know. She seems to enjoy my company as much as I enjoy hers." And she wasn't one to put on pretense like an overcoat. Her childlike openness was intoxicating. *"I'd hoped to see you here today."* Her easy laughter. Her glee when she saw the dollhouse. She was comfortable around him. But that could also be the behavior of a good friend, and nothing more.

Regardless of the depth of her feelings for him, he didn't wish to stir trouble between Emilie and her father.

∞

Emilie signed the delivery receipt and handed it to Mr. McFarland.

"Thank you, Miss Emilie. Greet your father for me, will you?"

"Yes sir. I'll do that."

He quirked a bushy eyebrow. "And I'll pass your greetings on to me son."

"Thank you."

When the McFarland Freight Company wagon rolled away from the store, she closed the door behind her and climbed the stairs to the home she shared with PaPa. He still hadn't come down. He may not appreciate her checking on him, but it wasn't like him to spend time upstairs during store hours. Especially on a day she was here and Quaid may have come with a delivery.

He wasn't in the living area, and the door to his bedchamber was closed. When she didn't hear any hint of movement, she tapped on his door. "PaPa?"

A snort. Then a stomp, where he'd apparently stepped out of bed, followed by footfalls on the wooden floor. The door swung open and PaPa stood before her, shielding a yawn with his hand. "I didn't hear the broomstick. You need me?"

"The order arrived."

"Ah. Then we have a lot of work to do, don't we?" He put his shoes on at the sofa.

"The senior Mr. McFarland asked me to pass his warm greetings on to you."

"I regret missing him today. He's a kind man."

So is Quaid. "They are a good and kind family."

PaPa nodded, then closed the door behind them on the way out.

She yearned to ask if he'd said something to Quaid to make him stay away, but she followed him down the stairs in silence. If PaPa wasn't feeling well today, it was best to wait for the answer. Besides, she'd know the next time she saw Quaid's father making a delivery to the college or to the store that PaPa had interfered.

Unless the newness of seeing her again had worn off and Quaid had simply moved on.

9

At the quilting circle late Thursday morning, Emilie pushed her needle into the flower petal appliqué and pulled the thread through. A few more petals to stitch and she'd have her quilt top finished. She liked the cheery pattern of the flower baskets. She'd also liked the new pattern she'd seen taking shape in her life—the one in which she was friends with Quaid and was seeing him fairly regularly. Until that day in the storeroom. She pushed the needle into the design, butting it against the metal thimble protecting her fingertip.

"My brother, Charles, has been spending a lot of time at The Western House Inn." Hattie removed the feathered crown from her head. "He's attending the meetings with Rutherford's friend Mr. Cowlishaw, the leader of the wagon train."

Garrett Cowlishaw was also the capable handyman who had mended Jewell's wagon and later come into the store asking about Caroline's husband. He'd said he wanted to help her find the answer to Colonel Milburn's fate, but that was nearly a month ago, and Emilie hadn't heard from him again. Another man discouraged by her father?

Hattie set her hat on the table beside her. "In fact, Charles went to a meeting first thing this morning."

Caroline squared her shoulders. "Your brother, who fought for the Union?"

"He did."

Caroline drew in a shuddering breath. "Your father died for the cause, and your brother fought for it, and yet he still thinks Mr. Cowlishaw is the best man to lead the caravan? He could well be a bushwhacker, for all we know."

Clearing her throat, Mrs. Brantenberg lifted her coffee mug from the table. "Even in our sorrow, especially in our sorrow, we must remember that God is Lord over all—the North, the South, and every mile surrounding them. God does not sow discordance."

Her lips pressed together, Caroline returned her attention to the quilt top on her lap.

"Your brother is taking a wagon west, Hattie?" Maren reached for her cup. "Are you planning to go with him?"

"Mother and I are talking about it."

Emilie's chest tightened. Could PaPa even make the trip? Not that she wanted to leave Saint Charles, but, like so many others, he'd talked about it. Now he seemed unable to make it through a day without a rest.

"Charles had brought home newspapers from San Francisco and Virginia City with articles written by our very own Sam Clemens from Hannibal." Hattie's voice rose with the thrill of adventure. "It seems there's no end to the opportunities there."

"Phillip talked about going west. Before the war." Caroline's last words squeaked out.

Mrs. Brantenberg returned her mug to the table. "Who will pray for our dear Caroline?"

"I will." Maren offered a heartfelt prayer, asking for God's comfort and peace for Caroline and for the Lord's divine stitching together of the scraps and remnants in her life.

"Thank you." Caroline blotted her tears with a handkerchief. "I am thankful for this circle, and for your prayers."

Emilie wiped tears from her eyes, then followed Mrs. Brantenberg into the kitchen, met by the sweet aroma of baking bread.

Mrs. Brantenberg stood at the stove, stirring a pot of onion soup while Emilie pulled a tureen from the shelf.

"What's on your heart, dear?" She'd spoken in German.

Emilie met the woman's tender gaze. "It seems quite selfish, given Caroline's situation."

"God sees you, too, dear."

Emilie nodded. "On harvest day, Quaid McFarland came with the freight wagon."

Mrs. Brantenberg pulled a loaf of bread from the oven. "I remember. The two of you seemed to enjoy each other's company."

Emilie moistened her lips. "We hadn't seen each other since he'd gone to war. Yes, I enjoyed his company, and he seemed to enjoy mine." Or he wouldn't have bothered to catch up to her at Lindenwood.

Mrs. Brantenberg's sigh waved the wisp of graying hair on her forehead. "Your father doesn't like it." A kindhearted look crossed her face.

Emilie shook her head. "No." She wanted to say more, but didn't wish to show disrespect.

"You care for Quaid."

"Yes ma'am, I do." Emilie set the butter crock on the table. "At first, I thought we were only old friends. Now I have feelings for Quaid that may run deeper."

Mrs. Brantenberg's thin eyebrows arched. "Sounds as if you may have stepped into a brier patch. Barefoot."

"That describes it perfectly." And it hurt, no matter which way she stepped.

"Without a doubt, a prickly place to be." Mrs. Brantenberg enfolded her in a warm embrace. "I'll remember you in my prayers, dear. Your father and Quaid McFarland, too."

"Thank you."

Mrs. Brantenberg set the wooden spoon on the counter. "In the meantime, the soup is ready."

Emilie laid a patchwork mat on the table.

A knock sounded on the back door, and it swung open. Garrett Cowlishaw stepped into the kitchen, his hat in his hand. "Rutherford said it'd be all right for me to come in."

Mrs. Brantenberg motioned him in farther. "I made enough soup for you and Rutherford."

"Thank you, ma'am. I didn't want to disturb your quilting, but..." He looked at Emilie. "I'm glad you're in here, Miss Heinrich. I wanted to talk to you."

Emilie's heart raced. "You have news?"

"For Caroline?" Mrs. Brantenberg pressed her hand to her mouth. Emilie didn't bother to ask the widow how she knew.

"Yes ma'am." His shoulders sagged. The message couldn't be more clear. It was bad news.

"I'll get her." Mrs. Brantenberg spun toward the door, quickly returning with Caroline.

Caroline planted her hands at her waist. "Mr. Cowlishaw? What right do you have summoning me like this?"

"My apologies, ma'am. I wouldn't trouble you, except that I have news of your husband."

Caroline looked at Emilie.

"Mr. Cowlishaw came to the store concerned that you hadn't received any word from your husband or the Department of War. He said he knew someone who might be able to obtain the answer you needed."

"And you didn't tell me?"

Emilie swallowed, breathing a prayer. "It was nearly a month ago, and I...we didn't want to get your hopes up."

"And now?"

Mr. Cowlishaw took a step toward her. "Ma'am, if you'd like to have a seat." He pointed to a chair at the table.

"I prefer to stand." Caroline stretched a red curl at her neck. "Thank you."

"Very well then." He reached into his coat pocket and pulled out folded paper. "The man who contacted me to master the train of wagons was a lieutenant in the Union Army. I told him of your plight and asked him to inquire about Colonel Phillip Milburn at the Department of War."

"But you don't know me. I wasn't even cordial in our first meeting."

"No ma'am."

"Then why would you trouble yourself?"

"It pains me to see a woman in distress."

Caroline blinked as if fighting tears. "You have my answer then?"

"This is the answer the lieutenant received." He held the paper out to Caroline. "My deepest sympathies, ma'am."

"You're making this up." Caroline grabbed Mrs. Brantenberg's arm. "I didn't feel it. Phillip *has* to be alive."

Mrs. Brantenberg patted Caroline's hand and gave Emilie a quick nod.

Emilie took the correspondence from Mr. Cowlishaw and unfolded the paper.

Department of War, Washington, District of Columbia

Dear Mrs. Milburn,

It is with deepest regret that I write you. Your beloved husband, Colonel Phillip Milburn, served our country well, earning the loyalties of his regiment and indeed the entire army.

Peril beset the good colonel in the Battle of Nashville, 16 December 1864, where the Union had suffered 387 killed, 2,562 wounded, and 112 missing. Colonel Milburn was instrumental in the taking of Shy's Hill, the source of much of the carnage. Though mortally wounded, he led his artillery unit to destroy the entrenchment and the cover it had provided the sharpshooters of the Confederacy. The Union ultimately prevailed in the battle, with no little thanks to the sacrifice made by your husband.

Caroline gasped. Emilie stopped reading while Mrs. Brantenberg guided Caroline to a chair at the table. With Mrs. Brantenberg seated beside her, Caroline looked at Emilie. "Is there more?"

"Yes."

"Then please continue."

Blinking back her own tears, Emilie fought to focus on the scrawling penmanship.

> *A brave patriot, your husband. He succumbed to his injuries the following day, 17 December 1864, and was buried with full military honors near Nashville.*
>
> *A box of the colonel's personals will be forthcoming. You may expect it to arrive shortly.*
>
> *With deepest sympathies,*
> *Major Augustus Shnebley, United States Department of War*

Caroline looked at her, tears streaming her face. "It's true then? Phillip is dead?"

Emilie nodded, about to bite through her bottom lip. Listening to Caroline's sobs, she thanked God for her small problems.

In the shadow of her friend's staggering heartbreak, her own heartache was slight.

10

Emilie walked up Main Street with Maren and Hattie. They'd been planning this Saturday outing for nearly three weeks. Long before Caroline received the news that she was indeed a widow.

"It doesn't seem right that I look for a wedding dress while Caroline mourns the loss of her husband." Frown lines furrowed Maren's brow.

Emilie had grappled with the same concern.

Hattie tucked a brown curl under her hat. "When my father died, I didn't want everyone moping about feeling sorry for me. Caroline wouldn't want that either."

"Hattie's right," Emilie said. "God has given you and Rutherford a second chance at love. That's a gift worth celebrating."

A slow smile lit Maren's blue eyes. "I do love that man."

Emilie refused to give in to her regrets. She was blessed with a father who was still alive and loved her, a respectable job, and a gaggle of wonderful friends.

Hattie hooked their arms as they strolled the cobblestones past the millinery, toward Gut's Saddlery and his daughter's Queensware Emporium.

The sound of a familiar Irish brogue drew Emilie's attention to the end of the block, where Quaid sat atop his parked wagon, visiting with a merchant. Her feet planted themselves. She needed to know if she'd imagined Quaid's interest in her, or if something or *someone* had interfered. What would she say? How did one even broach the subject? She watched as he flicked the reins and his wagon rolled toward her, a smile of recognition lighting his face.

He didn't look like a man trying to avoid her.

When the wagon stopped beside her, Quaid brushed the brim on his slouch hat. "Miss Jensen. Miss Pemberton. Miss Heinrich." His greeting was impersonal, but the intensity she saw in his gaze was not.

"Mr. McFarland." Her voice blended with the others.

"It's good to see you." He looked away, glancing toward the dry goods store. "But I can't linger. I need to buy wood for repairs to the Renglers' boat."

Emilie nodded. If only she could ask him if his glance toward her father's place of business was mere happenstance—or if PaPa was the reason he needed to flee.

When Emilie returned to the store, her father was engaged in a checkers match with Owen Rengler, while Oliver stood by looking on. She greeted them, then went upstairs to start the noon meal, welcoming time alone in the kitchen.

PaPa joined her within the hour. He clomped up the stairs as if his feet regretted each step. Seated at the head chair, he folded his hands on the edge of the table and offered the prayer of thanksgiving for their meal. Emilie recited the prayer with her father, but her mind was busy shaping questions.

"Amen." Emilie spread her napkin on her lap.

"Did you have a good time with your friends this morning?" PaPa looked a little better today, his eyes brighter.

"I did." Emilie scooped a potato cake and a schnitzel onto PaPa's plate, then onto hers.

"That's good." PaPa cut into his schnitzel. "The widow Brantenberg and her family deserve a bit of happiness, with all they've been through."

"*Ja.* Maren and Mrs. Brantenberg are enjoying planning the wedding." Emilie reached for her glass and sipped water. "Who won the checkers game?"

"Games. Six of them. Owen won a game. Oliver won two games. And your dear *Vater* won three."

"Good for you. Sounds like you had a good day."

"I did."

"Thank you for giving Maren and me time off today. She found a couple of dresses she really liked."

"I'm glad you enjoyed yourself." PaPa raised his fork to his mouth.

Emilie took another sip of water. "I saw Quaid today."

He bit off a hunk of bread, looking everywhere but at her.

"For some reason, he seemed in a hurry to get away from me."

"Oh?" He gulped coffee.

"I found it puzzling. At first, he looked happy to see me. Then he glanced this way and made an excuse to take his leave in haste."

Studying his plate, PaPa moved the food around with his fork.

"PaPa?"

He raised his head.

With PaPa feeling better today, there was no reason not to ask him if he'd said something to Quaid while they unloaded the wagon. "What did you say to Quaid?"

He straightened in his chair. "I told him you were completing your education."

"Did you forbid him to see me?"

"No."

Emilie crossed and uncrossed her arms, refusing to look away.

"I asked him not to encourage your affections."

She gripped the seat of her chair. "How *could* you?"

"It's my duty to protect you."

She leaned on the table. "And what will become of me when you're gone? Will I be trusted then to know what is best for me? And what of God, that you need to do His job?"

Her hands shook. She'd never spoken to her father that way. Why wasn't he yelling at her, defending his right to choose her companions? At the very least she expected a hefty scolding for disrespecting her elder. But he didn't have to reprimand her.

The knots in her insides were discipline enough for speaking to him in such an insolent manner.

She looked across the table. PaPa sat still, his hands cupping his coffee mug. "I'm sorry, PaPa. I know I'm all you have."

Sadness rimmed his eyes.

Emilie wiped her mouth with her napkin. "It's good this happened." She made a show of smoothing the napkin over her lap. "Anyone who could give up on me so easily isn't a true friend, after all. Quaid's avoidance of me is a sure sign he didn't care about me in the first place."

11

The new lumber still lay in the wagon as Quaid carried two cups of coffee to his father's office. Quaid had been greasing hubs ever since his return from the lumber mill. He didn't trust himself with a saw right now.

He stepped through the open door. His father sat at his desk, bent over a ledger. "You've been chewin' on the bookwork all afternoon?"

Chuckling, Father waved him toward the desk. "Mostly. I'm hoping one of your sisters'll take to working sums. And soon."

He remembered that Emilie did her father's bookwork. There wasn't much lately that didn't bring her to mind. Quaid set a cup at his father's right hand. "Thought coffee might help."

"Might not help with the numbers, but it'll warm me insides." Smiling, Father nodded for Quaid to sit across from him.

"You're a hard worker, Son. Glad you came back to be part of the business."

"Thank you. I'm enjoying makin' the rounds and catchin' up with everybody."

Father lowered his cup. "I'm proud of you."

Quaid swallowed the lump of emotion forming in his throat. "What for?"

"For one, letting me make the deliveries to Heinrich's. I'm proud of you for honoring his request, even though it's a difficult one."

"I saw Emilie in town today."

"Aaah." Father sat straight.

Quaid gulped strong coffee. "I greeted her and her friends, then made an excuse to leave. One of the hardest things I've had to do."

"I can't think of one thing worth havin' that's easy to come by. Not freedom. Not land. Not love." He rested his forearms on the desk. "If that's what you're feelin'."

"Emilie makes me smile more than I ever did. It hurts not to be able to spend time with her."

Father looked past him and stood. "Miss Heinrich."

Quaid rose from the chair, nearly upsetting it. Emilie stood in the doorway dressed like an angel in a dress the color of peaches and cream. A dainty reticule hung from her gloved wrist.

"Mr. McFarland. Please forgive my intrusion... I need to speak to your son."

"Of course." Holding his coffee mug, Father made a quick exit, pulling the door shut behind him.

Emilie looked at her gloved hands.

"This isn't a comfortable place for a conversation. But would you care to be seated?" Quaid pointed to the desk chair.

"It's an uncomfortable topic." When she finally met his gaze, he saw a thunderstorm brewing in her eyes. "I'll stand. Thank you."

This was his first encounter with Emilie's matter-of-fact tone, and he didn't like it. He hated hurting her. Of course she was angry with him. They had been friends growing closer, but lately he'd been avoiding her, practically shunned her this morning.

"I'm sorry we weren't able to talk earlier."

Even her sigh charmed him.

"Weren't able?" She pressed a gloved hand to a cabinet as if to brace herself. "If we were on Main Street now, in my father's line of sight, would you not run from me again?"

"You talked to him?"

"I had made such a fuss over the dollhouse that day I thought maybe you had decided I was still a child. But it was after you spoke to my father that everything changed between us. When I saw you this morning, I knew my father had interfered. At lunch, he finally confessed that he'd asked you to stay away from me."

Not to interfere with your education. Not to encourage your affections.
"I'm sorry."

Squaring her shoulders, she stood straight. "No, I'm sorry you're not the man I thought you were."

She couldn't have stunned him more if she slapped him. He blew out a long breath.

"The man I thought you were wouldn't cower…wouldn't abandon someone. Not someone he truly cared for."

He took deliberate strides toward her. When he'd closed the gap between them, he cupped her elbows, wishing her shawl was anywhere else. Her breath warm on his face, he lowered his lips to hers. Soft lips.

Welcoming lips. He made himself take a step backward, still holding her arms. Now, the lightning in her eyes was on his side.

"Does that feel like the kiss of a man who doesn't care for you?"

She shook her head.

"I'm not the man you thought I was if you thought I could toss proprieties aside, show no respect for your father, and risk damaging your relationship with him."

Tears brimmed her eyes.

"Like you, Emilie, I value family, and your father—"

"Is all I have." Her voice quivered, and his heart ached. He wanted to take her in his arms and make promises, say she had him too. But he couldn't.

"My mother told me not to chase my feelings, but to make them follow me."

A tear rolled from her bottom eyelid onto her creamy cheek. Bending forward, he wiped it away with his thumb.

"I can't trust my feelings if they mean I can't be true to myself… who I am deep inside."

More tears spilled onto her cheeks, and she pulled a handkerchief from her reticule. "I like your mother."

"Are you sorry I kissed you?"

"No." Strength had returned to her voice. "But I don't know what to do."

"You're a woman of faith."

"I try to be. Yes."

"Do you believe God could change your father's heart toward me…toward us?"

"I want to believe it."

"Then you need to trust me. More important, you need to trust God."

Her lips tight, Emilie nodded, then walked to the door.

Leaning on the office doorframe, he watched her walk past the wagons toward the door open to the street.

"God, help me trust You. I love her."

∞

Emilie sat in the armchair in her bedchamber. The light from her candle lantern cast a faint glow on the journal she held. Her Bible lay open on the small table beside her. Quaid's mother was a wise woman, and her son, a wise man. A man who seemed to know her better than she knew herself. And he'd been right; it would break her heart to go against her father. Quaid had refused to ask her to choose.

He was willing to wait.

Had he known she'd heard his prayer and confession of love for her, waiting would have been unspeakable. She'd felt the impatience in Quaid's tender, but certain kiss. She'd forced herself to maintain her gait until she left the freight house and rounded the corner.

Quaid had done the right thing giving credence to PaPa's concerns. She needed to follow his example—to honor her father.

Opening her door, she breathed a prayer for God's grace and the right words. Her father sat in his favorite chair in the sitting room, his nose in a newspaper.

"PaPa."

He lowered the paper and peered over his wire-rimmed spectacles. "I thought you had retired for the night."

"I thought so too. I've been reading and writing in my journal."

Light from the lantern on the wall above him showed the bald spot at the back of his head. Until recently, he'd seemed ageless. "I went to see Quaid this afternoon."

"I suspected as much." He laid the newspaper on his lap.

"I know you don't want me to see Quaid. I know you think you need to protect me from him." She clasped her hands. "You should also know that despite his affections for me, Quaid intends to honor your request that he stay away from me."

He hadn't done as well with not encouraging her affections, but it wasn't for lack of effort.

PaPa didn't respond, so she kissed him on the cheek. "I love you, PaPa." The weight from her shoulders lifted, Emilie walked away. She pressed her hand to her lips and returned to her bedchamber, prepared for sweet dreams.

12

Wednesday morning, Quaid loaded the last of the railing into the wagon and climbed onto the seat. He'd worked in his woodshop every spare minute since Saturday. Not seeing Emilie hadn't been easy, but knowing she understood the separation made the avoidance more bearable.

"Let's go, boys." A little flick of the reins, and the horses headed to Main Street. Heinrich's store was out of the way, but they'd received a small shipment. Since this was a school day for Emilie, Quaid had agreed to make the delivery.

He reined the horses to a stop at the storeroom door and climbed from the wagon. He'd only knocked twice when the door swung open.

"McFarland?"

Quaid shook Mr. Heinrich's hand.

He studied the full wagon. "My daughter ordered all of that?"

Quaid chuckled. "No. Just a barrel of nails and a cask of medicinal in your delivery."

Mr. Heinrich walked to the wagon. "And this woodwork?"

"That's the new railing I made for Owen and Oliver's boat. I'm on my way to install it."

"I remember them telling me about that over a game of checkers." Mr. Heinrich ran his hand across the lacquered beam. "S'pose I knew you'd done woodworking, but didn't realize you were so talented."

Not Emilie's exact wording, but the same sentiment.

"Thank you." Quaid leaned against the tailgate. "With all due respect, sir, I think there's a lot about me that would be a pleasant surprise."

Mr. Heinrich smiled. "I'm sure you're right. Emilie told me you practically ran from her on Saturday. Thank you for honoring my wishes."

Quaid nodded. "Later, she came to see me at my father's office."

"She told me that, also, and what you told her about doing the right thing by me."

"One of the hardest things I've ever been asked to do. I care deeply for your daughter."

Mr. Heinrich turned toward the wagon. "You get the barrel. I'll get the cask."

Quaid wasn't sure what had just happened here, but he felt good about it. Trusting God had brought him peace.

Despite the chill in the air, Emilie decided on a more leisurely stroll home from Lindenwood. PaPa hired Maren to help at the store two months ago, yet Emilie had continued to push herself. Today she'd take time to enjoy the sunshine before autumn fully gave itself to winter. Along the creek and up the hill behind it, evergreen pines mingled with the linden and sycamore trees that stood bare awaiting their spring revival. Maren and Rutherford would wed soon, while she and Quaid were forbidden to see each other.

Emilie sighed, longing for spring's resuscitation.

Pinching the sides of her skirt, she took careful steps on soggy leaves to the water's edge. Settling on a log, she laid her book sack beside her and stretched her legs. With the sun warming her face and the creek burbling, she watched a squirrel scamper across a patch of daisies and drew in a faltering breath. Oh, how she wished Quaid were here, seated beside her.

She admired his integrity and respect for her father. If only she possessed his patience. But she knew her father and his dependence upon her. What if PaPa were to never come to his senses and accept her and Quaid's...what?

She pressed her fingers to her lips, remembering.

Quaid had told God he loved her. Is that what she felt for him? If so, she didn't want to love him. Not if PaPa wouldn't change his heart. It would hurt too much.

Keep thy heart with all diligence; for out of it are the issues of life.

At the breakfast table that morning, PaPa had read the verse from Proverbs.

Issues like frustration? impatience? rebellion? She was battling them all.

She needed to trust God with her whole heart.

Lord, I know You are trustworthy. I do want to trust You. Why does it have to be so hard?

She breathed in the scent of pine and studied the patches of daisies along the banks of the creek. Some stood in direct sunlight while others waited in the shade, all of them leaning toward the light, bending toward the sun.

Tears stung her eyes. She was a daisy in the shade, waiting and stretching toward the sun for light and warmth.

Guard my heart, Lord. It belongs to You, first and foremost. She allowed herself to linger in her thoughts and prayers for a few moments.

Feeling refreshed, she picked up her book sack and resumed her walk home. She'd started down the hill toward Main Street when she heard her name.

"Miss Emilie."

Emilie turned to see Anna Goben rushing toward her. "Miss Anna." Emilie embraced her. "It's good to see you."

Anna held up a sack with both hands. "I was taking these candles to the store, so when I saw you—"

"I'm glad you caught up to me. We can walk together."

"Yes. I'd like that." Freckles bridged Anna's nose. Anna's father had left her family when she was a girl, and she'd lost her brother to the war.

Emilie set a leisurely pace. "I don't know if you've seen Mrs. Brantenberg lately, but we've missed having you at quilting circle."

"I haven't seen Mrs. Brantenberg, but on Sunday, Jewell Rafferty and her sister Caroline brought us a pot of stew and an apple pie. It was awful nice of them to come, especially so soon after the sad news of the death of Caroline's husband." Anna tucked a strand of straw-blond hair into her bonnet. "I do miss the quilting circle, but…between *Mutter* and *Großvater,* the grief hangs thick at my house. I seem to be the only one right now who can face the days."

Anna was the only one working. Emilie knew that much. The young woman was making tatting lace for the dressmaker, feather arrangements for the milliner, and beeswax candles for the dry goods store.

"I'm sorry."

"Thank you."

Emilie held her head high while they walked. She had so much to be thankful for, and like the petunias in the flower box they passed, she would bend toward the sun.

At the dry goods store, Emilie held the door open for Anna.

"Emilie? Is that you?" PaPa rushed in from the storeroom but stopped in his tracks when he saw Anna. "Miss Goben. It's a pleasure to see you."

"And you, Mr. Heinrich." Anna curtsied slightly. "*Großvater* sends his regards."

PaPa nodded. "You tell him I said it was high time he come in and beat me at a game of checkers."

"I'll do that, sir."

"Anna brought candles." PaPa followed them to the counter, and Emilie set her book bag on the floor behind it. He wouldn't normally involve himself in the purchase of candles, but he stood there as she and Anna lifted the sack onto the counter. She met his gaze. "Did you need me for something else? Is there a problem?"

"No. It can wait." PaPa swatted the air. "You girls tend to your business."

PaPa left to greet the banker's wife as Emilie went to the desk for the ledger. When she returned, a display of dipped candles lined the counter, laid out like felled trees.

"There's thirty of 'em."

Emilie wrote a voucher for Anna and handed it to her.

Anna's hands stilled, her eyes widening. "Did you hear that?"

Emilie shook her head. "I didn't hear anything. Suppose I was too busy concentrating. What was it?"

Anna slid the voucher into her sack. "It sounded like a distant explosion."

"We heard it too." His steps quick, PaPa carried a keg to the counter with the banker's wife at his heels.

Emilie set the bookwork down. "Where'd it come from? Could you tell?"

"From the river." The banker's wife pulled money from her woolen skirt pocket. "If you ask me, it was probably one of those dreadful steamboats. They're dangerous things, you know."

PaPa paled and rushed to the storeroom. Emilie and the others followed him out the back door. They looked downstream toward an umbrella cloud of smoke and steam. Shouts and screams filled the air, even at this distance.

A boy rushed up the hill shouting, "Renglers' steamboat blew up!"

She looked at PaPa, her stomach knotting. He was shaking. Oliver and Owen were more than his checkers buddies; they were good friends. She squeezed her father's hand. "Maybe they weren't there."

"That's what I wanted to tell you." Tears streamed his face. "Quaid McFarland was here. He finished making the railing for their boat."

She shook her head, fighting the storm building inside her.

"He had it in the wagon."

She stared at the billowing smoke. "No! Please, God, no!"

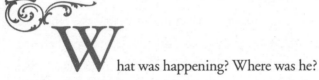hat was happening? Where was he?

Quaid sputtered. Choked. Fought to gain his balance.

A fire on the boat. He had to help the others. But he was being pulled away from them.

Muddy water stung his eyes, weighted his lungs. His legs could no longer kick, or his arms flail. A brawny arm pushed against his chest.

God, is that You?

"I've got ya." God sounded a lot like Captain Pete.

Safe, he gave in to the blackness.

"Took on a lot of water, he did." Pete?

"Got to clear his lungs." Doc Stumberg's gravelly voice.

"Quaid Patrick McFarland! Stay with us…stay with me, Son." Mother.

He was rolling. Draped over a barrel. Back and forth. Quaid gasped. His gut wrenching, he gagged. After he'd spit and sputtered, strong hands pulled him off the barrel and propped him against it. His eyelids felt leaden as he fought to open his eyes.

"His eyes. They're opening." Mother's voice again.

He blinked until a craggy face came into view. Doc Stumberg. Where was Mother?

Were the myriad sounds actually distant, or was something wrong with his hearing? He dug at his ears with his pinkies, dislodging wet dirt.

"You were underwater," the doc said.

Quaid tipped his head to drain the remaining goop from his ears.

"Thank You, God! Thank You, Jesus!" His folks' voices mingled.

He turned toward the prayer, where Mother and Father knelt beside him in front of a cheering crowd.

"A fire in the engine room, then the whole thing went up."

Quaid remembered. "Oliver? Owen?" Didn't sound like his own voice, forced and puny.

"We're here, buddy." Oliver said. "Your shouts got us all out in time."

"You're a hero."

"No lives lost."

"Explosion tossed you overboard like a rag doll."

"Captain Pete spotted you floating downstream. Dove in after ya."

Voices came from all around. Some he recognized. Others he didn't. None of them belonged to Emilie.

Johann Heinrich stepped forward. Was the man trembling? Kneeling, Mr. Heinrich looked Quaid in the eye. "Can you find it in your heart to forgive me? I was wrong."

Thank You, God! Thank You, Jesus!

Emilie dashed out the door. PaPa pulled it shut behind them, and they started down the hill.

"You saw him? He really is all right?"

"*Ja*. They were taking him home."

"You said the doctor was there?"

He nodded. "And going to the house with them."

"Quaid was walking?"

"Standing. His brother had a wagon."

"Quaid's wagon? His woodwork?"

"Gone."

Her heart raced. "I have to see him."

"That's why we're going. To make sure he's all right."

"But you said—"

"I'm sure he's fine. Dr. Stumberg wanted to be sure of his lungs. And I need to know you'll be all right."

She would be, if Quaid was.

Throngs of people were gathered at the river. The remains of the Renglers' boat smoldered offshore. Shattered timbers and mechanical debris littered the shoreline near the boat. The injured were being bandaged where they lay. Emilie's heart clenched. Quaid had to be all right.

The McFarlands' log cabin sat on a knoll two or three hundred feet above the riverbank. PaPa caught her arm and stopped her at the path to the door.

"Em, I told Quaid I was wrong. Asked him to forgive me."

Tears stinging her eyes, she pulled her father into a warm embrace. Now she just hoped it wasn't too late to tell Quaid what she should've said in the freight house.

"Miss Emilie." The twins jumped off the porch swing.

"Brother's been askin' for you." Mattie took her hand and led her up the steps.

Quaid's mother swung the door open.

"I hope you don't mind me coming, ma'am."

Mrs. McFarland shook her head, her eyes rimmed pink. "Not in the least. Me boy's about to set me nuts, askin' for ye." A smile thinned her lips.

Their hands clasped, the wisp of a woman led her through a modest kitchen to a small room packed with people. Quaid's brother and sister-in-law, his father, the Rengler brothers, and the doctor. The crowd around the bed parted. Quaid sat propped against the wall. The sight of his emerald green eyes and crooked smile weakened her knees.

"Emilie."

The elder Mr. McFarland waved his arms. "All right, all you gawkers, time to clear out. You, too, Doc." Quaid's father glanced at her. "Me and Mother will be right outside the door."

Silence, except for her thumping heart and Quaid's low whistle. "My, but you're lookin' good."

"I heard what you said to God."

He quirked an eyebrow. Had he forgotten?

"Outside your father's office door...when I was leaving."

"Ah. That." He swung his legs over the side of the bed and stood. "I meant every word—I love you, Emilie Heinrich."

She brushed a tear from her cheek. "I love you too. You really are all right?"

"I am now." He cupped her face and bent to kiss her.

Yes, he was fine. And she was feeling so much better.

When their lips parted, she gazed into his eyes. "PaPa said he told you he was wrong."

"Asked me to forgive him."

"Did you?"

"Yes." His smile quickened her pulse. "Our waiting is over."

Emilie sighed, certain she saw forever in his emerald eyes.

READERS GUIDE

1. After Emilie Heinrich's mother left, all she had was her father and his store. For many years, the two of them lived in a small apartment over the store. But now that she is a young woman, Emilie is experiencing a growing frustration or discontentment. What do you think is at the root of her discontent?

2. Quaid McFarland was one of the sons able to come home to Saint Charles after fighting in the War between the States. So relieved is his mother that she struggles with letting her son out of sight; never mind that Quaid is a grown man. How does he respond to his mother's need? What do Quaid's actions say about his family values?

3. The story opens with the apple harvest on Elsa Brantenberg's farm, where neighbors and friends come together for a community task. Some folks picked apples or worked with the cider press. Others used their abilities and gifts to serve in food preparation for the harvest celebration. Are you using your gifts and abilities in your community? In what ways?

4. Emilie has a full life with no room for romance. Yet while she may not have been looking for romance, when she begins spending time with Quaid, her heart tells her head otherwise. Has God

ever surprised you with a relationship you weren't looking for?
One you didn't think you had "the room" for?

5. When Quaid, an Irishman and freight wagon driver, steals
   Emilie's heart, her German father forbids their romance. Quaid's
   heart is what matters to Emilie, not his job or ethnicity. How do
   Quaid's principles guide his reaction to Mr. Heinrich's objections?
   Have you ever found yourself on either side of that scenario?
   What guided you?

6. In Proverbs 4:23, God instructs us to guard our hearts, for everything we do flows from it. What kinds of things do we need to
   protect our hearts from? How can we guard our hearts?

7. Mrs. Brantenberg, the host of the Saint Charles Quilting Circle,
   said, "Like a quilt is made up of remnants,...so is your life and
   mine." Do you agree with her statement? Are there scraps or
   remnants God has sewn into your life making it more beautiful?
   What would you say to someone who is staring at his or her
   mismatched remnants...waiting?

Mona is available for conference calls where she joins your book club or
reading group for a prescheduled conversation via Skype. When possible, Mona is happy to add an "in person" visit to a book club in a city
she's visiting. For more information, please contact Mona through her
website: www.monahodgson.com.

The Quilted Heart **3**

RIPPLES
ALONG THE SHORE

MONA HODGSON

*Caroline's story is dedicated to all of my
readers who have been widowed;
who have found themselves looking for a
new normal, one without the physical
presence of their beloved spouse.*

*Humble yourselves in the sight of the Lord,
and he shall lift you up.*

—JAMES 4:10

I

January 9, 1866

The side-paddles of the *New Era* churned the waters of the Missouri River while perplexing thoughts and feelings washed over Caroline. Standing on the crowded deck, she pulled her cape tight and looked toward the stretch of snowy shoreline that fronted Saint Charles. Her sister would be awaiting her return, along with her two nieces and nephew. It had already been two months since she'd received the letter from the Department of War with word of Phillip's demise. They were all the family she had left now that her aunt had passed.

Aunt Inez had bequeathed her home and worldly possessions to the sisters, and Jewell wouldn't have denied Caroline had she wished to stay in Memphis. But why would she stay? At least in Saint Charles, she had Jewell and the quilting circle—Emilie, Maren, Mrs. Brantenberg, Hattie, and all of the other women who had befriended her.

Caroline glanced toward the upper deck where the dapper fellow with a handlebar mustache stood. Looking her way, he brushed the brim of his white top hat. She smiled, then pressed her gloved hand to her warming face. Lewis G. Whibley had been the first man to flatter her since Phillip had left for the war.

And she couldn't escape the irony of the vessel's name for her voyage: the *New Era*. She had indeed been ushered into change. 1866. The New Year had dawned last week, and it was high time she had something—or someone—new to think about. Mr. Whibley seemed a perfect fit for that order; however, he had no plans to disembark. Caroline was more than a little tempted to remain on the boat herself. If she hadn't wired Jewell of her passage and return today—

"Yoo-hoo, Mrs. Milburn!"

Caroline recognized the voice of the woman who had seated herself at her meal table earlier in the afternoon. "Mrs. Kamden."

"We'll reach shore soon, you know." The woman now stood beside her at the gate.

Swallowing her amusement with the woman's knack for stating the obvious, Caroline tried to ignore the furtive glances of the stately man standing at the upper railing, a mere fifteen feet away. "Indeed, we will, ma'am. Will your son be waiting for you?"

Mrs. Kamden adjusted the hat that crowned her silver hair. "My daughter-in-law, actually. Ian is a wheelwright, which makes him a busy man."

"That makes perfect sense with so many folks readying wagons for the trail." It was contagious—now *she* was stating the obvious. More than a little distracted, Caroline turned away from her view of the deck above her, focusing on the approaching shoreline.

"You mentioned having a sister in Saint Charles?" The robust woman pushed round spectacles up the bridge of her nose.

"Yes. Jewell. She lives there with her husband and three children."

"Are they planning to go?"

"Go?"

"Why, west, of course."

Of course. Caroline hadn't discussed with her sister the possibility of going west. She'd left for Tennessee soon after the wagon train hub-bub started. No need to talk about it, anyway. Doing something so daring would require her brother-in-law to possess at least a small mea-sure of gumption. She scolded herself for her sour outlook on the man. He was, after all, married to her sister.

"I don't know that my sister and her family have any plans to join the caravan."

"I told you I'm going to Idaho with my son?"

Caroline nodded. That would be a cramped wagon...no matter how big it was. Her son and daughter-in-law had five children.

"It's a mite brisk out here, but I didn't want to miss the excitement of reaching the shore." Mrs. Kamden pressed her hand to the knit scarf encircling her neck. "It may be forward of me to ask, but what are you going to do...now that you're a widow?"

Caroline's stomach knotted. *Widow.* She'd always allocated that awful label to women for whom she felt pity.

The woman's question, however, did deserve thought. What was she going to do without Phillip? She'd been living with Jewell and Jack for nearly six months. It was one thing to stay with them while waiting for an answer concerning Phillip's fate, but now that she knew... She met Mrs.

Kamden's brown-eyed gaze and shrugged. "I haven't yet come to a decision. There was no time for such ponderings while caring for my aunt."

"But now that your aunt has passed—may the good Lord rest her soul in peace—you'll be ready for a change, won't you?"

Had her brother-in-law paid this woman to encourage her to move out? A juvenile notion, but he'd made it clear that having another adult taking up space in their modest house—and dividing his wife's attention—was a hardship.

Caroline sighed. She did need to do something with her life, but what?

"When Mr. Kamden died from the cholera, I wasn't as young as you. Nor was I as handsome." The older woman glanced upstairs. "You'll have no trouble turning the head of a suitable man. Why, you're already drawing such attentions."

The woman's nervous giggle tensed Caroline's shoulders. No one could take Phillip's place in her heart. "I'm not seeking a replacement for my husband."

"Perhaps you should, dear."

Perhaps she should. Unlike her forthright deck companion, Caroline didn't have a son to set her in a wagon and take her to Idaho.

Thankfully, Mrs. Kamden became distracted as the boat reversed its paddles. The *New Era* gently nudged the shore and the stage swung out to meet the riverbank.

Caroline's family awaited her at the edge of the mud. Emilie Heinrich stood with Jewell and the children, all of them waving. She directed the deckhand to her trunk and followed it down the stage. When the gangly young man set her trunk off to the side in the snow, she pulled a coin from her seam pocket and thanked him for his help.

"Auntie Carol-i!" Her skirt churning, Caroline's four-year-old niece darted across the muddy bank to the end of the ramp.

Caroline set her valise on top of the trunk and swung Mary into her arms.

"I miss you much." Caroline's youngest niece planted wet kisses on her cheek.

Resisting the impulse to wipe the wetness from her face, Caroline tapped Mary's button nose. "I missed you too. It's good to see you." That much was true. She hadn't said it was good to *be back.*

Cora latched on to Caroline's leg. "I thought you weren't coming home."

Jewell sighed, fluttering the wisps of hair on her forehead. "I said it time and again—your aunt Caroline was needed in Memphis to care for Aunt Inez." Her voice quivered. "Of course she came back."

"She has nowhere else to go." There, she'd finished Jewell's statement for her.

Jewell's eyes widened. "Saint Charles is your home. You needn't go anywhere else. This is where you belong."

Where she belonged. Another topic to add to the list of things she and Jewell needed to discuss. Later. Alone.

Eight-year-old Gilbert slid her valise off the trunk. "Aunt Caroline, lots of folks are forming a wagon train come spring. You could take a wagon west."

While her nephew's matter-of-fact suggestion made Caroline smile, a frown creased her sister's brow.

Jewell pressed her shawl to her middle. "Of all the outlandish things to say! Treks across the wilderness are for men with strong constitutions."

Not for widows, who apparently lack the disposition.

Before Caroline or her nephew could respond, Emilie cleared her throat. "I was on my way to the Queensware Emporium when I happened upon Jewell and the children."

Caroline smiled. "Looking for a wedding dress, are you?"

Blushing, Emilie clasped her hands at her chin. "The wedding is next month."

"I'm glad to hear you and Quaid are still getting along."

Emilie nodded, rubbing her gloved hands together.

"Quaid is actually the real reason Emilie came with us." Jewell cocked her head toward a cluster of freight wagons.

Caroline raised an eyebrow. "A-a-a-h."

"He's working in the woodshop today, not driving the wagon." Emilie stepped forward and enveloped Caroline in a warm embrace. "I really did come to see you. I was sorry to hear about your aunt's passing."

"Thank you. But with me living in Philadelphia, Jewell had spent much more time with her." Caroline reached out and squeezed her sister's hand.

Jewell glanced at the trunk, then at the riverbank toward her house. "I should've brought the wagon."

"I returned with a few of Aunt Inez's memorables."

Jewell nodded. "You managed to sell the rest of her belongings?"

"I did. And her house." Which meant she and Jewell would both have a bit of money...until Jack learned of his wife's modest inheritance.

"I wouldn't have known where to start." Jewell's eyes moistened. "The children and I will go to the livery and fetch the horse and wagon."

"We could be home and seated at the dinner table with the time that would take." Caroline grasped the leather strap on one end of her trunk. "It'd be easier and faster to carry it ourselves."

"I can make myself useful." Emilie lifted the other end and peered up at her.

Caroline smiled. She'd only been gone from Saint Charles six weeks, but she'd missed her friends from the quilting circle. For more reasons than their physical strength. Mrs. Brantenberg and the others had given her a shoulder to cry on and bolstered her faith when it had dwindled.

With Jewell and the children in tow, Caroline and Emilie stepped into the slushy ruts leading up the bank. They hadn't made it twenty feet when Caroline began to huff and puff. When her shoulder began to cramp, she stopped.

Emilie was accustomed to physical labor, working as she did in her father's dry goods store and grocery, and didn't seem burdened by the load in the least.

Gilbert stepped forward. "I can do it, Aunt Caroline." He wrapped his small hand around the leather strap and heaved. His end of the trunk hopped off the ground, then quickly went back down. "That's heavy!"

Caroline looked at her sister. "I brought the two brass elephant bookends you liked as a girl."

A smile bunched Jewell's cheeks. "I still like them."

"Good, because getting them home isn't going to be easy."

"If Quaid's brother is here, he would be happy to deliver the trunk to the house." Emilie glanced upriver. "Why, there's Mr. Cowlishaw."

Caroline's stomach knotted at the memory of their last encounter in Mrs. Brantenberg's kitchen. She followed Emilie's gaze to the brawny man seated atop a buckwagon.

Emilie waved at him like a woman without any sense, then looked back at her. "His timing is nothing short of perfect, wouldn't you say?"

If that was a romantic notion dancing in Emilie's brown eyes, Caroline would have no part in it. She'd be better off to walk away from her family, step back onto the *New Era,* and take her chances with Mr. Lewis G. Whibley.

∞

Garrett had been too distracted to notice the gathering of women and children—until Quaid McFarland's intended waved at him. That's when he'd seen Mrs. Milburn standing beside a trunk with a gloved hand perched on her waist. He returned Miss Heinrich's wave as he prodded the horses in that direction. Garrett stopped the wagon beside the shopkeeper's daughter and the young widow and her family. "Good day, ladies. Children."

"Good day." Miss Heinrich and Mrs. Rafferty were the first to return his greeting. The children followed. Mrs. Milburn seemed reluctant to speak, but when he looked directly at her, she finally did.

"Good day, Mr. Cowlishaw. I'm surprised to see you down at the river, with all the westward planning."

"That's precisely what brought me here today."

"Oh?"

He glanced back at Captain Pete's freighter grounded at the shoreline. "Can't go west without a proper wagon and supplies."

She studied the empty wagon bed.

"Neither were on the boat today. Delayed." Garrett set the brake and climbed down from the wagon.

"You're the man who fixed our wheel." The older of the two young Rafferty girls had the same wide-set eyes as Mrs. Milburn. She shifted her attention to her aunt. "Do you like Mr. Cowlishaw now?"

Heat seared Garrett's cheeks, despite the snowy blanket on the ground around him. The impetuous child's statement may have colored Mrs. Milburn's face too, but she'd turned away from him before he could see for himself.

"Cora, dear." The young widow tempered her voice. "It's not a matter of whether or not I like Mr. Cowlishaw. We are scarcely acquainted."

"We know him, Auntie. He's Mr. Rutherford's friend. He lives at Mrs. Brantenberg's farm."

The boy, Gilbert, shifted the valise to his other arm. "It's possible to like someone you just met, if they're likable."

The children clearly liked him. Problem was, in Mrs. Milburn's eyes he was entirely unlikable, and understandably so. He'd fought for the South, then delivered the news of her husband's death. He couldn't expect her to like him.

Her lips pressed together, Mrs. Milburn brushed a red curl the color of sunrise from her face. "You helped us with the wagon wheel last autumn, and it seems we are once again in need of your assistance."

"It would be my pleasure."

"I've been to Memphis to care for my aunt and returned with a heavy load."

He looked at the worn trunk by her side.

"Might you be willing to haul the trunk to my sister's house? It's up the bank a bit." Mrs. Milburn looked up the slope toward a row of small houses in the shadows of the main buildings downtown.

"Consider it done." Had her eyes always been that green? Like sycamore leaves in spring. "I hope she's faring well. Your aunt."

"She passed on."

He removed his slouch hat. "My sympathies. I'm sure you did your best."

"Will it ever be enough?"

A question he knew all too well. "Our best is all we have to offer, ma'am." That's what he'd told himself time and again.

She nodded, her lip quivering, and he had to look away. He darted past her and had the trunk and valise loaded onto the tailgate in no time. This more vulnerable side of the widow tangled his insides.

Caroline Milburn was easier to be around when she had her guard up.

2

The limp Caroline had detected in her first encounter with Mr. Cowlishaw didn't seem to bother him in the least. Within mere minutes of her request for assistance, the man had the trunk and her valise strapped into the wagon, and the children seated in the back beside them. Emilie chose to walk the short distance to her father's dry goods store. Caroline and Jewell shared the driver's seat with Mr. Cowlishaw. Since it would be improper for a married woman to sit beside a man other than her husband, and Caroline was no longer married, she sat in the middle. She would've walked, but whether she liked the man or not, she didn't wish to appear rude. Or ungrateful.

Her niece's and nephew's forthright comments came to mind. She may have been amused by their candor had she not been so uncomfortable considering the question.

Do you like Mr. Cowlishaw now?

She didn't want to like Garrett Cowlishaw. She shouldn't. He may not have killed Phillip, but a man wearing a uniform similar to his *had* ended her husband's life. Caroline straightened her spine against a shiver having nothing to do with the chill in the air.

Mr. Cowlishaw flicked the reins, and the horses lunged forward. Even with layers of trouser, petticoat, and skirt between them, there was nothing proper about their thighs touching. Phillip would be mortified.

If he were alive to care.

Caroline drew in a deep breath, hoping the exercise created more space between them.

"Mrs. Milburn."

The way he kept coming to their rescue, she should invite him to use her given name, but no amount of his chivalry could make that feel right. She angled her head to look at him. "Yes, Mr. Cowlishaw?"

"Ma'am, I neglected to welcome you back to Saint Charles."

He was nothing if not a polite Southerner. Swallowing another dose of regret, she met his gaze.

"Welcome back."

"Thank you." She hadn't noticed the dimple in his chin. "I hear you have a lot of folks interested in joining your caravan." Simple conversation seemed the least she should offer.

"Yes ma'am. A handful of families are already making plans. Others are still thinking on it."

She nodded, then held her breath while the wagon rocked and clunked up the bank. According to her nephew, she should be among those thinking on going west. The silly notion of an eight-year-old child, certainly not the consideration of a rational woman.

"How many months do you expect your journey will require?"

His hazel eyes widened, furrowing his brow. "Why do you ask?"

She hadn't a reason, except to make conversation. Should she say that?

He glanced at the children in the bed of the wagon. "Is your family contemplating a change?"

"No." Jewell's resolute response startled Caroline, causing her shoulder to brush against the man's firm upper arm.

She leaned into Jewell. Her sister's "no" was as deeply rooted as Jack was—immovable.

Mr. Cowlishaw finally answered her. "Usually takes four or five months, if there aren't any extraordinary delays. Taken as long as six months, when that's the case."

Leaving in April, six months would take them into fall. No, thank you. Perhaps Jewell was right—the journey west by wagon was for men with a strong constitution.

"This'll be my third wagon train company on the Oregon Trail. My first as the leader. Worked as a scout on the first two."

Not only was the man a Southerner, he was a vagabond...a wanderer. When his muscular thigh relaxed against her, she again pressed against Jewell. Mr. Cowlishaw definitely fit her sister's requirement for a trek in the wilderness. The man had to be strong to have been a soldier. If only Phillip had been the one to survive.

An awful thought, she knew. Especially after Mr. Cowlishaw had been nothing but helpful... Still, he wasn't Phillip.

When the wagon stopped to let a carriage pass, Caroline recognized the familiar "Yoo-hoo," then saw a gloved hand waving her direction. Mrs. Kamden sat beside a stick-thin woman, presumably her daughter-in-law, since five children filled the two back seats.

Caroline waved, thankful Mr. Cowlishaw was turning in the

opposite direction. The woman was nice enough, although a tad plain-spoken for Caroline's current sensibilities.

"That's our house. Up there." Jewell pointed to the square-cut log cabin. Melting snow fell in chunks from the shingle roof, forming a berm along the front of the house, although it looked like someone had shoveled the path to the front door that morning. Most likely Jewell.

Mr. Cowlishaw pulled up on the reins. "This is it?"

Caroline nodded. "It is." Before she'd left six weeks ago, she'd done what she could to help Jewell around the place, but there wasn't much she could do about the winter drab that had settled on it. Outside, or inside.

"Thank you." Jewell stepped toward the back of the wagon. "We can carry the trunk in from here, Mr. Cowlishaw."

The brawny man looked from Jewell to the roughhewn door. "Your husband?"

"He's in there. But he can't help."

"Pa lost a leg in the war." Gilbert worked to untie the strap securing the valise.

"I'm sorry about your husband's injury, ma'am." He helped Gilbert with the strap. "I'll be taking this inside for you."

Jewell sighed. "We're much obliged."

"Happy to help."

"That what happened to you? You get shot in the war?"

Mr. Cowlishaw heaved the trunk from the tailgate and looked at the boy. "Naw, I wasn't shot like your pa."

If Caroline wasn't curious before, she was now. But the man didn't offer an explanation as he followed Jewell's slow steps up the slushy walk toward the house. Caroline fell into step with the children, close enough to notice the muscles stretching his chambray shirt tight. Her sister wiped her shoes on the braided rug on the small porch and pushed the door open.

"High time you show up. Where you been?"

Jack's gruff welcome stiffened Caroline's spine.

Sadly, Jewell was accustomed to his growl and charged on ahead. "I told you I was going to the river to bring Caroline home."

"Didn't tell me you planned to lollygag. Woulda been nice to know."

Despite the heavy load he carried on a bum leg, Mr. Cowlishaw bounded across the slush and through the front door.

Caroline thought to take the children with her in any other direction, but followed them inside anyway. She couldn't leave her sister alone with the grizzly. And their good Samaritan's gallantry now piqued her curiosity. How would he respond to Jack?

"Mr. Rafferty?" A vein in Mr. Cowlishaw's neck jumped.

Jack glared at Mr. Cowlishaw, planting his hands on the arms of the wicker wheelchair. His crutch lay on the plank flooring beside him. "Who are you, and what are you doin' with my wife?"

Jewell motioned for the children to leave the room. The girls obliged, but Gilbert stood beside Mr. Cowlishaw, his grip on Caroline's valise turning his small knuckles white.

"A man who speaks to a woman that way—"

"What?" Jack scooped up the crutch and attempted to stand, finally hopping on his left leg. "Should have his leg blown off?"

Caroline stepped forward. "Jack, this is Mr. Garrett Cowlishaw. He's with me."

Her brother-in-law's hoot hung on the air like a midnight haunting. "You're takin' up with Southern men now, are you? I think Phillip would for sure have somethin' to say about that."

For Jewell's sake, and for the sake of decorum, Caroline swallowed the ire threatening to undo her and looked up at the man beside her. Clearly, a mistake. His jaw tight, Mr. Cowlishaw looked like a mountain lion ready to pounce on its prey. He'd have company.

Caroline rested her hand on his taut arm, hoping to calm him some. Couldn't know if it was effective, but she did feel her own shoulders relax a notch. She looked from the trunk he held to the single-pane window at the edge of the kitchen. "You can set it under that window, if you would."

Mr. Cowlishaw nodded and took long strides to the wall. As soon as the trunk touched the floor, he slid it to the wall, then stood and looked at Jack. Her brother-in-law's empty pant leg dangled as if expecting to be needed again. "I'm truly sorry about your leg."

"Not sorry enough to trade your limp." Jack sank onto the wheelchair. His scowl showed no hint of fading.

Garrett Cowlishaw looked back at her, a mix of emotions clouding his eyes: Frustration. Compassion. Questions. Restraint.

"Thank you for your help, Mr. Cowlishaw." Jewell walked to the door and opened it.

"Yes. Thank you." Caroline met his gaze, hoping he understood it was best that he leave.

"You're welcome." His chest expanded in a deep breath. Shifting his attention back to Jack, Mr. Cowlishaw exhaled through taut lips. "Very well." Glancing once more at Caroline, he turned and left the cabin.

Jewell pushed the door shut behind him and looked at her son. "Gilbert, take the valise to your sisters' room."

Gilbert opened his mouth, but just as quickly closed it and trudged out of the room.

"Didn't have enough junk settin' in my way that you had to bring more?"

Jewell jabbed the air between them with her finger. "Jack, my aunt is dead. All I have left of her is in this trunk."

Caroline followed her sister to the trunk and pinched the latch open. She should've stayed on the boat. At the least, left with Mr. Cowlishaw. She hated living here. Hated that her sister, nieces, and nephew had to live here.

And knew she was helpless to do anything about it.

What are you going to do...now that you're a widow?

Caroline wasn't any closer to having an answer to Mrs. Kamden's question. Now a bigger question hung thick in the stifling air. Why did God choose to take kindly men like Phillip and leave bitter men like Jack behind?

❧

It took all the self-control Garrett could muster not to yank that good-for-nothing out of his chair and whack some sense into him. History told him it would be a waste of energy. Instead, he marched to the wagon, snatched the reins from the hitching rail, and climbed onto the seat.

In one last look at the cabin, he caught a glimpse of the Widow Milburn standing in front of the glassed window, her porcelain face framed by a threadbare curtain. The desperation etched on her features knotted his stomach...awakened best-forgotten memories. Garrett looked frontward and signaled the horses to move him. Away.

Why had the widow returned to Saint Charles? To her sister's hostile home?

As soon as the thought formed, he knew why.

Some folks would do anything for their kin.

3

Thursday morning hadn't come soon enough for Caroline. Since her return from Memphis, she and Jewell had been sifting through the things she'd brought back and sorting childhood memories of time spent with Aunt Inez. Even the children engaged in reminiscing, remembering Aunt Inez's visit to Saint Charles while their father was away at war. But Caroline's heart had placed a limit on how much nostalgia and sentiment it could keep in check.

She was ready for a day away from the house and out of town.

As her sister sat silent at the reins, the wagon rolled up Brantenberg Lane toward the farmhouse. Caroline found herself glancing from the garden to the barn, and the granary to the orchard. She told herself she wasn't looking for Garrett Cowlishaw, but she knew better.

She'd seen a different side of the man two days ago when he'd carried her trunk into Jewell's house. Most impressive was the way he'd stood up to Jack. Even before that, the way he tried to comfort her when she told him of her aunt's death.

"My sympathies. I'm sure you did your best."

"Will it ever be enough?" A presumptuous question for a mere acquaintance.

"Our best is all we have to offer, ma'am."

Now, Garrett Cowlishaw had met her brother-in-law. He'd seen that the best effort she had to offer wasn't enough for Jewell or the children either. She'd felt helpless the past four years waiting for Phillip, and then witnessing Jewell's harsh home life since Jack's return. Caroline shifted on the wagon seat, feeling her chin lift. She would no longer stand by, waiting on those around her for change. It was time she took control and brought about reformation for herself.

Although she couldn't yet say how or what that would mean.

Jewell gathered the reins in her right hand and leaned toward Caroline. "Despite your protests, you like him." Playfulness blazed in her grin. Leaving the house today had been a boon to her sister as well.

"I do."

"He's an honorable man."

"I didn't think that possible of a Confederate soldier."

"And now?"

Now, she was looking for him. "I couldn't find such a helpful man for hire."

Jewell's giggle sent music into Caroline's soul. "Reason enough to like a man, I suppose."

Rutherford Wainwright stepped through the open barn doors, his little daughter beside him, and greeted them with a broad wave. Gabi jumped at the sight of their wagon and called to Mary and Cora, then to Gilbert. Caroline suspected her nieces and nephew looked forward to Thursdays for the same reasons as their mother, but the farm also afforded them what their cabin in town didn't—room to run and explore. Under Rutherford's watchful eye.

He motioned for Jewell to park beside Mrs. Pemberton's wagon. "It's a good day, Mrs. Rafferty." He extended his hand to her.

"It is indeed." Jewell accepted his offer of help down from the wagon. "Thank you."

Caroline set her foot on the metal step, then onto the ground. As she lifted the girls out, she couldn't help but wonder if Garrett Cowlishaw had told his friend about the encounter with Jack. But it didn't really matter, if he had. Despite Jewell's determination to keep her personal challenges private, Caroline had heard the whispers in town of folks expressing pity and judgment.

"Mrs. Milburn." Rutherford Wainwright's voice grounded her in the here and now. "I trust you are well today."

"I am. Thank you."

He watched as the children scampered across the snow and into the barn. "I thought Gabi might lose her mind waiting for your wagon."

"My children enjoy her company too." Jewell glanced at the muddy ground. "Jack didn't want us to leave this morning."

"Well." A shadow darkened his face. "We're all thankful you persisted." Looking away, Rutherford unbuckled the girth strap. "I'll unhitch the horses and put them in the barn with the others."

Caroline was tempted to ask after Mr. Cowlishaw, but didn't wish to stir that pot. Her sister and Rutherford were sure to add assumptions to her inquiry.

❧

Seated at one end of the hand-carved Biedermeier settee, Anna Goben soaked up the activity in Mrs. Brantenberg's sitting room. Maren Jensen and Emilie Heinrich talked about their double wedding, planned for next month. Caroline and her sister Jewell pulled quilt tops onto their laps, speaking in hushed tones. Sixteen-year-old Hattie Pemberton removed the pins from her green felt hat while she and her widowed mother bantered with the elder Mrs. Beck and her daughter-in-law, Lorelei, about the recipe for *Butterkuchen,* the "Joy and Sorrow Cake" dessert Hattie had brought to the farm today.

Mrs. Brantenberg took paper and pencils from a writing desk in the corner, then settled into a bentwood rocking chair. Steam rose from the coffee cup Maren had set on the side table beside her intended's mother-in-law. Their German hostess looked around the room, a smile deepening the creases at her eyes. "I am a blessed woman to have so many precious friends." She fixed her gaze on Anna. "And doubly blessed that you're back in our midst, dear."

"It's good to be here, ma'am." Such a satisfying truth. Anna felt as if she'd received a drenching rain after months of withering drought. Drawing in a refreshing deep breath, she reached into her sewing sack. The last time she and Mutter came to the circle, Anna had cut strips and squares, expecting to make a new quilt for her brother.

Anna pulled the fabric squares and her threaded needle from her sack. She'd make the quilt for her *Schrank* chest instead, although even on the best days, such a hope seemed far-fetched. Thankfully, no one had asked about Mutter. They didn't need to. Everyone in town knew that, upon news of her brother's death, *Großvater* had taken to his bed with sorrow...and her mother had befriended a flask.

"This morning, Hattie will ask for God's blessing upon our time together." Mrs. Brantenberg nodded in Hattie's direction, then bowed her head.

Anna folded her hands atop her quilting squares.

"Dear Father in heaven…"

The poor girl who was praying had lost her earthly father in the war.

Each of the women in the room had made sacrifices in the last five years, many having lost loved ones.

"We thank Thee, Lord God, for Thy loving presence in our midst. We thank Thee for one another…the bond we share, and we are most thankful You brought Anna back to us."

Anna pressed her lips against the emotion threatening to topple her composure. She should've returned to the quilting circle months ago. The lack of interest belonged to Mutter, not to her. As soon as Hattie started the amen chorus that circled the room, Anna gave Emilie's hand a squeeze. "Thank you for your persistence."

"You mean insistence, don't you?" Emilie smiled.

Anna nodded. She'd let Mutter's grief and her own embarrassment keep her from spending time with her friends. In a time when she most needed them.

Clearing her throat, Maren Jensen lifted a Bible off the side table and opened it. "Mother Brantenberg—" Her face pinked, and she looked at their hostess. "Apologies. Rutherford and I are not married yet. It's too soon to call you that in public."

"The day can't come soon enough for me."

"Or for me." Maren moistened her lips. "Uh, I will share a passage that holds special meaning. I will read it." She pulled a magnifying glass off the table and lifted the Bible to within six inches of her face.

A candle maker, Anna would deliver candles to Heinrich's Dry

Goods store, where she was able to become better acquainted with Maren. The Danish immigrant hadn't lost a loved one in the war, but she had suffered rejection from her betrothed as a result of her waning eyesight.

"I'll read the fourth chapter of James, tenth verse."

Thirteen months had passed since Anna and her mother received word of Dedrick's death in a battle. That's how long it had been since she'd heard Scripture read aloud in her home.

Humble yourselves in the sight of the Lord, and He shall lift you up.

Maren laid the Bible on her lap, then looked up. "Each of you knows my story...a mail-order bride suddenly without a groom."

Anna nodded with the others.

Maren looped strands of straw-blond hair behind her ear. "I had a plan. After a week in Saint Charles I was to marry. Make my own home. Having trouble was humbling."

Anna straightened, eyeing Maren. She knew about plans being abruptly changed. Before Dedrick left with his regiment, he'd promised that upon his return, the war and all its grief would be forgotten.

Maren's soft but sure voice pulled Anna's attention back into the present. "Since that day, standing alone in your father's store"—she looked at Emilie, then to Mrs. Brantenberg—"I've learned God had His own plan. This was to be my home. You and little Gabi, my family." She drew in a deep breath. "And Rutherford, my husband. Now, I am thankful for change."

Caroline, on the other settee beside Jewell, slapped her booted feet together. "What I've heard of the cad who walked away from you...

frankly, Maren, you were far better off without him. But what of us who have lost their husbands and fathers to the war?" She glanced at Mrs. Pemberton and Hattie.

The young widow's candor startled Anna, but she knew the question wasn't directed to Maren so much as it was to the God who allowed the war to happen. A question on Anna's heart that she had not dared to ask since her family's devastation in losing her brother.

Obviously nervous, Maren tucked another tuft of stray hair behind her ear and looked at Mrs. Brantenberg. When the older woman didn't open her mouth to address Caroline's question, the Danish immigrant took a deep breath and opened hers. "I am not a widow. Your life is not mine." She looked at the Bible on her lap. "But God is the same in all experiences. Faithful and true. He thinks thoughts toward us of peace, not of evil, to give us an expected end." Her blue eyes glistening, Maren caressed the onionskin pages on her lap. "God knows what we don't know. He sees the purpose in what happens. I don't know the good Lord's plan for you now that Colonel Milburn is gone."

Anna's throat tightened as she fought the urge to cry for Caroline, herself, Mutter. For everyone in the room—and those who were not.

"But the Lord said when we call upon Him," Maren continued, "He will hear. When we seek Him, searching with all our heart, we will find Him."

Caroline drooped against the back of the settee.

Anna hadn't realized she was wadding the squares on her lap until the needle pricked her fingertip.

Maren moistened her lips. "Mrs. Brantenberg taught me that when I humble myself, I step out of the way of God's plans."

Mrs. Brantenberg set her coffee cup in its saucer. "I didn't find it an easy task when my Christoph died or when my Gretchen died. Or when Rutherford left me and Gabi and I feared he would never return."

"Thank you, Maren, dear." Mrs. Pemberton pressed her hand to her knee. "Elsa, the thoughts you shared with the group last fall on scraps and remnants helped me."

Anna didn't know Hattie's mother well, but she was usually quiet, letting Hattie do all the talking. Now that her friend's mother had spoken, Anna was again sorry she'd missed the past few months at the farm. She was confounded by what cloth scraps had to do with grief.

Mrs. Pemberton looked directly at Anna. "Many of us will use pieces of fabric from tired or outgrown clothes in patches or appliqués."

Had the woman sensed her curiosity? "Yes. My mother has." She glanced at the mound of squares on her lap. "I'm using remnants from shirts Dedrick had outgrown."

"Another tragic loss. Dedrick was a good boy. My sympathies." Mrs. Pemberton's tender gaze warmed Anna's heart.

"Thank you."

"Last October, our faithful hostess talked about those scraps and how they are like the circumstances in our lives. Remnants to be reclaimed and used by God as He stitches our hearts together."

Hattie lifted a corner of the Crazy quilt spread on her lap. "A quilted heart is a transformed heart."

"As Miss Maren said, that comes when we humble ourselves before the Lord." Mrs. Pemberton looked at Anna. "Does that make a straight line, dear?"

Anna nodded. She'd forgotten how much she enjoyed the way Bette Pemberton turned phrases. But there were no straight lines in her life. Only jagged edges. She wanted to believe the scraps could be transformed…that her life and her faith could be restored.

After a sip of coffee, Mrs. Brantenberg returned her cup and saucer to the table and lifted the paper and pencils from her lap. "In light of the movement to the west, I propose that after today we postpone our personal projects to work on squares for two Friendship Album quilts. One quilt to remain with those who will rebuild their lives in Saint Charles, and one that will travel with those who intend to rebuild their lives out west."

Hattie clasped her hands at her chest, her eyebrows arching above blue-gray eyes. "What a wonderful idea!"

"Let's see who will work on each one." Mrs. Brantenberg stood and handed a pencil and one sheet of paper to Hattie. "You said your brother talked about taking you and your mother on the trail in the spring."

"Yes, it does seem my son has his mind made up, and we'll be going," Mrs. Pemberton piped in.

"And others of you? Are you remaining in Saint Charles?"

"We won't be going." Jewell Rafferty reached for the pencil and the second sheet of paper.

Caroline's eyebrows arched. She didn't look as if she shared her sister's certainty.

As Anna watched the two papers making their way around the room, she couldn't help but wonder which she should set a pencil to. The image of Mutter and Großvater making the trip caused her to shudder, but what else was left for her to do? She could no longer bear to watch them suffer. Her only hope seemed to hinge on another change.

To a place that didn't shout Dedrick's name in her memories.

4

ow that Rutherford had gone outside to help unhitch horses, Garrett was alone in the granary, remembering. He scooped wheat from one of several mounds and stuffed it into a sack. He'd been stuffing the memories harvested in his youth in much the same way. In the silence, the brick walls seemed to step toward him. Rutherford had told him the history of this farm. Before Mrs. Brantenberg's husband bought the orchard, the land belonged to a man who kept slaves.

Pulling the cord tight on the linen sack, Garrett glanced at the scarred stairs in the corner. The bulk of fifty slaves had slept in the loft. Those housed on his father's plantation in Richmond lived a similar life—impoverished and contained. Shaking his head, he added the sack to the pile headed for the flour mill tomorrow. He'd seen the tally of each year's crop carved into the back of every step, and didn't have to imagine the blood, sweat, and agony poured into those backbreaking years.

In contrast to those lean years for so many slaves, Garrett had enjoyed generous portions of victuals at Mrs. Brantenberg's breakfast table less than an hour earlier. He walked past two short barrels and lifted a heavy boot onto the first of the narrow pine steps. His footfalls thunderous in his ears, he climbed each plank as if he'd packed the weight of the world on his back. He had.

Familiar but distant voices called out to him. He paused, his head just inside the opening to the loft. He'd grown up around slaves, whom he'd counted among his friends. As Garrett looked from the A-frame rafters to the floor worn smooth by bare feet and imagined row after row of woolen blankets laid out as sleeping pallets, a recurring question draped him like a suffocating cloak. What would life be like if he hadn't been so compliant? Given the circumstances, he thought he'd done the right thing. Not according to the two men he'd tried most to please—his father and his older brother. And he would forever be a deserter or a coward, no matter his reasoning.

Garrett descended the steps. He'd tied shut another full sack when Rutherford returned to the granary wearing a smile as wide as the Missouri and probably just as deep.

"From the doe-eyed looks of you, Rutherford, I'd guess Maren rode out here for the quilting circle."

"She did." His voice sounded far away…as far away as Mrs. Brantenberg's sitting room.

"You two talked about the wedding, didn't you?"

Rutherford nodded, then removed his kepi. "Only three weeks now."

The man may as well be marking the days off on a doorpost.

Seemed all Rutherford talked about was his beloved Maren, his sweet daughter Gabi, and the day they'd officially become a family.

"You and me"—Rutherford walked toward the two short barrels—"we need to talk."

"Sounds serious." Garrett followed him.

Cocking an eyebrow, Rutherford sat down. "It is serious. I don't know how you feel about weddings."

Garrett gulped and sank onto the other barrel. "How I feel about weddings?"

"My wedding." Rutherford hung his hat over his knee. "Why so nervous? Should we be talking about your wedding?"

Garrett's laugh echoed off the upstairs rafters. "A guaranteed waste of time." He met his friend's concerned gaze. "At the very least, I'd need to have prospects in the picture. Which I don't."

Rutherford glanced toward the open door. "You like redheads, don't you?"

"She's here?"

"So, you have noticed her?"

"You'd have to be an ostrich with your head buried in the sand not to know Mrs. Milburn likes me about as much as she would a rabid skunk."

Rutherford chuckled. "Too fiery for ya?"

"The intensity, I can handle. But she's a recent widow."

"You're forgetting." Rutherford's eyes narrowed. "I buried my wife. I'm a widower myself, being given another chance at love."

His stomach knotted. "Yes, and I'm thankful you are."

"I doubt Caroline Milburn is any more content with being alone than I was."

A good point, but not one Garrett wished to entertain. He couldn't.

Even if she did like him, no woman could care for a man like him. Not if she knew the truth.

Especially that woman.

"It's not the same. I was her dead husband's enemy. Thus, her enemy too."

"Was." Rutherford slapped his hat onto his head. "We're all putting our divisions behind us. Starting fresh."

Even if that were true—

"She was looking for you."

The message tickled Garrett's ears. Felt good to hear it. Too good. He needed to put distance between the subject of marriage and his curiosity about Caroline Milburn. "Should I get back to work?" Garrett leaned forward, threatening to stand. "Or were we gonna talk about your wedding?"

Rutherford raised his hand as if to stop him, and nodded. "I'd be honored if you'd stand with me. In my wedding."

His breath faltered. "I'm not the best man."

"I didn't say you were." Rutherford's wide smile returned. "But tried-and-true friends are hard to come by."

Garrett's throat tightened with emotion while his secret gained weight, and he looked away.

"Quaid's brother is standing with him. I want you up there with me."

Garrett swallowed hard. "It'd be an honor."

An honor he didn't deserve.

Caroline stepped outside, onto the porch with Mary. The little girl's hand felt so small in hers. Her youngest niece had come into Mrs.

Brantenberg's sitting room crying, asking for her mother's help. Her siblings were apparently busy chasing the hibernating mice out of the milk cellar, but her brother hadn't been too occupied to tell Mary that five-armed monsters lived in that dark underground place. On the ride back into town, she'd have a talk with Gilbert about his storytelling.

Stepping onto the snowy path, Caroline looked toward the barn. Jewell had asked Mary to wait, as she was nearly finished stitching the last appliqué onto her squares, but Caroline told her she'd be happy to go with Mary in her stead to rid the farm of underground monsters so Mary could use the outhouse without fear. The two women both knew the truth—Caroline hoped to see Mr. Cowlishaw. Actually, the desire to see him made as much sense to her as chasing beasts with multiple appendages, but if Garrett Cowlishaw was on the farm today, she did want to thank him again for his help on Tuesday.

An innocuous and respectable reason to see the man.

"Auntie Carol-i?"

Caroline glanced at Mary. "Yes, sweet pea?"

"I'm sad you miss Unca Phillip so much."

Her lips pressed, Caroline nodded. She swung Mary into her arms and kissed the little girl's soft forehead. She needed to focus on something new. Everyone around her surely had to be weary of her grief. She certainly was.

"There's the wheel man."

The wheel man was Garrett Cowlishaw, and Mary was pointing at him. Smiling, Caroline pressed Mary's arm to the child's side.

"You didn't want to see him?"

"No." Caroline sighed. "Yes. But it's not polite to point." She watched as he and Rutherford walked out of the granary. Rutherford turned toward the barn while Mr. Cowlishaw walked directly toward them, wearing a shirt the color of an evergreen forest.

Mary tugged at the shoulder on Caroline's cape. "I need to—"

"Mrs. Milburn." Smiling, he reached up and tapped the brim on his white slouch hat. "Hello, Miss Mary. My, but you look handsome in pink."

"Thank you, Mr. Cow…" Mary looked at Caroline, her brow bunched.

"Cow-li-shaw. His name is Mr. Cowlishaw."

He held Caroline's gaze, his eyes more green than hazel today. "I'm fine with Mr. Cow, but I'd much prefer you call me Garrett."

"Very well, Garrett. Feel free to call me Caroline, if you wish."

"I'd like that." His chin dimpled in a knee-weakening smile.

Embarrassed by her puzzling reaction to the man, Caroline tugged her cape straight with her free hand, while holding Mary on her hip with the other. "Thank you, again, for your help Tuesday."

"You're welcome. Your brother-in-law—" He glanced at Mary, then back to Caroline. "Is he always like that?"

"Only when he's awake." Neither of them laughed.

"Auntie Carol-i!"

Immediately following Mary's exclamation, a rush of warmth soaked through Caroline's skirt and petticoat. This, when she was finally beginning to feel a measure of ease around the man. Determined not to humiliate Mary, she fought to hide her discomfort.

"If you'll excuse us, Mr., uh, Garrett."

"Yes ma'am." He brushed the brim of his hat. If he knew what had happened, he didn't let on.

Perhaps he was a kind man, after all.

5

Wood-slat chairs lined the center of the barn. Bunting and ribbons decorated the beams and stalls. Much effort had been made to rid the building of any evidence of its usual inhabitants. All of the stall doors on the downwind side were open to let in light. Twin lanterns hung from the posts at the front of the makeshift chapel. Despite the chill in the air, the barn was quite cozy. Caroline sat on the inside of the second row, fidgeting while she waited.

First, she fiddled with the lace on her gloves, then with her handkerchief. Waiting wasn't one of her strengths. Actually, she was hard-pressed to name a strength she did possess. If she were a good friend to Emilie and Maren, she'd be happy to be here celebrating their joy as they married Quaid and Rutherford. As it was, she'd almost rather be home moping with Jack. She was happy for her friends, and if this hadn't been the first wedding she'd attended since Phillip's departure, the waiting may have come easier.

Jewell laid her hand atop Caroline's knee. That's when Caroline realized she'd been tapping her heel against the packed earth floor. No doubt Jewell had meant to still her, but her sister's gesture also sent a calmness through her being. She looked into Jewell's warm gaze and smiled.

"You're going to be all right."

Caroline nodded, wishing she could say the same to her sister. Bearing her own sorrow was burden enough, but watching Jewell suffer was almost impossible to bear.

Music drew Caroline's attention to the back of the barn, set up as a stage this morning. Four-year-old Gabi stood atop a bushel box, her lips pursed on a flute. The child played "Home! Sweet Home!" for the quieted crowd.

A pastor in a long black vestment entered the barn from behind Gabi, with Rutherford, Quaid McFarland, and Brady McFarland at his side. The fifth man was the one who held Caroline's attention. His limp barely noticeable, Garrett Cowlishaw stepped onto the platform wearing a frock coat with a top hat, his head held high and his smile mesmerizing. She scolded herself for noting such things, but hesitated before looking away. She had no business paying that close attention to the man.

Nonetheless, she was. And Garrett Cowlishaw hadn't been the only man she'd noticed since Phillip.

Perhaps Mrs. Kamden from the *New Era* was right. Had the time come for her to consider the possibility that she could marry again one day? She hadn't thought her head could be turned again, or that she could still turn heads, but her time on the boat to Memphis and back had demonstrated otherwise.

Lewis G. Whibley was long gone, and she'd been anything but kind to Garrett Cowlishaw. Not that either of them would be interested in romantic matters. Certainly not the latter man, not with a caravan of wagons to lead west.

If she were the pillar of faith Emilie and Maren were, she'd pray about such matters of the heart. But given her history with God, she saw no reason to trouble Him with such notions.

❧

Garrett's knees weakened for countless reasons. The excitement in the air, for one thing. His best friend was about to marry, which necessitated he be dressed like a performing monkey.

As if all that weren't enough to topple him, Caroline Milburn sat perched on the aisle, looking like a fine porcelain doll.

It seemed a veil had lifted. He'd seen her as a grieving widow, a caring sister, and a devoted aunt. Today, though, she was something else entirely...

A fetching woman.

A lacy scarf draped her velvety dress, which was the color of cranberries. Pink tinged her creamy cheeks. Her fiery red hair, piled on her head, exposed a graceful neck.

She offered him a slight smile, then looked away. But not before he detected a spark in her green eyes. Something was different.

When the pastor cleared his throat, Garrett returned his attention to the ceremony at hand. "Miss Jensen will enter first. Then Miss Heinrich."

The two grooms nodded. Gabi played her last note, jumped down, and pulled the crate to one side. Rutherford walked to the rail of the horse corral where his zither awaited him. He picked up the flat instrument, then began strumming and plucking a halting rendition of the *Wedding March*. Good thing his fingers knew their way around the strings, for his gaze wasn't on the musical instrument but on his soon-to-be-bride. Miss Maren stood just inside the barn door with Mr. Heinrich at her side.

God had given Rutherford a second chance at love and marriage. Joy for his friend welled inside Garrett, mingling with regret in the memory of his own joyous wedding day.

He tugged his jacket sleeve straight. This day wasn't about him. Besides, he was better off alone. Oh, how he wanted to believe that.

❧

Her heart beat so fast Emilie expected at any moment it would leap from her chest and race into the barn without her. Outside the open door, she'd heard Rutherford play the zither and watched *PaPa* escort Maren to the man she loved. Now PaPa stood beside Emilie at the door of the barn while Quaid played a lilting tune on his harmonica. He looked resplendent in his top hat and tails. Overcome by her love for the Irishman, she lunged over the threshold.

PaPa joined her. "Is it time?"

Emilie nodded with care so as not to upset the wispy lace veil pinned to the braid circling her head. "I'm ready." Too ready to wait for the last refrain.

PaPa raised his bent arm, and, looping it, Emilie rested her hand on his woolen sleeve. Tears shimmering his blue eyes, he bent and kissed her on the forehead.

She faced the friends gathered before them and matched PaPa's long strides toward her future.

His smile widening, Quaid lowered the harmonica and struggled to finish singing the song, his cracking voice winging its way to her heart.

Emilie had little confidence her legs would've carried her the rest of the way to Quaid had her father not been supporting her.

Pastor Munson pushed his spectacles to the bridge of his nose and met her father's gaze. "Who gives this woman in holy matrimony?"

"I do. Her PaPa." He gently placed her hand in Quaid's.

When all four of them had recited their wedding vows and each couple shared a proper kiss, they lined up in front of the reverend for his introduction. That's when Emilie noticed the rest of the quilting circle had filled the first and second rows. Mrs. Brantenberg, Hattie, Mrs. Pemberton, Lorelei Beck and her mother-in-law, Anna Goben, Jewell, and Caroline.

She was indeed a blessed woman to have so many dear friends and to now be Mrs. Quaid McFarland. As she and Quaid embraced family and friends, Emilie smiled at Anna and breathed a prayer for the grieving candle maker and for the young widow—that they would one day soon be blessed by love.

ednesday morning, Anna strolled down the hill and onto Main Street toward Heinrich's Dry Goods and Grocery, still reveling in the merriment she'd experienced watching her friends wed on Saturday. The beauty. The music. The tears of joy. The warmth of friends gathered in celebration. The love filling the barn had defied the February chill in the air. She wished to always hold the memory close. Her witness to the festivities had hinted at a hope that one day she could find the kind of loving bond Emilie shared with Quaid, and Maren with Rutherford.

"Anna!"

Hattie Pemberton's voice stilled Anna's steps. She turned to face her friend. Hattie's knack for fashion made Anna smile. Today, Hattie wore a stylish two-piece dress that dusted her boots at her calves. A hussar hat with layers of lace and tulle sat atop her piled curls.

Anna smoothed her serviceable woolen skirt and shifted the sack of candles to her other arm. Careful to avoid a collision with her friend's rigid hat brim, Anna stepped into Hattie's warm embrace. "It's good to see you." Anyone cheery would be a boon, but Hattie's Christian joy, despite her father's death in the war, helped to lessen the throes of grief.

Hattie pressed her gloved hands together. Her eyes widened. "Wasn't the wedding divine?"

"It was so beautiful…charming." Hearing her own dreamy tone, Anna chided herself. She had family to take care of and couldn't afford to entertain romantic notions.

Hattie looked at the sack Anna carried. "On your way to Heinrich's?"

"Yes." She lifted the sack. "More candles."

Hattie raised her chin, her blue-gray eyes no longer hidden beneath the brim of her hat. "Wonderful timing! Mother asked me to stop in for border fabric for our square of the Friendship quilt."

Anna nodded. She needed to think on the quilting squares herself, but first she had to be sure her family was among those remaining in Saint Charles.

"Are you still making hats for the dress shop?" Hattie glanced across the street at the Queensware Emporium.

"Fewer than during the winter months. But I'm working on five new spring styles."

Hattie's generous smile warmed Anna's heart. If anyone appreciated fashionable hats, Hattie did. "I can't wait to see them."

"I'll make sure you're the first." Anna had gone so far as to design the hats on paper and was anxious to make them, but she'd need to sell a lot more candles before she could afford the materials.

Anna and Hattie strolled in comfortable silence up the cobbled brick sidewalk until a couple passed them arm in arm.

Hattie peered at Anna. "Do you think about marriage?"

Anna gulped.

"You're getting to that age, Anna."

"That age?" A nervous giggle bubbled inside her. "You make me sound like a spinster. I've just turned eighteen."

Hattie's eyebrows arched. "Surely you think about love and marriage and having a home of your own."

"Since returning to the quilting circle, it's been nigh unto impossible to think of anything else, with Maren and Emilie so enamored with Rutherford and Quaid."

Hattie's giggle overpowered the sound of the shod horse trotting past. "True. It has been about all they've talked about in recent months." She sobered, the lines at her mouth smoothing. "I think about it too. Wonder what it would be like to have a man look at me the way Quaid looks at Emilie...with devotion brimming his eyes."

Hattie Pemberton was definitely the incurable romantic in the quilting circle.

Outside the door to Heinrich's Dry Goods and Grocery, Anna glanced at the sack cradled in her arm. "I can't think about anything but work right now."

Hattie held the door open. "Life won't always be this hard for you."

"No?" Anna wanted to believe it. Some days, like Thursdays and last Saturday, she entertained daydreams of a different life, but most days she dared not allow herself the luxury.

Hattie reached for Anna's free hand and squeezed it. "God will make a way."

"For my mother? My grandfather?"

"For you."

"You are a sweet friend." Crossing the threshold into the store, Anna breathed in the warmth from the coal-burning stove.

Mr. Heinrich bent beside the checkerboard barrel with the Rengler brothers. At the sound of the bell, he looked toward the door. Doffing his top hat, he joined them at the counter. "Ladies."

"Good day, Mr. Heinrich."

Their words came out in unison.

"Good to see you both." He pushed his spectacles to the bridge of his nose.

"Mother sent me to look at cloth."

"Got in new patterns." He nodded toward the bolts of fabric.

"I'll take a look." Hattie strolled that direction.

Mr. Heinrich looked at the sack Anna carried. "I hope you've brought more of your bayberry and beeswax candles."

"I have." Anna had a feeling the man would cheerfully accept candles from her even if he had a storeroom full. She spread three dozen merry-colored candles on the countertop.

"You are a hard worker, Miss Anna."

"Thank you, sir." Anna smoothed her sack on the counter. Her hand hesitated at the redwork embroidery Mutter had done before Dedrick died: *Gleich und gleich gesellt sich gern.* It was a saying her brother was fond of: "Birds of a feather flock together." She'd made the sack for him, and it was one of the few belongings the army returned.

Mr. Heinrich pulled the money box out from under the shelf. "Your grandfather? How is he?"

"About the same."

"No need of another hank o' caning yet then?"

She folded the sack and looked up. "No, thank you. He has enough to finish the chairs he has."

"Don't imagine your mother is feelin' any better either?"

Anna shook her head.

"I'm sorry." He counted out payment for the candles and handed her the bills.

Anna tucked the money deep into her seam pocket and sealed it with the sack. "You and Emilie have been a tremendous help to us, Mr. Heinrich. I can't thank you enough for the work."

"We're happy to help. I grow weary feeling powerless to help those I care about."

When tears stung Anna's eyes, she looked away.

Mr. Heinrich returned the cashbox to its nesting place beneath the counter. "You know the Rengler brothers." He glanced toward the checkerboard and the men gathered there.

"Yes." She knew they'd lost their freight boat in an explosion last fall. Since, they'd been driving wagons for the McFarlands.

"They're joining the caravan going west this spring. The Kamdens and the Brenners are buying wagons to go too." He rubbed his clean-shaven jaw. "Maybe your grandfather should think about it."

When he won't even leave the house?

"Might be good for him, Anna, and for your Mutter."

If Großvater couldn't muster the energy to cane chairs, how was she to expect him to cross the country by wagon? And then there was Mutter.

"There's a meeting at The Western House Inn next Tuesday, thirteenth of February. Half past six, I believe. Flier's pinned at the post office."

"I'll think about it." Anna hoped her answer didn't sound as half-hearted to him as it did to her. "I best get back. Thank you again, Mr. Heinrich. Give my best to Emilie and Quaid."

"And you carry my regards to your family."

Family. Will we ever feel like a family again, Lord?

Hattie walked toward her holding a bolt of cloth in each hand.

Anna smiled, glancing toward the door. "However will you decide? I like them both."

"I do too." Hattie sighed, blowing a brown curl on her forehead. "Do you have to go?"

"Yes. But I'll see you soon." After waving good-bye, Anna stepped outside to go home to fix the noon dinner. If her mother was awake to care about eating.

The more Anna thought about going west, the more the idea of wide-open spaces and new opportunities intrigued her. But the building excitement collided with caution. Großvater's house was full of chairs they couldn't sit on. Chairs that belonged to his paying customers. Many of whom had been waiting a long time for new seats. He'd been doing a quarter of the work he'd done before falling sick with grief. Raising her hopes over a trip she'd never make wasn't good sense.

Anna started up the hill. She spent her walk talking to God about Mutter and Großvater, a familiar topic, although this time she added a few questions about the trail west. By the time she reached the ginger-bread-enrobed house, third from the end, Anna had mustered the courage to talk to Großvater. Her elder or not, he owed her the courtesy of hearing her out. And if Mutter was anywhere in the vicinity of sober, Anna had a few things to talk over with her as well.

Squaring her shoulders, Anna climbed the porch steps. She left her muddy boots outside and closed the door behind her. Großvater's voice, uncharacteristically cheerful, carried from the kitchen. A second male voice sounded vaguely familiar…

Robert? After all these years?

She quickened her steps through the empty dining room.

The moment Anna darkened the doorway, Robert Hughes jumped to his feet, leaving his hat on the kitchen table.

"Annabana—" He glanced at Großvater and quickly cleared his throat. "Miss Anna."

"Robert." The boy fond of dunking her braids into the inkwell in their one-room schoolhouse.

"Remember? My friends call me Boney."

Tears sprang to her eyes. She nodded, recalling the day her brother gave his friend that moniker.

His gaze tender, the now grown-up Boney took short steps toward her. "I've been in Saint Louis since the war. Just moved back to Saint Charles and came to pay my respects."

Großvater pulled a third chair from the table. "It's mighty good to see him, isn't it?"

"Yes." Though she spoke to Großvater, Anna kept her gaze fixed on Boney. "You heard about Dedrick?"

His blue eyes glistened. "I saw his name listed among the state casualties in the *St. Louis Dispatch*. I knew he would be the brave one." He shifted his weight and held out his hand to her. "I'm truly sorry about your loss, Anna. I was mighty fond of Dedrick."

She nodded, and he let go of her hand. "You were a good friend to him."

"What's all the racket?" Mutter dragged into the kitchen. One hand cradled her head while the other trailed the wall.

Anna pasted on a smile. "Mutter, you remember Robert Hughes, don't you?"

Leaning on the corner of the cupboard, Mutter brushed unruly hair from her bloodshot eyes. "Dedrick's friend?"

"Yes. He's moved back to town."

Mutter scowled, pulling her dressing gown tight at her waist. "Why didn't you tell me we had company?"

"I apologize if I disturbed you, Mrs. Goben."

Mutter waved a shaky hand. "Don't be silly. I was feeling a little ill this morning, is all."

Boney held his arm out to Mutter, and she accepted his escort to a chair at the table.

"Thank you."

Großvater was ready with a stout cup of coffee, nearly strong enough to overpower the stench of the previous night's rum on her breath.

"I'm feeling much better now that you're here."

While Mutter dominated the conversation, Anna busied herself at the cutting board, chopping potatoes for their dinner. So much for her reunion with Boney Hughes, the only other person who understood how much she'd lost when her brother died.

7

Caroline followed Jewell up the narrow porch steps of Emilie and Quaid McFarland's home on Monday. The newlywed couple had moved into a small cottage up the street from his father's freight company. Gingham curtains the color of sunshine hung in the front window.

Jewell had just raised her hand to knock when the door swung open.

"Welcome to my new home." Emilie's brown eyes sparkled with a pride that made Caroline's heart ache.

Jewell drew her hand back to her side. "You must have been peeking out the window."

"A little too anxious, I suppose." Blushing, Emilie pushed a strand of dark brown hair into the loose bun at her neck. "Please, do come in."

Just inside, Jewell sighed and removed her cape. "I'm sorry we're the last to arrive."

As usual, Jack had been hesitant to let Jewell leave. Caroline had stood up to him, causing a ruckus just before Mrs. Brantenberg arrived to gather the children. Their two newlywed friends were hosting a feast of celebration, and she and Jewell were sorely in need of the pick-me-up the gathering promised.

Emilie was closing the door behind them when Maren, Hattie, and Anna rushed out of the kitchen.

Maren—now Mrs. Rutherford Wainwright—reached for Jewell first, then embraced Caroline. "Thank you for coming. We're glad you're here."

The others each greeted them with an embrace, reminding Caroline of her first visit to Mrs. Brantenberg's quilting circle last year. The older widow had said hugs were a woman's way of drawing others into her circle of friends.

Nearly an hour later, Caroline sat at a dining table with her friends. She sank her fork into one of Emilie's applesauce brownies and happily crunched on a walnut in the sweet topping. And this delight, after eating delectable bacon popovers and a generous bowl of soup with pork ribs and potatoes. She and Jewell did their best to provide tasty foods for Jack and the children but hadn't the funds to fix such a fine meal. Trying not to lick her lips with each succulent bite, Caroline shifted her thoughts to Anna.

Whenever Caroline became overwhelmed by her life, she would think of Anna Goben. Just turned eighteen, and already she carried a burden of grief and the task of providing for her family.

Swallowing a sip of coffee, Anna lowered her cup to its saucer.

"When I was in the store last week"—Anna looked across the table at Emilie—"your father told me about a wagon caravan meeting tomorrow evening."

"He did?"

Anna nodded. "Yes. He thinks the trip may be good for us."

Caroline stopped chewing, her hearing perked.

Emilie raised an eyebrow. "I think PaPa would secretly like to go west. Hardly an evening goes by that he doesn't regale me with talk of the Rengler brothers' plans to join the train of wagons." She looked at Anna. "Are you interested in going?"

"I talked to my grandfather about it."

"And?" Hattie swirled her hand as if to pull more information out of her.

That's when Caroline realized that her curiosity had scooted her to the chair's edge.

"Grandfather told me my mother would never be able to make the trip. Wasn't sure he could, either."

"Charles and I will be at that meeting." Hattie brushed the brim of her unusually petite hat. "My brother has already caught the scent of California land."

"Rutherford plans to go to the meeting. Mother Brantenberg isn't yet convinced, but my husband is hearing a call to adventure."

"Most likely, Mr. Cowlishaw's voice." Caroline reached for her coffee cup. "The grand trek across the country is probably all you hear about with him living on the farm."

"It's true, although Rutherford said he and Gretchen had talked about going west ten years ago." Maren smiled. "I'm sure that Garrett, being the leader of the caravan, has given him a push that direction."

Anna straightened in her chair. "Robert Hughes is back in Saint Charles. He came to the house."

"Mother and I saw him at the post office yesterday." Hattie tilted her head in rhythm with the lilt in her voice.

Anna's eyes narrowed as if she, too, had detected the syrup in Hattie's tone.

"He told Mother he's planning to make the trip."

"Yes, I heard him tell my grandfather as much."

"I've heard about appeals for teachers to go to towns in gold and silver mining country, and several for the cities in the great valley and even San Francisco itself." Leaning toward her, Hattie whispered directly into Caroline's face. "Seems I remember you telling us at the circle that you were once a schoolteacher."

"I was." Before she married.

And, now that she was single again, the profession might be her ticket to a new life. In California.

✦

Garrett stood at the counter chatting with Johann Heinrich.

"Mr. Garrett Cowlishaw?"

Startled, he turned toward the self-assured voice. He'd seen twigs with more meat on them than was on this young man.

"Yes. I'm Garrett."

The younger fellow brushed the broad brim on his cavalry hat. "Robert Hughes, sir."

"The fellow who left the note for me at The Western House?"

"One and the same." He stuck out a sun-darkened hand for a shake. "Friends call me Boney."

Fighting the impulse to laugh at the boy's attempt to grow a beard was a definite distraction. Calling it *sparse* would be a compliment.

Boney cleared his throat, his eyes narrowed.

"Uh. Good to meet ya, Boney." Garrett slid a stack of jerky off the counter. "I planned to look for you at the boardinghouse when I finished here. Seein' that you found me first, you want to help me carry supplies to my wagon? Afterward we can talk over a coffee."

"Yes sir, coffee sounds good."

God may have skimped on the young man's build, but Boney Hughes was as strong as any oxen. That kind of strength could come in handy on the trail. When they'd finished loading the wagon, Garrett motioned for Boney to join him on the seat and drove the brick-paved road to The Western House Inn. Garrett pulled the wagon to a stop at the meeting hall and set the brake. As soon as they lowered themselves from the perch, he started the conversation. "Your note said you want a trail job."

"Yes, sir. Drover. Scout. Cook." Boney darted to the back of the wagon. "Whatever you need."

"Want to go west real bad, do ya?"

"That, I do." The young man reached into the wagon and latched on to a crock of lard.

"That stuff's going out to Mrs. Brantenberg's farm."

"Oh." He let go and backed away.

"You runnin' from the law?"

Boney chuckled. "No."

"A girl?"

"No sir." The wiry fellow hooked his thumbs in his trouser pockets. "Not runnin' from anyone, except maybe the war."

Garrett nodded and waved him toward the brick building. "Let's go in for that coffee." Inside, he led Boney to his usual table near the hearth.

"You ordering off the menu, Mr. Garrett?" The crisply dressed waitress looked at the slate board on the wall.

"No thanks, Millie. Just two coffees this time."

"Be right back with 'em then."

When she left, Garrett returned his attention to Boney. He liked the young man.

"Went as far as Arizona Territory with the cavalry, and I have a mind to see more of it. Land as wide open as the sky. And I ain't much for sittin' in one place."

"Fair enough. I've been with two wagon train companies that went west. Full of adventure, if you can take suffering in the hardships."

When the steaming coffee mugs arrived, Boney took a quick gulp, then wrapped his hands around the cup. "I saw your advertisement posted in Heinrich's Dry Goods and Grocery." He looked up, studying Garrett's face.

A good trait—being able to look a man in the eye.

"You think you might have a job for me? Folks say I'm good with animals. I was a mule skinner in the cavalry."

"Not good with people?"

Boney looked into the coffee cup. "They haven't said the likes, but I s'pose you could judge that for yourself."

"You've got an easy way about you." Garrett took a swallow of the bitter coffee. "Plain talker, forthright. Refreshing qualities."

"My ma didn't cotton to puttin' on airs."

"Wise woman."

"She was. She and my pa both died of the cholera. Been livin' with my aunt and uncle in Saint Louis."

"You'd be good to have on the journey. Consider yourself hired." Garrett raised his coffee mug in a sort of man-to-man contract.

"I'm much obliged." Dipping his chin, Boney lifted his cup till the two mugs clinked.

Garrett smiled. That gave him five hired hands. Folks were signing up to join the caravan. His wagon and supplies were ordered. Tomorrow night was the big town meeting, and he had the details ready for all who were interested. So, why did hesitation about leaving Saint Charles suddenly nag his gut?

A red-headed woman as lovely as a fine porcelain doll came to mind.

ranking the pump harder than she needed to, Caroline watched water splash into the metal washtub. The lye soap she'd added began to form bubbles, a perfect match for her boiling insides. Never mind that her sister hadn't felt well through the night. On Jack's orders, Jewell had just left the house with Mary to fetch a newspaper.

Caroline plopped a porridge bowl into the tub and watched suds take wing overhead. The man had lost a leg in battle, and he was letting it take his heart and mind too. Jack had been sour as vinegar for more than a year now. Fellow soldiers and others in the community had tried to reach out to him. Even his own family, but he wouldn't have any of it. Labeled it *pity*.

She dunked the dish and scrubbed. Mrs. Brantenberg would say the war had given Jack a ragged scrap of fabric, a remnant that didn't fit the pattern he'd laid out for his life. Caroline hadn't lost a limb, but she knew about scraps that didn't seem right for her quilt. Clearly, her brother-in-law had no intention of allowing God to have this piece of his life, to make something useful of it.

Gilbert and Cora were at school. Now that she was alone with Jack, she had a mind to hold a mirror up in front of the ungrateful man's face. Had Phillip lived, even if he'd lost a leg, he wouldn't have chosen to wallow in self-pity. At least Jack had his life. His family. A home, though it be humble. And crowded.

Dunking another bowl, Caroline blew out a long breath. Best she kept her opinions to herself. Jewell had enough troubles…didn't need her stirring a pot full of Jack's discontent. Caroline didn't blame him for experiencing melancholy. She'd felt it herself—grieved her loss, sank into despair. But he'd let it eat at him until he was just a shell of the man Jewell had married ten years ago. The worst part was that he didn't see it.

Or didn't care.

Shaking her head, Caroline recalled the support she'd received in her own distress. She was grateful for the love of her sister and her quilting circle friends. God had used them to help her see that He still had a plan for her.

Although, standing here with her hands in a tub of dishwater in another woman's kitchen, she didn't have a clue what that plan might be.

The scrape of colliding furniture in the next room pulled Caroline out of her ponderings. Jack's wheelchair was on the move, and the slap of his foot on the wood flooring told her he was headed her way.

Turning her back to the kitchen doorway, she busied herself with the breakfast dishes.

"Where's your sister?" Jack's growl sent chills up her spine. However did Jewell tolerate his gruffness? And why?

Caroline drew a fortifying breath and faced him.

His chair rolled to a stop at the sideboard.

"You sent Jewell to the store."

"Hours ago, I did." His eyes narrowed to slits.

Swallowing her frustration, Caroline walked to the table, but remained standing. "She has Mary with her, and it hasn't been twenty minutes."

"Should've gone myself. Would've been back by now." His hand shook on the arm of his wicker chair.

Water dripped from her hands, wetting the wood surface of the table, and she wiped them with her apron.

"It wasn't a newspaper you really sent her for."

He spun the chair to face her. "You got somethin' on your mind?"

Caroline pulled a chair from under the table and seated herself.

"You women think you have all the answers."

A vein in her neck throbbed. He was the one who had made the mistake of asking, and she wasn't one to turn down such a rare opportunity.

"You gonna tell me what a rotten husband I am? And a rotten father?"

He knew and hadn't done anything to make amends. Her stomach soured. "I don't know why Jewell stays with you"—she raised her hand, hoping to stop his canned response—"and it has nothing to do with you having one leg." She pressed her hand to her queasy stomach. "Nothing directly, that is."

"Is that so?"

Caroline fussed with the edging on the plaid table runner she'd given Jewell at Christmas. "You're not the only one who suffers, Jack." Countless folks flashed in her mind. Anna. Mrs. Brantenberg. Hattie. Mrs. Pemberton. The Rengler brothers.

Jack planted his hands on the arms of the chair and hoisted himself from the seat. "You may have lost your husband, but you have both of your legs." His face hardened. "You can go most anywhere you want to." He slammed back into the seat, then spun the chair into the doorframe. "I suggest you do that. Go!" He'd hurled the words over his shoulder.

Now *she* was shaking. When Caroline heard the wheels of the chair in the distance, she stood on weak legs, thankful neither Jewell nor the children had been here to witness their heated exchange. She returned to the cupboard and the dirty dishes.

She was only making things worse, staying here. She wouldn't be like Jack—hopeless and aimless.

When she'd finished cleaning up from breakfast, Caroline opened the kitchen door, then pulled the tub off the countertop. Outside, she stepped off the back stoop and flung the dirty dishwater onto the matted remains of last year's garden.

She didn't mind housework, but she needed something else to do. She needed to teach.

Garrett rested his arms on the table and studied the man seated across from him. Father would've been about Mr. Otto Goben's age had he...lived. "You said this was your granddaughter's idea? You comin' to see me?"

"Yes sir."

Father's cheeks were never that hollow. This man looked like he didn't spend much time at the meal table.

"Long about last week, Anna Mae sat me down...said she was tired of dodging all the chairs I wasn't gettin' caned." His cheek bulged, and Garrett knew his tongue was rolling a wad of chew.

"Dodging chairs?"

"That's my work. Folks bring 'em to our house, and well, I haven't been gettin' much done."

He had doubts the man could weather a windstorm, let alone survive walking across the country. Garrett pushed back in the slat-back chair. "Mr. Goben, the trail west is hard. If you've been sick..."

Mr. Goben rubbed his gray whiskered jaw. "Not exactly. But Anna says I'm makin' myself sick with grief. Her brother died in the war. Her mother hasn't taken the loss well." He scratched a balding spot at the center of unruly gray hair. "Truth is, neither have I."

He needed strong stock for the trip. Folks who could tend to their livestock and family. Do the upkeep on their wagons. Ford rivers. Garrett drew in a deep breath and blew it out. "Your granddaughter thinks joining the wagon train...going west will help?"

The waitress set Garrett's plate in front of him, teasing him with the scent of braised pork chops and potato pancakes. "Thank you." He glanced at Mr. Goben. "You sure you don't want anything to eat?"

"Ate at home." He looked at the waitress. "Thank you." As soon as the waitress left, the elder man waved for Garrett to eat his meal. "Anna's the kind that when she speaks, you're gonna want to listen. The girl isn't one to waste words on the wind."

"Does she go out to Mrs. Brantenberg's farm for the ladies' quilting circle?"

A shadow darkened the man's eyes. "When Anna's mother stopped goin' more than a year ago, she stopped too. Started up again last month. You know the widow?"

"Met her at the farm." Garrett scooped another forkful of potato.

"I'm not sayin' we'll go, but Anna made a point worth listening to." Mr. Goben reached for his glass of soda water.

The man's pauses were almost more than Garrett could tolerate. Probably raw nerves about tonight's meeting. That many people in a confined space. The open trail would suit him better.

"Anna said you can't get anywhere stuck in the mud."

Garrett shook his head, betwixt laughter and a holler.

"Apparently, she's thinking me and my daughter's been stuck in the mud. Thinks us all going with you will pull us out."

"And what do you think?"

"Anna's the smart one. Told her I'd talk to you."

"You should come to the meeting here tonight at 6:30. I'll have the contracts for signing up and a supply list for every family." Garrett raked his hair. "Four to six months' worth of hard travel through mountain passes and desert, sir, fording rivers with wagons and women. It's a long walk."

The man's cheek bulged again. "Sounds like you're trying to discourage me."

Garrett laid his fork on his empty plate, swallowing his last bite of pork. "I have an obligation to discourage anyone who might be at risk due to ill health or a frail constitution."

He'd been on the trail. Knew the hardships of traversing an unforgiving land. He'd heard death's cries; seen the heartache. This was the first time he was the one making the decisions about who went and who stayed…

And he didn't want to make a mistake.

9

Caroline held a candle lantern in one hand and pulled her cape tight with the other. Thankfully, The Western House Inn was positioned just a few blocks up, at the corner of Boone's Lick Road and Main Street. Not far from the center of town, but still it wasn't proper for a lady to be out alone after dark. Jewell made sure Caroline had heard that twice, at the least.

It wasn't like she'd planned to go out. She'd only decided to attend the meeting after the confrontation with Jack. She'd spent the bulk of the day avoiding the man. For that matter, she'd avoided Jewell as well, spending most of the time in the room she shared with Mary and Cora. The keepsakes she'd kept from Aunt Inez's trunk were now well polished and organized. She'd cleaned each one, bringing back the good memories of her world before the darkness of war. The mother-of-pearl cameo hung around her neck, swinging between her shirtwaist and her cape, calming her with each step. Aunt Inez had never married, fancied herself an independent woman. Caroline was drawing confidence from the memories of her aunt…until she heard wagon wheels slowing behind her.

Her pulse quickened. Perhaps this wasn't a good idea, after all. She lengthened her stride.

"Caroline?"

Hattie Pemberton's voice relaxed her like a warm blanket placed over her shoulders, and she turned to greet her friend. Hattie's brother, Charles, held the reins while Hattie sat in the backseat of the surrey with Anna.

"Mrs. Milburn." Charles doffed his bowler, obviously dressed in his Sunday best for the meeting. "Wherever are you going this time of day?"

She frowned at his scolding tone. "I imagine it's the same place you're headed."

"The Western House?"

"Yes. To the Boone's Lick Wagon Train Company meeting."

He glanced behind her. "Your sister and brother-in-law?"

"I'm alone." The words stung her tongue.

"No, you're not." Hattie's hand fluttered in the glow of her candle lantern. "Join us." Holding her flowered hat, she scooted to the far edge of the seat.

"I'd like that. Thank you."

Charles wrapped the reins around the brake lever, stood, and faced her.

Since the wagon was lit, Caroline blew out her candle lantern and handed it up to him. She pinched her skirt, lifting it above her boots, and settled her foot on the step.

Charles offered his hand. "I'm pleased we came along when we did.

It's not safe for a woman to be out at night *alone.*" The phrase was becoming downright tiresome.

"You can be certain it isn't my first choice." Letting go of his hand, she squeezed onto the seat beside Anna. "I do thank you, Mr. Pemberton."

"I'm happy to oblige." He seated himself, then turned to look at her. "Please. Call me Charles."

When they arrived at The Western House Inn, Charles helped them down from the surrey and shooed them inside. "I'll park the wagon and join you momentarily."

Hattie didn't respond. Instead she looked at Caroline, her eyes as wide as turkey platters. "You're going west?"

"I'm thinking about it."

Anna's mouth dropped open. "You are?"

"I have to do something."

Anna nodded. "That's how I feel. I talked to my grandfather about making the trip, and he talked to Mr. Cowlishaw earlier today. Doesn't like crowds, so he told me to find a ride and come."

Hattie slid her reticule onto her arm and looked at Caroline. "Your sister knows you're gone? However did you slip away?"

"Jewell knows. Mary told her I was dressing for church instead of for bed."

Anna tittered. "You do look well put together."

Proof that looks can indeed be deceiving.

Hattie nodded toward the peacock-feathered creation on Caroline's head. "Is your hat new?"

"It belonged to my aunt. Jewell said the hat was too gaudy for her."

"It becomes you." Stepping to one side, Anna viewed the back. "I may need to use it as a pattern for my collection next winter."

A young man opened the door and stared at them. When they didn't budge, he cleared his throat. "Good evening, ladies." He doffed his hat. Although it had been stripped of its sabers and cord, it was a Union cavalry hat. "You're here for the meeting, are you?"

"We are indeed, kind sir." Hattie inched closer to the open door.

"Boney?" Anna pressed her gloved hand to her mouth in a failed attempt to stifle a laugh.

"Since when does The Western House have a butler?" Hattie pressed her gloved finger to her chin. "Or are you standing guard against hostile attack?"

"I work for Garrett Cowlishaw now." His shoulders squared. "Hired me to work the wagon train."

Anna jerked her gaze to Caroline. "Forgive our poor manners. Boney, this is our friend, Caroline Milburn."

"It's my pleasure to make your acquaintance, ma'am." His smile revealed a gap between his teeth. "Robert Hughes. My friends call me Boney, and any friend of Anna's is a friend of mine."

"Thank you." She couldn't help but smile. "It's a pleasure to meet you."

"Boney lived in Saint Charles when we were all in school." Anna looked at Hattie. "He was good friends with our brothers."

When a line began to form behind the ladies, the charming young man ushered them inside, then leaned toward Anna. "We didn't have much opportunity to visit the other day. Think we could talk after the meeting?"

Anna's face paled. "That depends upon my companions. We came together." She nodded toward Hattie. "Charles escorted us."

At the mention of Charles's name, a shadow crossed the young man's face, piquing Caroline's curiosity. Was Mr. Hughes sweet on Anna?

Perhaps so. He didn't seem to notice Hattie's attentions.

"I don't mind waiting." Caroline sidestepped two children in a chase.

When Anna nodded, Mr. Hughes waved them through the door.

The hum of chatter filled the meeting room. Men straddled the benches on either side of three rows of tables. Men and women competed for attention while getting acquainted and talking about wagons and provisions. Children scrambled up and around the aisles between the tables.

If she joined the caravan, she'd be traveling with all these folks. Rowdy children that weren't her nieces and nephew. For months. What was she thinking?

Caroline had all but convinced herself to leave when Charles walked through the door. Hattie waved her gloved hand, signaling their whereabouts, and Charles escorted them to the second table in the far row. Seating herself on the end of a bench, Caroline glanced to the single table at the front of the room. Garrett Cowlishaw stood fumbling with a stack of paper, dressed in the style of a frontiersman, not of the dandified leaders of the city. Four men of varying size and age stood beside him.

Anna's lean friend—Caroline wasn't sure she could politely call a man Boney—sprinted toward the front, joining the other men. That's when Garrett looked up. His ready smile quickly faded, his brow pinched.

"Here! Here!" The thunder-boom voice belonged to a bear-sized man.

The klatsches dispersed and folks scurried to fill nearly every bench seat in the room.

"Let us commence this meeting for the assembly of a train headed west." As the crowd quieted, Garrett looked everywhere but at her. "This expedition brings with it hardship and heartbreak. Only the most committed among you should consider making the passage." Yet another side to this Confederate-soldier-turned-wagon-train-leader. In charge. Confident. "Everyone will be expected to grant aid and support to each of the members of this undertaking, including tending the sick and burying the dead."

A woman behind her gasped.

"I have printed lists of required provisions and equipment for each family present." He waved the stack of paper. "You will be expected, at a minimum, to procure these provisions. I will leave several copies of the list at Heinrich's Dry Goods store. Johann Heinrich, the shopkeeper, will be ordering in anticipation of your need."

"You got wheel grease on your list?" The question came from the back of the room.

Caroline looked that direction. Mrs. Kamden waved at her from beside the man, apparently her wheelwright son.

"I do. With instructions and information on taking care of wagons and wagon wheels on the trail." Garrett raked the dark blond waves above his ear. "Furthermore, my men and I will inspect every rig for its worthiness for the trip. Have the doctor check your livestock and your team." Men mumbled while Garrett ran his finger down the stack of papers in his hand. "Be sure to have a Last Will and Testament done and filed at the state capitol."

Caroline's breath caught in the collective gasp that rippled through the room. Living in the same house with a man who didn't want her there suddenly seemed much less of a hardship.

A woman in the next row tugged her husband's coat sleeve while rattling off in French. Two young boys and a girl about Hattie's age squirmed beside her. "Mister Cowlishaw, your gloom and doom is scarin' my wife, it is." He stood, pulling a beret from his head. "I seen there's miles and miles of fertile land out west. Land o' plenty. That's why we go."

"Any of you interested in joining the Boone's Lick Wagon Train Company need to know you're not signing up for a holiday or a picnic." Garrett seemed to shift his focus to the fresh-faced, well-scrubbed children scattered in the crowd. "The journey is hard on families."

Another man stood. "Others have made the trip, and they're picking up gold nuggets right off the ground!"

"I don't deny there's wide open spaces and opportunities in the West for farming, cattle ranching, and even gold prospecting, but you take a hundred folks—men, women, and children—two thousand miles on foot through hostile, untamed country, some...many will suffer illness. There will be deaths. I've seen the markers...fresh-dug graves." He paused until the murmurs quieted. "I will be regarded as captain of this expedition and my decisions and guidance will be for the benefit of the entire assembly. My men here"—he regarded the five men flanking him—"will provide assistance where needed. But we will all be expected to assist one another in this endeavor. Undue burdens cannot be tolerated, as they will be a burden to all. Heavy objects such as pianos are best sold before departure."

"What about bathtubs?" The bearded man seated across the table from Caroline looked at his wife, who was now the color of Christmas bows.

"No bathtubs. No kitchen cupboards. Not if you want your mules and oxen to survive. Not to mention the wagons. My men'll bring the provisions lists to the tables." The capable captain dispersed the lists among his men. "There's a roster here on the table." He pointed to an inkwell and paper. "You plan on going with us, you'll need to sign up on the roster."

Caroline watched Robert Hughes saunter toward their row. She had her money from Aunt Inez and could make do with very little. She'd be traveling with a big group, many of them friends from the quilting circle. She was no longer a wife expecting to start a family. She needed a fresh start. Opportunities to teach. A renewed purpose.

And she now had no doubt Garrett Cowlishaw was a leader who could get her there.

10

Garrett watched his men deliver lists of provisions to each table, forcing himself to avoid looking in the direction of the second table in the far left row. Why was Caroline Milburn in attendance at his Boone's Lick Wagon Train Company meeting? He'd heard for himself from her sister that the family had no intention of leaving Saint Charles. Probably only came to accompany her friends, or out of curiosity. Certainly wouldn't blame her for wanting to leave that house for an evening's respite.

When folks started flooding to the front, he had them form a line at the sign-up roster. From the looks of it, they could have ten or more wagons going. Wouldn't want many more than that. Garrett seated himself on a bench behind the table and pulled the quill from the inkwell.

Rutherford tentatively signed up for his family—Maren, Gabi, and Mrs. Brantenberg. A Mr. and Mrs. Kamden, with five children and his mother, enlisted for the trip. A big group—good thing the man intended to take two wagons. The Rengler brothers and their family. And five or more other families. Others stepped up to say they were still thinking on it.

He could no longer avoid Caroline Milburn, for she now stood on the other side of the table looking as handsome as she did at the wedding.

"Mr. Cowlishaw." Even formal, his name sounded like a song on her lips. Out at the farm, they'd agreed to call one another by their given names, but now they were in public.

He stood. "Mrs. Milburn." She held a paper, presumably a provisions list, at her side.

"That was quite an impressive speech you gave."

"Thank you." The compliment warmed his ears, and he felt his resolve to leave Saint Charles and the complex widow begin to weaken. Again.

When she reached for the pen in the inkwell, he laid his hand on her arm.

She stilled, her green eyes widening. But she didn't object or pull away.

"Given your brother-in-law's condition, do you really think he could make the trip?"

"I don't. My sister has not changed her mind about going." She drew in a deep breath. "I'm not here on their behalf."

She'd waited at the end of the line. There was no one with her, or behind her. "Someone else asked you to sign the roster in their absence?"

Clearing her throat ever so modestly, Caroline stared at his hand, still resting on her arm.

He withdrew his hold on her and shoved his hand into his trouser pocket.

"I'm signing for myself. I'm going west."

His heart pounding, he fought to keep his voice calm. "You're not."

"Pardon me?"

He gripped the edge of the table. "My apologies. What I mean is... with whom would you travel?"

"Myself, and judging by that long wait to get up here, I'd say dozens of other folks."

His throat went dry. He swallowed hard. "You're single."

"Widowed." Her eyes narrowed, a brighter green than he'd seen them. "What does that have to do with this?"

"Everything." A vein in his neck pulsed. "Single women have no place on the trail."

"I have several friends intending to go. Maren, Mrs. Brantenberg, Anna Goben—"

"The sea offers more comfortable travel and doesn't take much longer."

"I don't wish to travel by ship." She pressed her fingertips to the table. "I want to provision a wagon and make the trip with people I know."

"You can't go."

Her shoulders squared.

He pulled the roster from the table. "I'm the captain, and—"

"What you say goes." She crinkled the provisions list. "Even if it's wrong. Unfair. And vindictive." She spun around and marched toward the door.

Vindictive? Someone had to be sensible. Certainly wouldn't be her…thinking she could up and drive a wagon through hill and dale, mile after mile.

Boney joined him at the table and let out a low whistle. "Looks to me like you've got lady trouble."

"Not anymore." Garrett glanced toward the stiff-backed red-head. "She's a war widow. Told her she couldn't take a wagon west by herself."

"Sounds to me like she might have something to prove."

"Well, she won't do it on my watch." He'd have his hands full with all the little ones riding along. Didn't need her distracting him…worrying him.

❧

Caroline didn't bother to mind a ladylike pace. Her neck burning under the heat of ire, she marched toward Anna, who stood alone near the back.

If Caroline had her druthers, she'd walk straight out the door, not look back. But she didn't have a say in anything. She was a widow, and that changed everything. Without a man, she couldn't go west. Not in a wagon, anyway. On a ship, she'd have no escort. No friends accompanying her.

And no Garrett Cowlishaw in sight.

That suddenly seemed reason enough not to go on the caravan come spring. Five or so months with that man would be more burdensome than fording rivers or facing a bear. Six months under his leadership would be the death of her.

"You look like you've swallowed a frog." Concern narrowed Anna's blue eyes. "You told Mr. Cowlishaw you wanted to add a wagon to the train, did you? What did he say?"

"No." She refused to follow Anna's gaze to the man. Whatever she did, she wouldn't give Garrett Cowlishaw the satisfaction that he'd won his first battle as captain of the company. "He said no."

Anna didn't look the least bit surprised. She opened her mouth as if to say something, then closed it.

"Mr. Cowlishaw doesn't want widows on the trail."

"He said that?" Anna's eyebrows arched.

Guilt dried Caroline's mouth. "Not in those words, exactly." She moistened her lips. "But he did say a single woman couldn't travel alone…in her own wagon. He thinks every woman going should have a man." Grudgingly, she did too. Elsa Brantenberg had Rutherford. Mrs. Kamden had her son. Anna had her grandfather.

All options she didn't have.

"Life's not that easy." Anna's statement carried a wistfulness that Caroline understood.

She knew Anna expected the trip to invigorate her grandfather's spirit and pull her family together.

Caroline swung her shoulders, settling her cape. She wouldn't be a wet blanket putting a damper on her friend's hopes. "Speaking of men, has Mr. Hughes talked to you yet?"

"Ha! Mr. Hughes. I can't make myself think of him so formally. My brother called him Boney." Anna shook her head. "Not yet. But he's busy talking with Mr. Cowlishaw right now."

"No doubt about addle-headed women who don't take the dangers of the trail seriously and think they have the constitution to make the trip west."

"We can leave any time Charles is ready." Anna looked about the room. "Have you seen him or Hattie? Boney and I can catch up on another day."

"Yoo-hoo, Mrs. Milburn."

Caroline's shoulder's tensed. She was hardly in the mood for polite conversation, but she turned toward the familiar voice anyway. Mrs. Kamden waved a gloved hand and rushed toward her, the littlest of her five grandchildren in tow.

Anna raised her hand to her mouth. "The woman you told us about from your trip home from Memphis?"

Caroline nodded. "Hello, Mrs. Kamden." She regarded the little girl with the big brown eyes.

"This is Maisie, the youngest of my Ian's children."

Following the introductions, Mrs. Kamden laid her gloved hand on Caroline's arm. "Dear, I saw you at the table with your friends, then in line behind us. Are you going west with the caravan?"

"I had hoped to."

"With your sister and brother-in-law?"

"They're not going."

"Oh." The woman's lips formed an elongated O that shrank, while her eyes did the same. "Well, with all that man's talk of death and peril"—Mrs. Kamden looked at the little girl—"I'm having second thoughts about going." Her ability to whisper hadn't improved in the least.

Caroline noticed Anna's attention drift away from their conversation, then saw that Boney Hughes was approaching.

Mrs. Kamden glanced down at Maisie. "It's time we return to the rest of the family." She looked up. "The Lord bless you and keep you, dear. And you, too, Miss Goben."

Caroline smiled. "And you, Mrs. Kamden."

"Thank you." Anna's gaze darted to the woman, then back to the young man now standing at her side.

"Have a pleasant evening, Mrs. Kamden. Miss Maisie." Boney Hughes tipped his hat, and the woman shuffled away.

Caroline needed to do the same. "If you two will excuse me—"

Anna grasped Caroline's cape. "No need for you to leave. Please stay. We don't want to make it difficult for Charles to round us up when he's ready to leave, now, do we?"

"All right." She looked at the young man, feeling like a third wheel on a pushcart.

Boney cleared his throat. "About the other day…"

Caroline looked down at Anna's hand, which still had a firm grip on the edge of her wrap. "I don't wish to intrude."

Anna drew in a deep breath. "Please stay. Any friend of mine is a friend of Boney's. He said so himself."

"I did indeed." He removed his hat and faced Anna. "I saw the chairs he ain't fixing, Anna. And I saw the way she is. I've heard how hard you've been working since Dedrick died."

"Großvater has been under the weather. Mutter too."

"You don't have to hide the truth from me."

"They're my family."

"Marry me."

Caroline barely heard Anna's gasp over her own.

"Come with me on the wagon train as my wife. You deserve to be taken care of."

Tears stung the backs of Caroline's eyes and she turned away. Since when had she become such a romantic?

"I…uh." Anna held firmly to Caroline's cape. "You've been gone for five years. We're not children in the schoolyard anymore."

"No. We're not." He stepped forward, his gaze tender. "Anna, you're a beautiful young woman with lots of life left in you. If you don't squander it."

Letting go of Caroline's cape, Anna reached for Boney's arm. "You are a dear to notice and to care." Her shoulders rose and fell. "This is so sudden."

Boney nodded. "Will you think on it?"

"Yes." Her hand swung to her side. "I will think about it."

An idea dawned…

Yes, Anna would think on it. And so would Caroline. If she had a man willing to marry her, that would put an end to Mr. Cowlishaw's concerns about her going west with the caravan.

Caroline couldn't help herself.

She smiled.

II

Braying donkeys woke Garrett on Wednesday morning. Or was he awake? Perhaps he was dreaming.

Rolling, he pulled the wool blanket back over his face. After all, he had behaved like a donkey last evening. Caroline Milburn lived in a hopeless house. She obviously dreamed of starting a new life out west. He'd puffed up under the guise of captain and crushed her hope of a new beginning.

"For her own good."

Yawning, he tossed to his other side, tangling himself in the blankets. Rimming the edge of the cot, he rolled out of bed. His covers went with him. "What a mess!"

"Couldn't, in good conscience, approve of her foolish plans." He had a responsibility to protect those who couldn't protect themselves. Garrett swatted at the blankets anchoring his feet, then stood. "What kind of a leader would I be if I caved in because she was a charming woman?" If she had simply been a charming woman, he would've slept better. "Caroline Milburn. Of all people." He cringed at his reflection in the washstand mirror, then splashed his whiskered face with cold water. It didn't matter who it was that he'd turned down, he'd made the right decision. Although, he agreed with the mirror that he could've been more diplomatic in dashing her dreams.

The sound of hooves and more braying jerked Garrett out of his daydreaming.

The animals were real. And close by. Inside the granary!

Garrett scrambled down the shallow steps, nearly toppling off of the last one.

Rutherford stood near the door with a smug smile on his face. Three donkeys stood at the end of the lead ropes wrapped around his friend's hand.

Garrett blew out a long breath. He obviously hadn't latched the door last night, leaving an invitation to a grain feast.

Rutherford glanced up the staircase. "Who you talkin' to up there?"

"I was talking?"

Rutherford nodded, wagging thick eyebrows.

"What do you think you heard?"

"Only that you're smitten with Caroline Milburn."

He brushed his woolen sleeves out to full length. "I didn't say that."

Rutherford shrugged. "Some things don't need spelled out."

Garrett swatted the air. "You're a newlywed, hearin' romance everywhere you eavesdrop."

Rutherford's laugh boomed.

Whether he was attracted to Caroline or not, he couldn't let the young woman risk her life. Surely, there was something else the widow could do. Something safer. More comfortable.

Rutherford cleared his throat. "I'd ask you to help me take these well-fed jennies back to the barn, but"—he looked at Garrett's bright red union suit—"there are ladies on the property."

Garrett looked at the open door, then darted up the steps. "See you at breakfast."

Tomorrow was quilting circle day on the farm, and he'd make it a point to be here. The perfect opportunity to make things right with Caroline. With another day for her to calm down, she'd surely be ready to listen to his explanation and have a better understanding of his position.

aroline pulled a sedate brown hat from the wardrobe. She stood in front of the wavy mirror that hung above her dresser and placed the hat on her upswept hair. Mary sat on the bed watching her every move.

"Why you go away to church?" Her niece's stocking feet dangled just above the rough wood flooring.

"Sometimes it's good for me to get out." Caroline pushed one of Aunt Inez's pearl-tipped hatpins through her hair. She hadn't been to the quilting circle the past two Thursdays. Since her run-in with Garrett Cowlishaw at the Boone's Lick Wagon Train Company meeting, she hadn't been anywhere but to the grocery. Jewell conducted a Sunday service for the children in their home, but it wasn't the same. Today Caroline needed more. She'd not attended a formal church service since leaving Philadelphia.

Most of her friends here were members of German-speaking congregations, but Maren had invited her to visit the Presbyterian meetinghouse that she and Rutherford attended—the type of church Caroline had grown accustomed to in the East. Placing the last pin in her hat, she looked out the sunlit window. Her burdens seemed to lift with the promise of warm sunshine. A perfect day for a nice long walk. And an inspiring worship service.

"You were out yesterday. Remember?" Mary slid off the bed. "You washed the windows."

Caroline giggled. "I did." She lifted her Bible from the bedside table. "But I meant I need to be out among other people."

"Oh." Freckles dotted Mary's round cheeks. "Then you'll come back?"

"Yes." Thanks to Garrett Cowlishaw's sensibilities about single women on the trail, she may be here forever. Unless she found a man to marry.

And what better place than in a church?

Mary followed her out of the bedroom and into the kitchen. Caroline had invited Jewell to come along this morning and suggested it would be good for the children, but her sister preferred to stay home. No doubt hoping that if Jack heard enough Scripture, he'd shed his nasty cocoon and become a new man. Caroline sighed. She didn't have that kind of patience. She may not be a part of the wagon train come spring, but she was determined that things would be different for her. Soon.

Jewell looked up from the table where she sat with her Bible. "You don't have to go. Are you sure you want to?"

"I'm sure. It'll be good for me." Caroline kissed Mary's forehead, then patted her sister's shoulder on her way to the back door. "I'll see you this afternoon." The moment the door clicked shut behind her, the tension in her shoulders eased. Her neck warmed by the sun, Caroline crossed Main Street and walked up the hill. A cardinal chirped among the new leaves in a mottled sycamore. All signs that spring already had a foot in the door.

A red brick building on the corner of Jefferson and Boone Street housed the Northern Presbyterian Church, its bell tower and steeple a welcoming sight. It was a smaller version of the Presbyterian meeting-house that she'd attended in Philadelphia. Men, women, and children dressed in their Sunday best mingled in the wagon lot and congregated at the hitching rails in front of the stained-glass windows. Colored families rushed past, down Boone Street, as the bell on their meeting hall called them to worship.

As Caroline approached the front steps, she studied the crowd looking for Maren. "Pastor Munson." Rutherford Wainwright's voice caused her to turn toward him. Maren was standing beside her husband, her arm looped through his. Gabi held her other hand.

"This is our friend, Mrs. Caroline Milburn."

Caroline smiled.

"Welcome to the meeting of our church, Mrs. Milburn. I'm pleased you chose to join us this morning."

She was pleased too. "Thank you, Pastor."

After their greetings, Caroline followed Rutherford and Maren through the arched foyer and into the narrow sanctuary. Rutherford paused beside a pew that was uncomfortably close to the front and motioned for her to step out of the aisle first.

Caroline obliged him. She picked up the book of Psalms and hymns before seating herself in the middle of the pew. She returned the smile of the girl she sat near, who was about Gilbert's age, but left a space between them in case either of them needed a little elbowroom.

Maren scooted in to her left. When Gabi was settled between her and Rutherford, Maren faced Caroline. "What a pleasant Sunday surprise to see you here. I'm so glad you came."

"I am too." She meant it.

It was her own fault she'd been cooped up. Except for the quilting circle, which she'd only joined at Jewell's insistence, she hadn't had any outside involvements. She'd considered getting a job to supplement her army widow's pension, but she'd not had the energy. She'd been despairing, looking for any cave to crawl into. Not all that different from Jack.

But today was a new day. Tinted light streamed in through the arched stained-glass windows lining the sides of the sanctuary. Caroline relaxed her back against the smooth oak, letting her hands rest on the Bible and songbook on her lap. She saw a few people she recognized from town, but no one she really knew. And most of the men were seated with women. Didn't seem single men were able to get themselves to Christian meetinghouses. Phillip had stopped attending before he met her.

Caroline scolded herself for such a self-centered focus in the house of the Lord. She was here for a boon to her faith, not for a husband. A musical prelude returned her attention to the front. A generously proportioned woman sat at the piano while a more petite woman stood in front of a simple lectern with an open songbook. The pastor walked in from the back, his long black vestment billowing slightly, and ascended the curving stair to the pulpit to the left of the chancel.

"Alas! And Did My Saviour Bleed." The woman's voice was not petite. "Hymn 85."

A memory of Aunt Inez's off-key voice plucked at Caroline's heart. This had been one of her aunt's favorites. One she often sang at the clothesline.

Caroline rose with the congregation and joined in the singing, remembering.

Alas! And did my Saviour bleed, and did my Sovereign die?
Would He devote that sacred head for such a worm—

Before she could finish the refrain, Maren tapped her arm and motioned toward the aisle. Caroline followed Maren's gaze, pressed her hand to the bench in front of her, and leaned forward. Garrett Cowlishaw stood beside Rutherford, offering her a small, close wave that stiffened her spine. Leave it to Mr. Cowlishaw to challenge her conclusion about single men and church attendance.

She scooted her Bible down the bench and sidestepped toward the young lady to make room for Garrett, her elbowroom gone. She hadn't seen him since the night he'd told her she couldn't travel west, and she wasn't too keen on seeing him now. Even in the house of the Lord.

❧

Stepping out of the aisle, Garrett accepted the open songbook from Rutherford. His mind should've been on God, or the song and the singing. On anything but Caroline Milburn. When, at the last minute, he'd decided to finally darken the doors of a church again, he hadn't considered she'd be here. Smiling.

Rutherford was right. Garrett was at the least fascinated by the

Widow Milburn. And he really needed to get over it. He was leaving Saint Charles.

She was staying.

He set his hat on the bench. Facing the song leader, he mouthed the words, listening intently to the soprano standing on the other side of Maren.

Thus might I hide my blushing face while his dear Cross appears;
Dissolve my heart in thankfulness, and melt mine eyes to tears.
But drops of grief can ne'er repay the debt of love I owe;
Here, Lord, I give myself away—'tis all that I can do.

Caroline being a single woman wasn't his only reason for not allowing her to join the caravan. How else was he to protect his heart?

13

Dressed in a green cotton skirt and a shawl draping her shoulders, Caroline left the house on Wednesday morning. Puffy white clouds formed uneven rows across the blue sky. A slight breeze teased the lace collar on her pleated shirtwaist. She couldn't apply for a teaching job until spring, which she intended to do since it would no doubt take an act of God for Garrett Cowlishaw to change his mind about her joining the wagon train.

She needed to do something with her time and energy. Something besides finding fault with her brother-in-law and frustration with her sister's plight. Since Maren wed and moved back to the farm, Johann Heinrich was short-handed at the Dry Goods and Grocery. Emilie was still trying to help her father despite her own new marriage and classes at Lindenwood, but she couldn't keep up with the demand of all the westbound folks coming in with their lists for provisions. Clerking in the store was a job Caroline could do, and it would give her the income she needed to move into her own room at the ladies' boardinghouse.

Although the day seemed warmer, sweet smoke from hundreds of fireplaces still scented the air. Deciding to take the long way around for a nice leisurely walk, Caroline strolled up the dirt path along the river. Her reticule swung at her side. Memories of her return to church two Sundays ago splayed across her mind. The sense of belonging. The music. The teaching. Garrett Cowlishaw's warm smile. How could she stay mad at the man?

A shrill steam whistle broke through her thoughts, drawing her gaze to the river's edge and the large side-wheeler docking there. The *New Era*.

Caroline stilled. Seemed fitting that the boat would return just as she was attempting to embark on a new era of her own.

Had Lewis G. Whibley made another round trip from Memphis?

He was obviously a man who embraced adventure and didn't mind traveling. Perhaps he would consider a wagon caravan west an intriguing proposition. People had married for less noble reasons.

Caroline shook her head. Those were not the thoughts of a sensible woman. She'd met the man once. On a boat. He'd been the first to flatter her since she'd lost Phillip. That's all. But even Mrs. Kamden had noticed the man's attentions on that January day.

He'd told her he would welcome the day she agreed to run away with him. Even when she'd laughed and refused, he'd remained a gentleman, continuing to see to her every need on the boat. She would simply see if he was aboard. And what could it hurt to greet him if he was? A cordial greeting would afford her the opportunity to see if Mr.

Whibley's interest in her remained intact. After all, he knew she'd gotten off the boat in Saint Charles and was living here. Had he returned with the intention of finding her?

She chuckled. Her desperation for change had her fishing without sensible bait. More than two months had passed since their friendly encounter. A lot could've happened in that time.

Doubtful the man was even on the boat.

But despite her doubts and reservations, Caroline slipped the handle of her reticule over her arm and tugged her sleeves straight. She took careful steps toward the river. A week of sunshine had done a good job of melting the snow and drying out the bank between town and the river, but it was a far cry from being without rocks and ridges.

The waterfront teemed with activity. Wagons lined the bank down to the freighter. Folks crowded around the lowered stage of the *New Era*. Since she wasn't there to meet a loved one, Caroline moved to one side of the crowd and slowed her steps. Keeping watch for Lewis G. Whibley, she studied the passengers pouring off the deck. Couples disembarked. Women and children greeted husbands and fathers. Men came ashore dressed in fine suits—some in full military regalia. But no sight of a particularly dapper fellow in a white top hat and tails. When the crowd dissipated, Caroline approached the uniformed steward.

"Ma'am." He raised a thick hand. "We won't be boarding until tonight. Starts at eight o'clock for a ten o'clock departure."

Caroline moistened her lips. "I apologize for the misunderstanding. I'm not a passenger."

"I see." His bushy eyebrows waggled. "What business do you have here?"

"I, uh, I'm here to see a Mr. Lewis G. Whibley. Is he aboard?"

"He is." The man was as tall as he was square. "You his sister?"

"An acquaintance." A very uncomfortable one.

"This way, ma'am." He stepped aside, leaving room for her to enter through the louvered door. "Last I saw him, he was in the dining room."

She waited just inside the door, then followed the square man down a corridor, past the door to the kitchen. The pungent aroma of smoked meat floated in the air, making her hungry for lunch and the adventure the riverboat promised.

Approaching an open door, Caroline recognized Mr. Whibley's smooth baritone voice. Her escort halted his steps. So did she, listening.

"God created woman for man, not for widowhood." Mr. Whibley paused, no doubt for emphasis. "The war is to blame for that injustice."

Pressing her hand to her mouth to suppress a huff, Caroline took a quiet step into the dining room. Lewis G. Whibley sat at an intimate two-seat table, his back to her. His hand draped over that of a young woman with blond curls and exquisite lace framing her shoulders.

"A lovely woman such as yourself, Penelope Reinhart, should not for a moment have to suffer alone."

To the letter, the exact words he'd sprinkled on her ears.

Setting the huff free, she marched toward the man. Of course he'd flattered her. That's what he did. Apparently, that was his job. "You, sir, are a scoundrel and a scavenger."

Rising to his feet, Lewis G. Whibley turned to face her, his movements characteristically calm and calculating. "Caroline." He looked past her. "Where is your nurse?"

"My nurse? Ha! Mr. Whibley, you are a forager preying upon wounded women."

He took quick but composed steps toward her. Cupping her elbow, he twirled her toward the door and spoke over his shoulder. "Please excuse me, Penelope. I must attend to my sister, lest she harm herself."

His drivel numbed her ears as he escorted her past the steward, to the deck.

∞

Garrett walked around the rig, looking at the new harness in the bed. Wasn't a fancified prairie schooner like Kamden ordered, but Garrett's new wagon suited him fine. At least it would, once Harry over at the Wagon House added bows and a canvas bonnet.

"I thought about checkin' with you today but got lazy." He shook Captain Pete's hand. "Thanks for sending the messenger."

Pete gave a wheel a good shake. "Long time gettin' here, but it should take you to California right comfortably. Can't do much about the other stuff that might get in your way, though." He chuckled, showing holes where two teeth had gone missing. "You stocked up yet on ammunition and jerky?"

"I am." Garrett shuffled the harness, picking up the collars and inspecting them. "Even have a poke of willow bark for staving off headaches."

"Too many women goin' along, are there?"

Garrett laughed, but his heart wasn't in it. The one woman he cared about seeing on the journey was staying behind. Remembering his first encounter with Caroline Milburn this year, he glanced upstream at the *New Era* he'd seen making waves minutes ago.

He yanked his hat off his head. Blinked feverishly. Couldn't be her. Feeling gut-punched, he looked at Pete, then nodded toward the passenger boat. "You see a redhead there on the deck?"

"That's Jack Rafferty's sister."

"In-law. Caroline Milburn." Garrett stepped away from his wagon for a better look. "You know the dandy she's with?"

"Yep." Captain Pete scratched the white swirl of hair on his head. He let out a long, pained breath. "Thought everybody knew about him. Name's Lewis G. Whibley."

"Has a reputation?"

"Gambler and confidence man. Heard he could sell a plow to a sea captain." Pete spit a brown streak on the sand. "What's a fine eastern lady like her doin' with a rogue like him?"

Garrett rubbed the back of his neck. "Good question." And he'd make it his job to find out. Apparently, Caroline Milburn would require less looking after if she was on the trail.

He slapped his hat back onto his head. Since when was it his job to care for her, anyway?

Didn't matter. His job or not, he probably began to care for the young widow the moment she rejected him at the wheel of her sister's wagon, his punishment for having been a Confederate soldier.

aroline jerked her arm from the man's hand, then slapped his smug face. Gloves would've protected her fingers from the sting but robbed her of the assurance that Lewis G. Whibley had felt pain too.

She took quick steps down the deck, her boot heels tapping the teakwood in rhythm with her staccato heartbeat. So much for her leisurely stroll to Heinrich's store. She'd definitely taken the long way—seemed the only path God allowed her. No shortcuts. No easy way out of grief.

Or imprudence.

Standing at the bottom of the ramp, Caroline noted the freighter docked beside the *New Era*. Then she saw the wagon parked at the end of its stage, with two men standing beside it, one of them being the seemingly ever-present Mr. Garrett Cowlishaw. He wasn't smiling. And neither was she.

Not only did life not afford her any shortcuts, but she was forced to battle demons at every turn. Looking straight ahead, she kept a steady pace until she turned up Jackson Street to Main. Shopkeepers swept the boardwalks outside their doors. Flower boxes brimmed with fresh soil. Businessmen scurried to and fro. Caroline dodged a fully harnessed stuffed horse in front of the saddlery shop. A few doors down, she stepped into Heinrich's Dry Goods and Grocery.

The bell jangling overhead seemed intent on fraying her last nerve. Drawing in a deep breath, she made certain her hair was in place. Emilie's father stacked canvas duck overcoats at the end of the counter. Another item she recognized from Mr. Cowlishaw's list of provisions.

Straightening his back, Mr. Heinrich peered at her over the wire rims of his spectacles. "You're a welcome sight, Mrs. Milburn."

"As are you, sir. Thank you." She looked toward the office. "Is Emilie working today?"

"Not this morning. She needed a book from the college library, so she's studying at Lindenwood. Married life and higher education are keeping her busier than ever."

Caroline nodded, noting the piles of merchandise needing to be put away.

"Is there something I can help you with?" He glanced at her reticule. "Did your sister send you with a list?"

"No sir." She swallowed her hesitation. "I mean, yes. I think you can help me. No, I don't have a list."

His white eyebrows arched.

"I wondered if perhaps you might have work. For me."

"Might I?" A generous smile deepened the creases at his blue eyes. "When can you start?"

The bell drew her gaze to the door. Mr. Cowlishaw stepped inside, his face stormy.

In no mood to receive any comments on her presence at the waterfront, Caroline nodded a greeting that she hoped told Garrett she was busy, then returned her attention to Mr. Heinrich.

"Tomorrow?" When Garrett Cowlishaw was nowhere in sight.

"Tomorrow is Thursday." Mr. Heinrich seemed as distracted as she was by Garrett's apparent pacing. "What about the quilting circle?"

"I need the work."

Mr. Heinrich looked past her. "Do you have unfinished business with Mr. Cowlishaw?"

"It can wait." He could wait.

"Tomorrow, it is." Mr. Heinrich held his hand out to her, and she shook it. "You, Mrs. Milburn, are a godsend."

"So are you, Mr. Heinrich. So are you." Her a godsend? A burden, yes. And apparently an equal annoyance to the man expelling hot air behind her.

"Mrs. Milburn."

She slowly turned to face Garrett Cowlishaw. He held his hat to his chest. "Yes, Mr. Cowlishaw?"

"Might I have a word with you?" Garrett tipped his head toward the door. "Outside, perhaps?"

Caroline drew in a deep breath. The man was nothing if not persistent. If he'd followed her here, he wasn't about to be easily dismissed. She may as well listen to what he thought she needed to hear, then be on her way. She had chores to do before she'd be ready to start her new job come morning. "Yes, a word would be possible. If you don't mind waiting outside for a moment or two."

He gave her a quick nod and waved at Mr. Heinrich before taking long strides out the door.

When the bell silenced, Mr. Heinrich slid his spectacles down the bridge of his nose and looked at her. "He's a good man, that Garrett Cowlishaw."

A good man for another woman.

"Is eight o'clock tomorrow morning suitable?"

"Yes. Thank you." On her way out the door, Caroline breathed a prayer for patience with the man pacing at the street's edge.

She'd no sooner closed the door behind her than Garrett motioned for her to join him at the far end of the building. When she obliged, he folded his arms, then unfolded them and shoved his left hand into his trouser pocket.

"Do you have something to say? If not—"

"I saw you."

She lifted her chin. "You have nothing better to do with your time than to spy on me?"

His hazel eyes were more brown than green today. "I like you."

"You pity me."

"Now that makes as much sense as a…well, it doesn't make any sense." He swatted his leg with his hat, sending dust into the air between them. "Why would I pity a woman as fetching as a sunrise and as strong as a Virginia oak?"

Fetching? Caroline pressed her lips together against a wall of emotions. *Flattery.* She'd had her fill of it.

"No. I don't pity you. I truly like you."

She watched his Adam's apple bob in a swallow.

"But I don't like being called 'vindictive.'"

Caroline squirmed, recalling the moment she stormed from The Western House Inn.

"I assure you, I hold no malice toward you. Do you really believe me to be a vindictive man? Cruel and unkind?"

Despite the mid-March chill in the air, the back of her neck warmed. "No."

His arms relaxed at his side.

"I shouldn't have said it. I was angry."

They both took a step closer to the brick building to allow room for an older couple to pass them.

"You were doing your job." But she didn't have to like it. Or him. As a matter of fact, she'd rather not.

Thankfully, he was a man who would, in two months, ride out of town with a ragtag collection of wagons while she created store displays of barrels of salted meats and tins of condensed milk.

"You seemed upset. At the river." Garrett drew in a deep breath and blew it out. "I only wanted to make certain you were all right."

She nodded and glanced down the street. "I best return home before my sister sends out a search party."

He smiled. "Of course." The smile deepened as he doffed his slouch hat.

"Good day." Caroline turned and took slow steps toward her sister's house.

How could she be all right if Garrett Cowlishaw was bent on being kind to her—and then leaving her? Phillip had done that.

And she was weary of being left behind.

Garrett watched the chunk of blue cheese melt into the flaky crust on his piece of apple pie. He pulled two forks from the white maple tray in the center of the kitchen table while Mrs. Brantenberg poured steaming coffee into two generous mugs. She returned the pot to the cast-iron stove and joined him at the table. Rutherford and Maren had gone upstairs to tuck little Gabi into bed for the night.

In boyhood, Rutherford had always been more sensible…less of a rebel. It figured that Rutherford would be the one with the family.

Mrs. Brantenberg rested her elbows on the table and peered over the top of her steaming mug. Mist beaded on the wisps of silver hair on her forehead. "Rutherford seems to have his heart set on going west."

Garrett nodded.

She set the mug down. "Rutherford and my Gretchen had talked about going to California when they first married."

"And you? How do you feel about the wagon train?"

"Finally, he's like a son to me again. Maren, a daughter. And Gabi…" She lifted her cup to quivering lips.

Garrett scooped another bite of pie, sweeping his fork to catch a crumb of cheese. "I know Rutherford, ma'am. He wouldn't leave you behind. You're a family—the four of you."

She nodded. "If he decides it is best that we go, we will. But…" The threat of rain moistened her gray eyes. "Life was bad in Germany. Gottfried Duden came to America desperate and returned to our homeland a dream spinner. He wrote a book about the wide expanses of land…the freedoms in America." She wrapped her hands around the coffee cup.

Garrett swallowed another bite of pie.

"My Christoph dreamed of owning farmland in America and raising our Gretchen in its freedoms. In '48, we boarded a ship that brought
us here. Saint Charles has been our home…my home." She looked toward the darkened window. "I know the good Lord will provide, but it's
not easy to think of leaving."

"The war changed everything, ma'am." Memories tugged at Garrett's shoulders. "Reconstruction here will take years. You'll have military rule in Missouri for a long time. Folks want away from the
bushwhackers and jayhawkers. You and your family can start afresh out
west." He hoped the same encouragement was true for him.

Mrs. Brantenberg raised a forkful of apple pie. "Do you still have
family in Virginia?"

"No ma'am. My folks both passed." Garrett straightened the stack
of knives in the tray on the table. "My only brother is married with
children and living in Florida." Well, he was, last word Garrett had
from the postmaster. Garrett was nearly ready to tell her why he didn't
know this for himself—and why he wasn't present when his folks died.
But instead, he just stared at his empty fork.

"Wide open spaces can only do so much for you, son. Don't you
want a wife and children?"

"I did."

"Not any longer?"

"I was married."

Compassion softened the line that framed her mouth. "Did she
pass?"

He shook his head. "It wasn't like that."

"The war?"

He scraped the rest of the apple filling into a pile. "Mostly me." He never did measure up. Not in his father's eyes, nor where his former wife was concerned. He'd also let Caroline Milburn down. On more than one occasion.

No, he was better off alone.

"War can surely divide a family. And in many different ways."

Giving in to resignation, he lifted his shoulders and let them fall.

"I'm sorry."

Garrett drew comfort from the compassion he saw on her kind face. "Thank you. I haven't told Rutherford."

"You will. When you're ready."

Her way of saying it was their secret until then. He couldn't believe he'd told her and not his best friend. But the widow had a way about her. A mother's way that his own mother hadn't possessed, not in his childhood.

If she'd ever had it before that, his father no doubt squelched it.

aroline had lain awake much of the night. When rain wasn't tapping the roof, she listened to Cora and Mary's sleep-breathing, a chorus of soft snores and gentle whistles.

Her mind no less active than the night's sounds, Caroline considered the events of the past several months. Her stagecoach ride to Saint Charles from Philadelphia. Her first tentative ride to the farm to join the quilting circle. Garrett Cowlishaw delivering the news of Phillip's death in Mrs. Brantenberg's kitchen. Coffee-time conversations with Jewell, Mrs. Brantenberg, Maren, Emilie, Hattie, and Anna. The children's laughter. Her vigil at Aunt Inez's bedside. Gilbert's suggestion that she go west with the caravan. Mr. Cowlishaw's resounding "no." Hearing the same man recite the prayer of confession in the church service. Lewis G. Whibley's disdain when she'd caught him preying on another widow. Her job...

So many thoughts swirling with the raindrops.

She'd completed her first week of work for Johann Heinrich. Emptied crates of new shoes and boots. Filled out vouchers for folks bartering with eggs and milk. She'd even managed to play a couple of games of checkers with her employer. All in all, a good job for her until she could teach again.

When sleep still refused to pay Caroline a visit, she lit a candle lantern and propped herself on the bed. After reading the fourth chapter of James, she finished her square for the Friendship quilt that would travel with those leaving Saint Charles come April.

Thankfully, Thursday morning dawned without clouds. Emilie didn't have classes and had chosen to work with her father, which meant Caroline was free to go to the farm today for the quilting circle.

First, she needed to fetch the sorrels from the livery. Two curled lead ropes swung at her side as sunlight and shadow guided her steps around water puddles and pools of mud. Thanks to heavy wagon traffic, both were plentiful on Pike Street. Caroline waited for a freight wagon to cross in front of her and returned the driver's wave. Emilie's husband, Quaid McFarland, tipped his hat in a quick greeting, then pulled into line behind a couple of other wagons.

Within twenty minutes, a gangly livery hand brought the two horses to her outside the corral gate, sparing her a mucky walk through the wet manure that coated the ground.

"Thank you." She took the two leads from him.

He brushed the brim of his cap and spun toward the corral. When the gate chain clinked behind her, she settled between the sorrels, one rope in each hand.

"Mrs. Milburn?"

Caroline looked into the friendly face of the young man she recognized from the wagon train meeting. "Good day, Mr. Hughes."

"Please. Call me Boney. Any friend of Anna's is—"

"Is a friend of yours." She smiled. "Thank you. Boney." There, she'd used his nickname. But she didn't expect to ever grow accustomed to the relaxed comportment on this side of the Mississippi.

"Mr. Cowlishaw told me of your intention to provision a wagon and go west with the company."

"It's true." Polite airs obviously didn't concern Boney Hughes. "Did your boss also tell you what he said?"

"Yes ma'am, he did."

"Well, I'm a woman who takes *no* to simply mean *not now*." She squared her shoulders. "I still intend to go west, Mr. uh…Boney."

He scrubbed the shadow of a beard. "I see."

She swallowed a giggle. "You needn't trouble yourself though. I won't be making the trip this spring with your wagon train. I've already made other plans."

"No hard feelings, then?"

She smiled. "No hard feelings." Except when she grew frustrated with her living conditions. Still needed to work on that. Soon, she'd have a place of her own, which would help immensely.

The young man's marriage proposal to Anna nipped at her curiosity, tempting her to ask him about it. Unfortunately, her eastern proprieties were still intact and forbade inquiry.

Boney dug the toe of his boot into the wet ground, then looked up at her. "I called on Miss Anna and her family this past week."

"Oh?"

He nodded, bobbing his hat forward as if it were too big for his head. "She hasn't answered my question."

"About your question, Mr. Boney… it didn't seem hasty to you?" If he wasn't willing to entertain her curiosity, he shouldn't have brought up the subject.

"Anna did look a bit flabbergasted, didn't she?" Boney chuckled. "Her jaw dropped so suddenly that I feared she might bruise her chin. I hadn't thought on it long, but it ain't my nature to stew. Just don't take me long to make up my mind about somethin'."

Yes, well, she'd tried throwing caution to the wind last week. Had to hope doing so turned out better for this likable fellow. And for Anna.

∞

Less than an hour later, Caroline and Jewell had the horses harnessed to the wagon and were on their way to Mrs. Brantenberg's farm. Mary squirmed on the front seat beside her mother while Caroline sat in the back with Anna.

Anna leaned forward, her shawl fluttering in the light breeze. "Did you tell your sister?"

Turning slightly, Jewell glanced over her shoulder. "Tell me what?"

"I didn't say anything." Caroline looked at Jewell. "Didn't feel it was my place."

"Do you remember the boy named Robert Hughes…Boney?" Anna asked.

Jewell nodded. "He lived with his aunt and uncle over the old cobbler's shop."

"Yes." Anna leaned forward. "He's back in town. I saw him at the Boone's Lick Wagon Train Company meeting last week. And…he up and asked me to marry him."

"He *what*?" Jewell's voice rose an octave, causing them all to giggle.

"After the meeting, Boney proposed marriage."

"He had a reputation for being a tease. You're sure he wasn't pulling your leg?"

"I was there. He seemed plenty serious to me." Caroline looked at Anna. "As a matter of fact, I saw him this morning at the livery. Mentioned he had called on you last week but had yet to receive your answer."

"He's very sweet. Said I deserved to be taken care of. I told him I'd think about it."

"And have you?" Jewell faced the road in front of them.

"It's all I've thought about. Ruined about a dozen candles in the distraction." Anna wrung her hands. "What would you do?"

Caroline shook her head. "You won't hear me tell you what to do. I'm not even listening to myself anymore."

Anna giggled. "What about you, Jewell? You're married. What do you think I should do?"

Jewell looked at the road, then back at Anna. "If you don't know for certain it's what you want to do, I think you best not be rushing your thinking."

Anna blew out a long breath. "I—"

Mary twisted onto her knees. "I know." Her little hands grasping the back of the seat, she peered at Anna with big green eyes. "Does he have a horse?"

Anna startled. "I believe he does, and a wagon."

"Marry him then."

When Anna's shoulders began to shake with laughter, Caroline could no longer hide hers behind her hand. She remembered those childhood days...when everything seemed so simple and matter-of-fact. Days when she and Jewell skipped through grassy meadows and dreamed of dressing up like lovely princesses to marry charming princes.

Those days were gone. So were the dreams.

Humble yourselves in the sight of the Lord, and He shall lift you up.

Recognizing the words of Scripture that echoed in her heart, Caroline folded her hands on her lap. *Show me how, Lord. Show us all how.*

16

Saturday afternoon, Caroline was the acting shopkeeper while Mr. Heinrich went to the bank. She pulled a tin of peaches off of a high shelf behind the counter and dangled it for her customer to reach. Concern creased Oliver Rengler's brow.

"You shoulda let me do the climbing, ma'am." He set the tin on the counter and steadied the ladder.

Her knuckles white, Caroline planted her booted feet on one wrung, and then another. She didn't wish to lose her footing. Nor did she fancy tangling the heels of her boots in her skirt with two men nearby.

She'd counted two more steps when Oliver held his hand out to her. She gladly accepted his assistance onto the solid floor.

"Thank you."

He nodded, but didn't let go. Caroline glanced at her hand in his, which looked like a teacup inside a serving bowl.

His face tinted red and he jerked his hand to his side.

Caroline smoothed her work apron and returned to the ledger. A lot of folks were using store credit to gather provisions for their trip west, planning to pay off their debt after they'd sold their property and belongings. The Rengler brothers were counted among those. She picked up the pencil and continued listing their supplies. Like she and Jewell, the brothers were as different as a pencil is from a hammer. Owen favored the costume of a city businessman while Oliver seemed content in sailcloth trousers.

Oliver added a poke of tobacco to the pile they were accumulating at the end of the counter. "A lady like you, Miss Caroline, should be sipping tea in a parlor."

She smiled. Oliver's flattery was different…innocent. "I like the way you think, Oliver." *A parlor in San Francisco.* "But sipping tea doesn't pay the rent."

"No ma'am." Oliver chuckled. "Playin' checkers and gulpin' old man Heinrich's coffee don't neither."

Owen set a sack of dried beans in front of her. "Looks to me like my brother's sweet on you, Miss Caroline."

Color flooded Oliver's face again. Was he *sweet* on her? No. Everyone in the store was friendly, that's all it was. He was simply being sociable.

Oliver met his brother's impish gaze. "That ain't the way it is, Owen. I'm tellin' the truth, is all." Hooking his thumbs on the suspenders holding up his trousers, he turned to face her. "Unless you'd like that, ma'am." His eyebrows arched, his childlike expression sweet. "You want me to be sweet on you, Miss Caroline?"

Her mouth went dry.

"Wouldn't do either of you any good, Ollie." Owen clapped his brother on the back. "Miss Caroline is staying in Missouri."

Oliver sighed. "You were at that meeting about the wagons. With Hattie and Miss Anna."

She nodded. "I went to the meeting, but I won't be going west." And right now, saying so was a considerable relief. "It's a fine offer...you being sweet on me, and if I were looking for a husband—"

The doorbell's jingle stopped her midsentence. She faced the door. The grandmother of five seemed intent on tracking Caroline's every move, but Caroline couldn't have been any happier to see the woman. "Good morning, Mrs. Kamden."

"Dear." She dipped her chin. "Misters Rengler." A smile bunched her cheeks.

Oliver chuckled, and pointed to his brother, then to himself.

"Mrs. Kamden." Owen doffed his bowler. "The pleasure is ours."

Caroline set her pencil down and stepped out from behind the counter. "Did you need help finding something?"

The older woman waved her gloved hand. "Ian said we'll do our shopping next week. We came to see you."

Caroline looked at the door. She didn't see anyone waiting outside.

Mrs. Kamden fanned herself. "I meant to say...the others are on their way."

"The others?"

"Why, my son and his family, of course."

Of course? Caroline nodded. Somewhere along the way, she'd apparently missed an important piece of the conversation.

Davonna Kamden waved for Caroline to return to the brothers. "You go right ahead with your business, dear. I am in no hurry."

While Caroline finished adding the Renglers' goods to the ledger, she couldn't help but entertain a puzzling question: Why would Mrs. Kamden and her family come to see her if they weren't there to shop?

∞

Caroline stepped onto the cobblestone walk in front of the dry goods store. As she strolled down the hill toward her sister's cabin, the late afternoon sun cut a swatch of light across the road in front of her. That's how Caroline viewed the news she'd received today—a light illuminating a dark path.

But Jewell? That's not at all how she'd see Caroline's opportunity.

With supper behind them, Caroline and Jewell tucked the three children into bed while Jack lounged in the sitting room, smoking his pipe like that was all in the world there was to do.

First, Caroline smoothed the quilt over Mary, tickling her youngest niece's belly as she went. Her heart warmed and wrenched in the reward of joyful giggles she received. Jewell came behind her tucking the quilt in at the sides, then Caroline followed with a nose tap and a kiss. They repeated the routine with Cora. But since such silliness was far beneath Gilbert's eight years, they settled for tucking and a kiss on the forehead.

Jewell claimed the tradition of praying over her children every night and every morning. The only difference on this night was that Caroline knew her role in the rite would soon come to an end.

Sighing, she added her own amen to her sister's.

"Sweet dreams, children." When Jewell lifted the candle lantern off its peg near the door, Caroline glanced longingly at her own bed in the far corner. She was ready to retire, to lie in bed and think about her future, but she could no longer delay the conversation she needed to have with her sister.

Caroline followed Jewell out of the room, clicking the door shut behind them.

"Hot tea?" Her sister's invitation came out on a whisper as she led the way to the kitchen.

Caroline pulled their favorite teacups from the hooks beneath the shelf and set a ball of sassafras leaves into each of the cups. "On the porch?"

Still holding the candle lantern, Jewell nodded and poured water from the kettle, filling the small kitchen with steam.

Caroline wiped her damp cheeks as if the kettle were to blame for her tears. She added a pinch of sugar to her cup and then followed Jewell past the man in the wicker wheelchair and out the front door.

The porch wasn't anything to boast, but it did house two slat-back armchairs and afforded them a quiet reprieve. Sister time. Together. Alone.

Another tradition Caroline would sorely miss.

Jewell set the candle on the low railing and looked at Caroline. "You're real quiet this evening. Have been ever since you returned from work." She lifted her cup to her mouth and took a sip. "Did something happen at the store today?"

Caroline rested her cup on the arm of the chair and met her sister's gaze. The glow from the candle set at their knees was enough to illuminate Jewell's pinched brow. Caroline opened her mouth to speak, but the words didn't come.

"You're going, aren't you?"

Caroline nodded, swallowing hard against the lump of emotion clogging her throat.

Jewell looked away, her hands wrapped around the teacup, and shook her head.

Caroline lifted her cup to her chin, letting the droplets of steam on her face mingle with the tears.

17

I can *read* English, too."

Seated in The Western House Inn, Garrett slid the provisions list across the table to the oldest of the three Zanzucchi boys. At age ten, Alfonzo Junior was already well into manhood. His father sat beside him while his mother and two brothers stood behind them. The family had arrived in Saint Charles that afternoon from New York. They'd journeyed by train with their wagon on a flatcar, then across the Mississippi at the confluence of the Missouri on a paddle-wheel barge for the daylong trip upstream to Saint Charles. "Tell your father he will need to have the wagon stocked and ready to go on April 11. We'll line up the wagons out on the River Road."

Junior looked at his father, then rattled off in Italian what Garrett assumed was a translation.

"Candles, a water keg, chains, a sturdy rope, flour, rice…it's all there." Garrett pointed to the paper.

Junior spoke Italian to his parents and tapped the list.

Mr. Zanzucchi nodded, responding at several points in Italian.

Mrs. Zanzucchi cut in with what sounded like a question.

"Ermalinda!" Her husband shook his head, his look as stern as his voice.

Despite that, she let fly with what sounded like a diatribe. Her hand motions as fast as her Italian, the woman studied Garrett, her lips pursed and her gaze steady.

Garrett shrugged, waiting for his English explanation. Did she want to take a piano? A set of fine china?

Unfortunately, Ermalinda Zanzucchi didn't look like a woman who could be easily dissuaded.

"Papa said we'll be ready." Junior folded the paper.

Garrett pulled the roster from the chair beside him. The Boone's Lick Wagon Train Company would be a multilingual community. So far, he had Americans, Germans, Scots, French, and now Italians. Fortunately, each group had at least one member who could communicate in English.

Leaning forward, Mrs. Zanzucchi rolled her open hand in front of Junior, then pointed to Garrett.

Junior's shoulders rose and fell. "Sir, Mama wants to know if you have a wife."

Garrett swallowed hard. "Why would she want to know that?"

The two younger boys giggled.

"It's Aunt Mia. She is traveling with us." Junior's dark eyebrows lifted. "She has no husband."

"Ah."

Junior fanned his fingers out in front of him like his mother had done. "So *do* you?"

"Have a wife?"

The boy nodded.

"No. And I don't—"

Another outburst in Italian from the woman who apparently had no problem understanding his *no* but didn't care to hear his explanation.

Junior pointed his open hand at Garrett as his mother had. "Mama says, 'She is a good cook, my sister Mia. Not afraid of work.'"

Garrett looked at Mrs. Zanzucchi. "Ma'am. I'm sure your sister is a fine woman."

Junior dutifully translated.

She dipped her chin and pursed her lips.

"It would not be right for me to marry anyone at this time."

He waited for Junior to translate.

Her eyes narrowed to slits.

"I have a job to do. A difficult job."

Junior added hand motions in his translation this time. Garrett hoped they were convincing.

Straightening her back, the woman rattled off Italian. Even in a foreign language, it was a universal message of *Mama knows what's best for you.*

Before Junior could translate, Garrett rested his arms on the table. He clasped his hands and looked her in the eye. "Mrs. Zanzucchi, your sister is welcome to join you on the journey, but I do not want a wife. And I have a cook."

Five of them, although his bet for best cook was on Boney.

Junior was quick with his translation.

Mrs. Zanzucchi raised her thick eyebrows. They were fully arched by the time her son finished speaking. She answered in heavily accented English. "Some men don't-a-know what they *need*."

Choosing to ignore the remark, Garrett held the roster out to Junior. "You'll need to read the information at the top to your parents. It is an agreement to abide by the company's rules. If he still wishes to join the caravan, your father will need to write his name—all of your names—and then sign his name. It is an agreement to abide by the company's rules."

Junior set the roster in front of his father. The boy was translating the instructions into Italian when Caroline Milburn walked into the room. Her bustled green skirts swished with each step. She drew the attention of the waitress and had a short conversation. She'd gestured toward him, then to an empty table. The waitress looked at Garrett, then led Caroline to a table in the corner.

Why else would she be there but to see him?

Garrett pushed his chair back. "Will you kindly excuse me for a moment?" He waited for Junior to translate. When the boy's parents nodded, Garrett walked to the table in the corner and removed his hat.

"Mrs. Milburn."

"Mr. Cowlishaw. Do you have a moment?" She motioned to the empty chair opposite her.

He seated himself. He hadn't seen her since they'd agreed he wasn't a vindictive man. "You came to see me?"

"I did." Her sly smile added a shine to her emerald-green eyes.

Had she come to try her charms to get him to change his mind? Would he be able to resist? Did he really want to?

She tilted her head a tad. "The Kamden family came to see me at the store."

That didn't sound the least bit threatening, or of any concern to him. "Is there a problem with the supplies? Johann said he ordered in all the dry goods. If something hasn't arrived, I'm sure—"

"Ian Kamden asked me to go with them."

"Go with them?"

She nodded toward the west, bobbing a fiery red curl at her forehead.

"West? With them?"

"They have two wagons. I would go as their nanny to help with the children and, well, the elder Mrs. Kamden."

"I think that's a fine idea."

"You do?" Her lips curved into a small O and seemed frozen there. "I do."

Her smile faded. "You don't want to argue about a single woman traveling through the scary wilderness?"

He shook his head. "And your sister? What does she say about this plan?"

Caroline shifted in the chair. "It wasn't so much what Jewell said, but what she didn't say that pierced my heart."

Garrett had met the ill-tempered Jack Rafferty and had no problem imagining the desperation his wife must feel in losing her sister to the west.

The beguiling redhead drew a deep breath, drawing his heart in with it. "Needless to say, my sister doesn't like the idea. But she understands that I must establish a new life…a life of my own. At least, I have to hope she understands."

He nodded. "And how did your nieces and nephew take the news?"

Tears pooled her eyes. "I will tell Mary, Cora, and Gilbert after supper." She blinked hard and straightened. "I have to do this."

"Very well then," Garrett said. "I'm glad you're going. Seems to me that you've secured for yourself the means required to make the trip. So, a trip you shall make."

"Yes, I shall." She stood, and so did he.

Now, the burden of guilt he was wont to carry for leaving her to her fate could be lifted.

A remarkable company indeed—Germans, Scots, French, Italians, and one unpredictable redhead.

∞

Excitement swirled around Caroline as she carried a tray of chilled apple cider into the dining room, the room's seams about to burst. On this last Thursday of March, Mrs. Brantenberg's Saint Charles quilting circle had convened for one last time. Their hostess had called the children in to join them for a celebration. Mary and Gabi stood at one corner of the table working their patchwork dolls like puppets, their giggles sinking deep into Caroline's soul. The elder Mrs. Beck and her daughter-in-law conversed with Emilie while Hattie and Bette Pemberton engaged in an animated conversation with Mabel Webber. Maren held Jewell's hands, speaking with her in hushed tones.

Those who were going west mingled with those they were leaving behind.

The Beck women seemed the easiest to separate. "Pardon me, ladies," Caroline said. Irene and Lorelei parted like the Red Sea, allowing Caroline access to the table. She set her tray down, and Anna had managed to do the same at the other end, with a second tray.

Mrs. Brantenberg seated herself, then set her Bible and the stack of quilting squares on the table in front of her. When she clapped her hands, the chatter quieted and the chairs quickly filled, including the extras they'd placed on the perimeter. That's where Jewell settled and pulled Mary onto her lap.

Fanning the quilting squares on the table, Mrs. Brantenberg pressed her lips together as if to hold back tears. She'd made a Shoo-Fly doll square in remembrance of her daughter, Gretchen, and for the joy of her granddaughter, Gabi. Anna honored her brother, Dedrick, with a Soldier's Cot square. Mrs. Pemberton's Remembrances square peeked out from under Maren's. On her Double Hourglass square, Maren had embroidered "Our times are in God's hands" above her new name—Maren Wainwright. Emilie had chosen a red and green Special Blessings pattern for her square.

"In my lifetime, I've said many hellos and many good-byes." Their beloved hostess tucked a spray of white hair into the braid circling her head, then looked around the room. "We all have. No matter our age. Life's changing seasons are as persistent as the ripples along the shore."

Caroline nodded in accord with Anna and Mrs. Webber.

Mrs. Brantenberg moistened her lips. "While parting will be difficult, I'm so thankful God brought us together for a season."

"I am too." Hattie glanced at Caroline, then to Mrs. Webber. "For our seasons of sorrow."

Maren turned her tender gaze toward Mrs. Brantenberg. "For seasons of joy."

"For seasons of planting." Mrs. Brantenberg looked out the window, toward the apple orchard.

"For seasons of harvest." The dreaminess in Emilie's voice reminded Caroline that Emilie and Quaid had reunited here on this farm during the apple harvest.

Hattie pressed her hands over her heart, her hat wobbling as she giggled.

Smiling, Mrs. Brantenberg opened her Bible. "The Lord has quilted our hearts together in those seasons of love and loss, sorrow and joy."

A round of gentle nods circled the room.

Mrs. Pemberton set her weathered hands on the table. "And now we are in a season of plucking and uprooting."

"Yes." Mrs. Brantenberg nodded, her lips pressed together. "In two short weeks, most of us will set out on a long journey to rebuild our lives farther west."

Emilie snatched Maren's hand. "While a few of us will remain to see Saint Charles rebuilt."

"Yes." Mrs. Webber looked at Emilie. "I'm moving into town to work in Heinrich's Dry Goods and Grocery."

Caroline gave the woman a broad smile, supported by relief. "That is good news. I had only just started my job there when it worked out for me to leave with the Kamdens."

Emilie nodded. "We will miss you, Caroline, but we are all seeing God at work in this change of seasons." She looked at Mrs. Brantenberg. "Quaid and I are buying this farm."

They all looked at Mrs. Brantenberg, who nodded and smiled.

"That's wonderful!" Jewell shifted Mary on her lap.

"It is indeed a blessing. It pleases me so to know that our dear

Emilie will raise her family here." Mrs. Brantenberg looked at Maren. "The four of us will move into town until our exodus day."

"We move into the house this weekend." Sheer joy lit Emilie's brown eyes.

Jewell cleared her throat. "Emilie, will you continue the quilting circle for those of us who remain?"

"What a splendid idea." Mrs. Brantenberg's eyebrows arched as she pinned Emilie with a questioning gaze.

"I suppose I could. With help."

Jewell nodded. A heartwarming smile curved her mouth.

Emilie's eyes widened. "Let's continue." She looked at Mrs. Webber, then to Jewell. "We can recruit other women looking for sisterhood in the seasons of their lives."

Mrs. Brantenberg wiped a tear from her cheek.

"There's still more news," Anna said.

Hattie jumped. "You've given Boney an answer?"

Blushing, Anna shook her head. "I'll see him Saturday. But it is good news that Jewell is taking over my candle making."

"I help Mama." Mary beamed.

"The children are excited to help." Jewell lifted a teasing eyebrow. "Thankfully, Anna will be showing us all how to make her pretty-colored candles before she leaves."

Again, Caroline's heart warmed. Jewell had chosen to remain with her husband who hadn't changed, but Caroline was seeing God provide for Jewell in other ways.

"We are seeing God's grace at work." Mrs. Brantenberg lifted her Bible from the table. Pointing a gnarled finger to a page, she began reading. "He giveth more grace."

Tears stung the backs of Caroline's eyes.

Wherefore he saith, God resisteth the proud, but giveth grace unto the humble. Submit yourselves therefore to God. Resist the devil, and he will flee from you. Draw nigh to God, and he will draw nigh to you.

Because of Caroline's involvement in this group, the teaching from James was now familiar to her...had become her prayer. A prayer God had answered in a surprising way, against all odds. Or at the least, against Garrett Cowlishaw's judgment. She was counted among those added to the wagon train company.

She joined the other women in reciting the verse that had become their theme that year. *"Humble yourselves in the sight of the Lord, and He shall lift you up."*

Mrs. Brantenberg nodded toward Maren, Gabi's new mama.

"Today we have gathered in celebration of the Lord's good work." Maren picked up a glass of cider and passed it to her left, doing so until everyone had a glass, including the children. Caroline wrapped her hand around the coolness, breathing in the sweet scent of apple.

Mrs. Brantenberg raised her glass first. "In celebration of the Lord of all of our seasons."

"To the Lord of our quilted hearts." Tears streamed Jewell's face.

Nodding, Caroline blinked back her own tears. "To the Lord of our journey...here *and* there."

1. Caroline Milburn's worst fears had been confirmed—her beloved Phillip had indeed been killed in the War between the States. All hope of a life with him had been crushed. What do you think you might have done in Caroline's situation?

2. Garrett Cowlishaw was a Confederate soldier, wounded both physically and emotionally. In his attempt to stand for justice, Garrett put himself in harm's way against his own regiment and was rejected by his family because of actions they considered disloyal. Because of it, he had no place to call home after the war. Have you ever had to make a choice—a decision that wasn't popular with the people you care about? What did it cost you?

3. Not only did Caroline dislike Garrett upon their first meeting and on several subsequent meetings, she considered the man her enemy. Why did Caroline have such an instant disdain for Garrett? Have you ever judged someone on an assumption or a first impression and discovered you'd been very wrong about that person?

4. Holidays can be especially difficult for those who have an empty seat at the meal table. Mother's Day can be painful for those women who haven't been able to conceive or have had to bury a child. Recently widowed, Caroline found herself attending a double

wedding. Have you ever been called upon to celebrate with friends or family when your heart was torn? What did you do?

5. In anticipation of the impending separation as some of the members planned to head west, the women in Elsa Brantenberg's quilting circle make two Friendship quilts—one that will remain in Saint Charles and one that will travel with the members who will rebuild their war-torn lives elsewhere. Quilt patterns usually tell a story about the maker or the time and place they were made. If you were working on a quilt block for a Friendship quilt, what pattern would you choose?

6. When Caroline finally accepts that her life as Phillip's wife has ended, she must make a decision: remain in Saint Charles under her sister and brother-in-law's roof, try to find a livelihood that would allow her to set up housekeeping near her family but not under their roof, or pack up and start over elsewhere. Caroline choose to go west with the caravan of wagons. Do you think she did the right thing? What would you have done?

7. *Ripples Along the Shore* doesn't conclude with Caroline and Garrett professing their love for each other. Why do you think that is?

Mona is available for conference calls where she joins your book club or reading group for a prescheduled conversation via Skype. When possible, Mona is happy to add an "in person" visit to a book club in a city she's visiting. For more information, please contact Mona through her website: www.monahodgson.com.

DANISH GLOSSARY

Fader—Father
Moder—Mother
Takke—Thank you

GERMAN GLOSSARY

Bitte schön—You're welcome
Bleib hinter mir—Stay behind me
Brötchen—Bread
Currywurst and Rotkohl—Brats and red cabbage
Danke—Thank you
Der Apfel fällt nicht weit vom Stamm—The apple doesn't fall far from
    the tree
Geteiltes Leid ist halbes Leid—Trouble shared is trouble halved
Gleich und gleich gesellt sich gern—Birds of a feather flock together
Großvater (the ß is pronounced as a double *s*)—Grandfather
Gut—Good
Guten Morgen—Good morning
Herzliche Grüße—Friendliest greetings or warm wishes
Hunger ist der beste Koch—Hunger is the best cook
Johann (the *J* is pronounced as a *Y*)—John
Liebling—Little one, little darling
Meine—My
Milchbrötchen—sweet rolls
Mir geht es gut—I am very well
Mutter—Mother
Oma—Grandmother

PaPa—Father

Schnitzel—a breaded cutlet dish

Schrank—a piece of German furniture, usually tall and used as a
clothes closet or wardrobe

Tochter—Daughter

Unsinnig—Nonsensical

Zimtsterne—Cinnamon stars, a classic German Christmas cookie

AUTHOR'S NOTE

Thank you for joining me on The Quilted Heart adventures with Mrs. Brantenberg's quilting circle in Saint Charles, Missouri, a city brimming with compelling, real-life characters and historical institutions.

The Historic Main Street District of Saint Charles charmed me during my first visit in 1999. My return in 2012 deepened my fascination with its rich historical past and modern-day charm.

If you've read The Sinclair Sisters of Cripple Creek series, you know I like to include real-life women from the time and place in my stories. In the Quilted Heart novellas, you'll hear about Mary Easton Sibley, the founder of Lindenwood University—known as Lindenwood Female College in 1865.

Also, I'm not writing my personal or family history in my fiction; however, bits and pieces of it do make their way into my characters' journeys. That's the case with Maren Jensen's experience with losing her eyesight. Her blindness is hereditary with the symptoms of what we now recognize as retinitis pigmentosa (RP), a disease that caused my mother's father to go blind. Three of my mother's four sisters and several of her nieces and nephews are also affected by RP.

The unusual letter ß (*Esszet*) you see in the word, Großvater, translated as Grandfather, is the letter used for the double S sound in the German language.

While I enjoy featuring actual cities and places in my books, in keeping with my commitment as a storyteller of historical fiction, I'm required to play with facts and actual locations to best meet the needs of my stories.

Are you ready to roll your covered wagon into line with mine? We'll keep company with some of our Saint Charles friends as well as others who are going west on the caravan. Please join me in my next series, Hearts Seeking Home. Book 1, *Prairie Song*, is now available!

Love and hugs.

Your Friend,

Mona

ACKNOWLEDGMENTS

On many levels, writing is a solitary undertaking. But it is also a process requiring a team of supporters. Many people rallied around me in the various stages of this story.

- My hubby, Bob, who takes care of everything else
- My agent, Janet Kobobel Grant of Books & Such Literary Agency
- My editor, Shannon Hill Marchese
- The entire WaterBrook Multnomah/Random House team
- Dorris Keeven-Franke, archivist, Saint Charles County Historical Society
- Carol M. Felzien, director of communication, Greater Saint Charles Convention & Visitors Bureau
- Robert "Bob" Sandfort, PhD, past president, Saint Charles County Historical Society
- Paul Huffman, university archivist, Lindenwood University
- Dr. Gary McKiddy, Saint Charles County German Heritage Club
- The Historic Main Street business owners for making me feel so welcome
- My prayer partners

A big thank you to all who are listed and to all who aren't, for making it possible for me to accomplish my dream of writing fiction for you.

Now unto the King eternal, immortal, invisible, the only wise God, be honour and glory for ever and ever. Amen.

—1 TIMOTHY 1:17

About the Author

MONA HODGSON is the author of nearly forty books including The Sinclair Sisters of Cripple Creek series, The Quilted Heart novellas (*Dandelions on the Wind, Bending Toward the Sun,* and *Ripples Along the Shore*), *Prairie Song,* Book 1 in the Hearts Seeking Home Series, and twenty-eight children's books. Her writing credits also include hundreds of articles, poems, and short stories in more than fifty different periodicals, including *Highlights for Children, Focus on the Family, Decision, Clubhouse Jr., The Upper Room, The Quiet Hour,* and the *Christian Communicator.* Mona speaks at women's retreats, schools, and conferences for librarians, educators, and writers and is a regular columnist on the *Stitches Thru Time* blog and the *Bustles and Spurs* blog.

Mona and Bob, her husband of forty-two years, have two adult daughters, two sons-in-law, and seven grandchildren.

Learn more about Mona and her speaking ministry, and find Readers Guides for your book club at her website: MonaHodgson.com. You can also find Mona here:

Mona's Blog at MonaHodgson.com.

Facebook at Facebook.com/pages/

Mona-Hodgson-Author-Page/114199561939095

Twitter at Twitter.com/monahodgson

Pinterest at http://pinterest.com/monahodgson/

The Sinclair Sisters *of* Cripple Creek

Four sisters, each seeking their own place in the world, travel to the booming mining town of Cripple Creek, Colorado, in the late 1890s. Kat and Nell Sinclair arrive only to discover their husbands-to-be have abandoned them. Ida follows her sisters West with dreams of big business, not of finding a beau. And Vivian, the youngest, flees a shameful past, hoping to find redemption in the hills of Colorado. Will the four sisters find the promise of God's love in the bustling mountain town?

Read excerpts from these books and more at
www.WaterBrookMultnomah.com!

Continue the adventure with the Boone's Lick Wagon Train in book 1 of the Hearts Seeking Home series.

Anna Goben is praying for a fresh start. Caleb Reger is a man running from his past. As these two tenacious hearts follow a pillar of hope through the American wilderness, they learn that the first step in a challenging journey is often the one that means the most.

Read an excerpt from this book and more at www.WaterBrookMultnomah.com!

The Quilted Heart
A Women's Retreat and Conference Series

PRESENTED BY
Mona Hodgson
Author and Speaker

"If Mona is part of your program, she will have you laughing while quickening your heart to seek God." –Connie

This retreat series of talks served as the inspiration for the three novellas by the same title: *The Quilted Heart*.

God cares about transforming hearts. Quilters are transformers. *The Quilted Heart* is a transformed heart.

Quilts have a top, batting, and backing bound together by thread. Using that imagery, Mona offers a fun and poignant examination of a Christ-centered faith, a heart surrendered to God's design and His divine pattern for stitching our hearts together.

God can take the remnants from our circumstances and past experiences that we'd rather hide and stitch them into our transformed heart for our good and His glory.

The topic of *The Quilted Heart* lends itself well to one, two, three, or four presentations of 40–60 minutes each in Mona's most popular Women's Retreat Series.

Mona speaks for a variety of audiences and in various venues, including Christian Women's Retreats, Writers' Groups and Conferences, Schools and Educators, and Book Clubs. To discuss your group and Mona's fees, visit Mona's website: www.MonaHodgson.com.